JEROM

MW01133304

PALMETTO PARDON

A CODY HOUSTON SERIES NOVEL

outskirts
press

CHAPTER 1

The early morning air felt heavy and damp as the long-legged, lean man loaded the saddle bags with a few provisions for his trip that included several bottles of high SPF sunscreen, a bag full of cigars, lighters, and a cutter, and a big bottle of Jack Daniel's. The sun was an hour away from rising and the darkness enveloped all but the strong beam of the three-light headlight assembly on the front of the bike. The v-twin motor carried on its lilting idle chorus with a throaty rumble as the man wiped down the seat and grips with a terry cloth rag. The long leg swung over the saddle and engaged first gear with a loud, solid clunk. The 800-pound bike was awkward and hard to handle at low speed but seemed almost light and nimble as he took the top gear and rumbled through the early morning darkness. The motor made a purring sound as it hit its torque curve as if expressing happiness to finally be in its element.

Although there were many bikes made that were faster than the big Harley, there was no bike equal to it for cruising and touring. At speed the motor vibration stops, and the power curve opens up at relatively low rpms and makes the bike easy to ride. Riding double felt almost no different than riding solo on the big roadster. The ninety-six-cubic-inch motor has a long legacy of reliable service that had been fine-tuned over decades of producing the same basic engine with continual refinements. Once on the road, it gave the feeling of being a living and breathing beast connected with its rider in a way that is impossible to explain to those who hadn't experienced it for themselves.

Against all common sense and good judgment, he never wore a helmet, which detracted from his sensation of freedom and connection with his surroundings. He didn't want to survive a bad crash anyway. He chose to take his chances and insured that he rode carefully and defensively. The air felt heavy, clean, and fresh against his face as he cruised through the darkness.

The rider was a lean, rugged man with piercing blue eyes, chiseled facial features, and short dark hair slightly graying at the temples. He had a short list of good friends. Universally, they described him as the most independent, free-spirited individual they had ever known with an uncanny ability to focus and concentrate. They said that getting caught in the stare and focus of his eyes was enough to wilt the unprepared. He was a man born of the wide-open, hard-baked, wind-blown Texas prairie. His father had been an independent oil man with huge swings in his business fortunes. Through boom and bust he was constantly on the lookout for the next strike. His life had been comprised of always hustling the next grub stake to fund another hole in the ground, looking for the next mother lode of West Texas crude on the latest mineral lease that couldn't miss. His father had lived life on his own terms and had enjoyed the best and worst of times. Through it all, he had a big laugh and a good word for anybody with time to spend listening. His mother had died shortly after he was born, and his father was all he had known growing up except for the countless girlfriends and mistresses. His father's death had hit him hard several years ago, and for some reason this morning, the man was smiling to himself and thinking about his father as he rode the big chrome machine through the morning mist. He was riding east and watching the sun peep over the horizon.

The day was heating up already as the sun claimed its place in the sky. The July morning was starting to give signs of the oncoming heat and humidity in store for all those who made

Florida their home. The summer weather pattern brought brutal heat and humidity every day, with showers almost every afternoon. Most parts of the state get more than 100 inches of rain every year. Those who knew, understood, and loved the beautiful state understood how vital the rain is for the delicate ecology and never cursed it.

Thoughts of the man's father passed as he rolled smoothly along the back roads on the big bike. He was on his way to meet his best friend for a weeklong lobstering and fishing trip in the Keys. They went down every year for "mini-season" to catch a limit of lobster and fish for the abundant mahi-mahi in the brilliant blue waters. The lobster season closed every year to recreational and commercial harvest. Before the season was re-opened again to commercial harvest, recreational divers were given the opportunity to dive for the spiny lobsters before their population was decimated again by the commercial fishermen with their mountains of wooden traps. The mini-season always created a Roman orgy of sunburnt, hungover, maniac lobster hunters dragging on ski ropes behind small boats and chasing the crustaceans out of every hole, coral head, and rock ledge they could find. The mini-season is the last Wednesday and Thursday of July every year. Most true sportsmen avoided the weeklong craziness at all costs, but the two old friends had continued the yearly sojourn out of pure stubbornness and tradition.

His father had taught him how to lobster as a teenager off of his boat that he kept moored at the Faro Blanco marina in the Middle Keys town of Marathon. Many good memories of those carefree times came flooding back as he thought about the days of diving, fishing, and lazing around the pool at the marina, and coming back each year for mini-season was his way of celebrating the good times of young adulthood spent with the friend he was riding to meet.

Cody Houston had spent a lot of time during the summer unsupervised on his father's boat in the Keys both as a teenager and young adult passing time there during summer breaks in college. He met Dillon Luther his first day at the marina after his father decided to dock his new boat in Marathon. Dillon was holding down a summer job at the marina and the two were almost inseparable from that first day. Being the same age, same size and build, and fearless swimmers, divers, and fishermen, they had bonded as close as two friends could during those long summers in Marathon. Eventually, his dad had lost the boat in one of the eventual downturns in his volatile business, but the two had remained fast friends. Cody had served as a junior officer in the Navy Special forces after graduating from college. After college, Dillon had gotten into computers, landed a job with NASA, and now lived in Titusville in a soulless subdivision featuring a golf club and street after street of the same houses painted similar pastel colors. Dillon had gone on to get married and had two young sons with Laura, a girl he had met at NASA and married after a brief and intense romance.

The annual trek to Marathon was just as important to Dillon as it was to Cody. Having grown up in Marathon and loving the water as he did, the trip was a chance for them both to reconnect on familiar territory. They had made a solemn vow to never miss a year of time together stalking the wily crustaceans. Although they had included others on their annual trips before, over the years the trip had dwindled down to just the two of them getting together to relax, catch a few "bugs," and fish offshore in Dillon's center console boat he called the *Jacques Crusteau* in parody of the name of the famous French diver and the primary use of the boat for hunting crustaceans. They had called the boat that for so long now that neither could really remember how the name came together. Dillon had re-powered the twenty-five-foot boat with two new Mercury four-stroke outboards and he was anxious to run the boat offshore for an extended time to see how his new motors would work out.

Laura Luther was standing outside on the front lawn with the family's pet Labrador retriever as he glided up to the house with his motor off to keep from waking up the two sleeping kids with the bike's rumble. She was a slender, pleasant, attractive woman who was completely devoted to her husband and family. She had come to know Cody through countless stories of raucous exploits that he had with her husband from a long-ago time before she was part of her husband's life. She was wise enough to know that Cody the carefree bachelor was an important person to her husband, but she always viewed him as a possible threat to her happy suburban home life because he was untamed and led an unencumbered life that her husband might envy. Cody's relationship with her had always been cordial but distant as a result. Cody chalked it up to her natural instinct to be wary of any potential threat to her home life and never held it against her. She loved his best friend, and Dillon loved her; they were happy together. They had produced two hard-headed, rough-and-tumble boys together who worshipped their father like a rock star idol. In private conversations that men have together at times after a full day of fishing and lobstering and too much tequila, Dillon had confirmed how much his wife and kids meant to him. Women rarely completely trust their men, many times for good reason. In Dillon's case, he was completely devoted to his wife and family at a level that she couldn't know because she would never be there when Dillon spoke of her before his best friend with no reason to not tell the truth. Laura viewed Cody with suspicion only because she saw him as untamed, uncommitted to a home life like her husband was. Two kids, a dog, mortgage, minivan, and four-door sedan in the garage. Dillon had fully converted from a carefree bachelor life to a tee-ball coaching, minivan driving, computer systems specialist living in a suburban subdivision full of kids.

Cody pulled the kickstand down on the big bike and leaned it over as he swung his leg over the saddle. Laura came up and hugged him while the friendly lab sniffed at his boot.

"Dillon is getting the last few things together and putting them in the boat. I swear he is so anal about this trip," she said. "He has hardly been thinking about anything else for the past month. Just what is it that you guys do down there that is such a big deal anyway? By the time you pay for this trip down there and back for the week, I could have bought twenty times as much fish and lobster tails at the grocery store." She smiled bravely when she said it, knowing it would never change anything.

"Don't you worry, Laura. I am personally guaranteeing a record catch this year. No messing around, we are going to put the silly grocer in his place this year. We'll have our hunt and feed the whole neighborhood upon our return. Your neighbors will celebrate us at campfires throughout the neighborhood for years to come. *Kumbaya* will resonate through your suburban paradise in celebration of the memory of our return."

"It's not so bad, you know." The petite woman looked seriously into his face. "I have some friends that would love to meet you and move your stubborn carcass into four bedrooms and a double-car garage. If you weren't such a loner you might see how nice it is to be with someone and maybe start a family yourself."

The tall man's eyes twinkled when he smiled at her and said, "How can I get serious about meeting someone when you are already married to my best friend? Every time I met somebody I would always compare them to you and I could never be happy. You have ruined my only chance at ever experiencing true happiness."

"Typical man response to a serious comment," snorted the

woman as she grabbed the big Lab's collar to keep him from getting into the food bags on the ground.

Just as Cody pulled out the cigars from the leather saddle bag, he looked up to see his friend rounding the corner of the house with tickle sticks, nets, ski ropes, snorkels, masks, and fins in one hand and a 100-cubic-foot aluminum tank in the other. The exertion was making his face ruddy as he set the tanks and gear down in front of Cody.

"Well, it looks like Laura is keeping you fed," Cody remarked about the heaving paunch around his friend's midsection.

"That is what good living does to a man," said Dillon while grinning from ear to ear and rubbing his stomach. "When we got married, Laura couldn't heat soup. Now I can't keep her out of the kitchen."

Laura wrapped her arm around her husband's waist and said, "I like him this way. He is my big stud lobster man. You never seem to even gain a pound though, Cody."

Cody chuckled at Dillon, who kissed his wife's forehead and opened the box of cigars. "Fernando came through for us, buddy. Twenty-four box-cut Padróns fresh off the line in Dominica. Just the way you like them."

Dillon picked one up, sniffed it, and said, "We might have to spark a couple of these bad boys up on the drive down."

"Speaking of the drive down, you bad-ass hunters better get on the road if you want to get out of here before the fan club gets up," Laura said in reference to Dillon's two boys. "You know if they see you here, you are never going to get out of town on your sacred schedule. It will be bad enough on me when they see their favorite uncle's motorcycle here and the boat gone."

The two men took turns hugging the slight woman and quickly packed the remainder of the gear on the boat the way they had countless times before. As she usually did, Laura had packed them a cooler of water, fruit, beer, and snacks for the drive down to the Keys. Dillon had fueled the truck and boat, and stowed the gear on board the night before so that they could make an easy early morning getaway.

Dillon was driving the big Ford F-250 up the I-95 onramp when Cody turned around to check out the boat to see how it was riding on the triple-axle trailer. "The *Crusteau* is looking good, buddy. New canvas in the T-top, new motors, good wax job. We are going to look like we know what we are doing. We look like a professional operation now compared to last year when I thought we looked like Sanford and son."

"Yeah, I spent some money on the old barge this year." Dillon chuckled. "I got some bonus money that Laura did not already have spent, and she let me put it in the boat without complaining too much. I had to promise to start taking the boys next year on our trip, though. What do you think about that?"

Cody took a long pull on the Padrón and reflected about the fact that this would be the last time he and his friend would be taking this trip without being loaded down with the "ankle biters" as he affectionately referred to them. The two boys were complete animals most of the time and they fought like most brothers do over just about anything. They listened to their father, though, and they revered their motorcycle-riding, quiet uncle with the intense stare that completely intimidated them.

Dillon looked over at his friend again and said, "That was a question, Chief. What do you think about it?"

"I think it is high time that those two boys learned how to do something besides play video games," said Cody. "They are both great swimmers, neither gets seasick when we go fishing, and they have been talking about catching lobster since they could open their mouths. I don't think we can drown them, and they are too ornery to leave at home with Laura without you around, so maybe we should bring them along."

"Okay, buddy, if you insist." Dillon grinned. He looked like a little boy himself, thought Cody. Cody could take or leave the trip except for spending time with his friend. Dillon got so damn excited about it every year that Cody could never let him down and miss the trip. "I'll keep the boys in line," said Dillon. "They are little hellions but they still listen to their dad, because they know I'll fire up some butts if they don't."

Cody laughed uncontrollably at the ridiculous statement. "You are the biggest softie I have ever seen with those boys, man. They run all over you and, for the record, I don't think that you have ever fired up either of their little asses."

His friend laughed indignantly. "So what if I've never spanked them. They still listen to me because they think I might." He then launched into a full download about every detail of the school fights, baseball practices, soccer games, homework, school achievements, and fishing trips that made up his happy life with his beloved wife and two boys. He had a good and full life and he was as happy as anyone that Cody knew. Hearing Dillon talk made Cody feel like he had a superficial and lonely existence with no future to look forward to when he aged. Three hours later they were pulling into a gas station in Homestead to get fuel, and Cody had gotten completely caught up on everything that his friend had been doing since he had seen him last.

After switching drivers and grabbing some coffee, they got back on the road. Cody looked over and chuckled at his friend, who had almost instantly dropped off to sleep while the well-worn CD with Jimmy Buffet tunes floated around the cab of the truck. Cody checked the way the big center console boat was riding on the trailer, took a sip of hot black coffee, and settled in for the remaining two-and-a-half-hour pull down to Ramrod Key. After the long download from his friend, Cody was glad for the quiet time while he enjoyed the beautiful water views down the narrow ribbon of asphalt known as A1-A that ran the length of the string of islands they call the Florida Keys. Cody had decided that he was going to break some news to his friend during the trip, and he wasn't sure how Dillon would react. Dillon had the coffee clutched on his lap with both hands as his head drooped down on his chest. Cody reached over and gently pulled the cup out and put it in the drink holder. He hoped his friend would understand what he was going to tell him later that week.

CHAPTER II

The calm, brilliant blue water of the Caribbean gave little opposition to the big center console as it pulled the five bait
pattern through the mid-morning sun. Some gentle tunes floated
out of the storage box mounted speakers in the boat's T-top. The
T-top had special rotating outrigger mounts that, combined with
the three rod holders in the transom, allowed for up to five rigged
ballyhoo baits to be trolled behind the old but sturdy Mako center console.

Beers had been cracked open, cigars had been lit, and the
nonstop back-and-forth between the two old friends had com-
menced as always. At the moment, Cody was doing his best to
ignore Dillon as he was giving Cody grief over the rather large
girl at the pool last night who had unsuccessfully been trying to
talk Cody into slow dancing around the pool deck after the two
had returned from a hard day of lobstering at the ancient mobile
home park resort where they always stayed for lobster season.

"I thought she was going to elbow drop you in the hot tub,
drag you out, and then make you do the bear dance to that Barry
White song. I was afraid, man, for your physical safety. As big as
she was and with as much as she had to drink, if she had fallen on
you it could have broken something. You could have been hurt
and all that flesh could have gotten all up in your face and smoth-
ered you." Dillon was looking at him with mock seriousness with
his ridiculous fishing sombrero that he wore to minimize the sun
on his upper body.

Cody was staring intently at the weed line they were following and hoping that his friend would tire of giving him the red ass over the big girl and change the subject. Since it had been going on for the last five minutes, Cody knew that the subject was going to play out soon. He had so far refused to acknowledge the remarks, but it was not discouraging Dillon from carrying on with his fun.

"I mean, next year we can get separate rooms so that you can have your little tryst with your big mamma without worrying about whether or not I am going to report back to anybody about your pathetic fetish for the big ladies. I mean, Jesus, Chief, I knew you liked 'em curvy, but you could not see the bottoms of that girl's bikini for all the fat rolls. You would have needed crampons and rock climbing gear to get up in there and hit that pussy."

"How about getting me another beer?" Cody asked without responding to the comment.

Just as Dillon was bending over in the cooler and starting to launch into another barrage, they got a strike on the starboard outrigger line, and the reel started singing as the line stripped off it. When they looked back, a big beautiful bull dolphin broke the surface thrashing wildly. Both men instantly knew that they had a potential for a double hookup since dolphins usually run in mated pairs. The two old friends were silently efficient, with Cody at the helm keeping the boat running forward slowly and Dillon retrieving lines and spooling out the one remaining bait to run close to the bull. Just as Dillon was taking over the rod and reel with the big bull dolphin hooked up, the bull's mate hit the remaining bait and Cody left the helm to take over the rod and reel and make sure that the hook was set. They were both smiling broadly as they battled their fish in and eventually gaffed and pulled them into the boat. At least the hookup got his friend off the subject of the big girl, Cody chuckled to himself. Together with the wahoo they had landed earlier while high-speed trolling, the lobsters they had caught over the previous two days, the grouper they speared while checking out all their lobster holes, and the snapper they had speared while diving the Thunderbolt wreck on their first day, they had a full ice chest of meat to deliver back and justify the trip to Dillon's wife for their annual seafood cookout in their neighborhood.

Once the two big dolphins were in the iced locker in the floor of the boat, the two recovered their beers and sat down to look at each other. The sun was almost straight up in the sky and they were still drifting down the weed line they had been fishing for the last hour and a half. Cody lit up the torch and puffed on his cigar until the tobacco lit up and began to smoke again. He passed it to Dillon, who did the same.

For that moment in time, the world was right for the men. They rehashed the dolphin hookup and the earlier wahoo landing while munching on a sandwich and fruit. They had taken a lot of sun over the past week and both had developed their deep-water tans. Dillon was beginning to plan his big neighborhood cookout.

"It wouldn't hurt you to attend my cookout this year. Laura's friend Shirley got divorced a few months ago. She nailed her husband for some new titties, though, before she moved his fat ass out of the house. You ever notice how quickly people get divorced once the wife gets new titties? It never fails—within two months of talking the idiot husband into paying for the new titties, the woman is letting some other guy play with 'em. And all the good husband ever has left is the balance on his credit card.

"Anyway, this girl Shirley keeps asking about you since she saw you over at the house last year unloading the boat with your shirt off. Now I know she might be way too slender for you since you are all into this pathetic new big girl program of yours, but I think she might be worth coming over to check out. She never said two words to me over the last five years and since she got her titties she keeps talking me up so that she can ask me about you. If you don't do something about it, Laura is going to think I have something going on with her and she is going to divorce me. That is how serious this is, Chief. This girl Shirley called me on my *cell* phone last week to ask me when we were coming back. I think she is planning to be there so that you can admire her new chest. You have to come over this year or it's going to cost me my marriage, it's just that simple. You know what would happen to me if Laura found out her newly divorced friend with big new titties was calling me on my cell phone."

Cody looked at his friend in the goofy sombrero while he waved his cigar around and talked about the perils of his suburban existence. He passed the torch to Dillon and pointed at the built-in seat by the transom and said, "Sit down for a minute; I need to talk to you about something serious."

The goofy smile left Dillon's face and he put the unlit cigar in his mouth without looking away from Cody. "Now you are scaring me, Chief. Tell me what's going on with you. I knew you haven't been acting right this trip," he mumbled over the half-smoked cigar.

The two friends sat facing each other with a long silence. For once, Dillon kept quiet until Cody got ready to speak. Cody felt the sense of dread in his stomach intensify. He was tired of this tightness in his stomach that he had felt since deciding to tell his friend about his secret life, and Cody could not stand waiting any longer.

"The life you think I lead is not real," Cody blurted without any fanfare. "I have led a lie for a long time and I have to come clean with you so that you know who I really am and what I do." He was speaking a little faster than he normally did, trying to get this over with. "I am going to be making some changes."

Dillon studied his friend and said, "Chief, I have known you since you were seventeen years old. The last time I counted that was quite a few years. What kind of lie could you be living?" The look on his face showed real concern.

"You think that I make my living making furniture in my shop," said Cody. He stared at Dillon through his sunglasses and paused. Dillon stared back silently.

"The truth is I've been working for a long time for an organized crime syndicate out of Spain on a contract basis. The woodworking I do is only a cover. I haven't made much money selling furniture or doing finish carpentry in a long time. Most of what I make there I give away to people I know and don't get paid for it. I really don't work that hard at that business."

Cody knew that the windup on this was getting to his friend. The punch line to this story was going to hit hard and he had no idea what kind of reaction Dillon was going to have to the truth.

Dillon met his friend's stare and took a long pull on the cigar. "What are you doing for them?" he asked. Dillon now felt a strange feeling in his stomach as though he was about to lose his friend to a truth he had never suspected.

"I kill people who they want killed." Cody took a long pull on the cigar and slowly released the smoke into the air. "When I was going on all those trips to Mexico and Europe, I was going to take someone out. They hire me to move in quickly and quietly from outside the country to take someone out and disappear. Sometimes they want it to look like an accident, a suicide, or a revenge killing, and other times they want it done in public to make a statement. I've had it though, man. I can't do it anymore. I've turned down the last three assignments. I told them that I wasn't going to do any more jobs for them. I've done more jobs than I can remember in the last fifteen years and I can't do it anymore. I can't live this lie anymore and I can't look at myself in the mirror. I want to get back to who I really am and quit living like that."

"Why are you telling me this now if you are quitting? For Christ's sake, Chief, I just thought you liked to travel a lot. How the hell did you get started doing that anyway?" Dillon took a pull on the beer and pulled the sombrero off to wipe the sweat from his head.

Three hours later, Cody had shared the long story of how he had been approached by the only contact he had ever known from the syndicate. His name was Carlos, they always met in public, and they always paid up front in cash. He never saw them after the job was done, and they never had any contact in between jobs. Carlos was a slender, Ducados-smoking smallish man with intense brown eyes and a thick mustache. He was always immaculately tailored and very well mannered. Carlos had sought him out at the mixed martial arts academy where he had been teaching and training after he got out of the military. After visiting with the head instructor at the academy under the guise of finding bodyguards, they had sought him out in private to interview him and find out more about his military sniper training, weapons knowledge, family background, and willingness to travel. He had been trained in Spanish in the military, which made him appealing since most of the assignments took him to Spain, Mexico, and South America.

As a young man recently out of the Navy and full of himself, for Cody the allure of the fast money and excitement of the hunt seemed irresistible. He had no sympathy for the victims. They were all crime lords of one sort or another who had gotten on the wrong side of his employers and had stolen money or drug territory from the syndicate that hired him. It was all seedy business; the majority of his kills were shady characters and they took place in low-rent places where nobody wanted to know anything about anybody else's business. All of the assignments took him out of the country, and he traveled in and out with as low a profile as possible.

He always traveled to his destination country through another country first and then back out through a different country to hide his trail. His employers trusted him to work out the details of the event based on his review of the circumstances of his target's environment and the effect desired. Sometimes they wanted it to look like suicide, sometimes public murder, robbery, car accident, or romantic jealousy. They grew to trust the slender, rugged American for the toughest of assignments and they readily paid for the results. They never asked him to work in the United States, they never had any written, phone, email, or other traceable contact with him, and they never discussed the last job when discussing the next. They provided complete dossiers on the victims with recent pictures and all personal data needed to put together a good plan.

Within a few days of following his target, Cody generally had a workable plan pulled together. Every plan included bail-out and escape contingencies. Cody never recovered any cash or property; he did the wet work only and got away from the scene. Others came in behind him to recover any property, drugs, or cash that was in dispute. When there was an assignment, Carlos showed up unexpectedly and quietly. He would find a nondescript note with a time and place for a public meeting and the two would meet and exchange bags. The one Carlos took would be full of newspapers; Cody took one with money and information on his target. No more contact, no more questions or discussions. They verified the results separately and never bothered him for details. Cody knew they had others watching and verifying his kills but they never interfered or got in his way.

Cody always delivered on his part of the job and for that he was rewarded with all the jobs that he could handle. Once finished, the assignment never came up again. Cody silently left the country and made his way home through another country so that no discernable direct trail could be pulled together from a computer search. Cody generally used either a Soviet-made Dragunov sniper rifle or an AK-103 assault rifle for his assignments if a weapon was required. Cody shipped the weapons into the country in advance packed in metal woodworking tools, and they were always left behind in some swamp, river, lake, or other unrecoverable location. He had never encountered a problem with his carefully planned escapes. He planned his hunt, made his kill, and then slipped out with as little noise and fanfare as possible. He never did his business in his own country and he never had any connection to the people he killed. Unless he were caught in the act, it would be virtually impossible for the police to catch him. There had never been any suspicion shown by anybody about his life or how he made his living.

There were very few people in his life who were close enough to get suspicious about his frequent trips or the fact that he paid for almost everything with cash. Too much cash was hard to disguise from someone with intimate knowledge of your life. Except for the few rarely used credit cards he kept, Cody was almost entirely off the conventional modern radar. No debts, no mortgage, very few transactions that could be traced to him, and almost all purchases in cash. He was in the process of carefully taking the cash that he had been paid for his assignments and cleansing it through many smaller deposits at scattered fake business accounts at banks across the area.

Each deposit was carefully planned to be less than the $10,000.00 cash maximum allowed before the bank was required to report it to the federal agencies. After depositing it into his furniture business account in any of several smaller local banks, he paid out the money to a fake lumber supply business that he owned. From there, he consolidated the money and wired it in larger transactions to another lumber supply company that he had set up out of state. From there, he purchased small commercial real estate properties in the name of the lumber supply company. All the property he purchased was located in a fairly tight radius of the area where his father had lived and where he grew up. He later transferred the properties into a limited liability company that his father had made him an officer of before his death. At some reasonable interval afterward, the property would be sold and the money sent to an out-of-state account in the name of the LLC.

Almost none of the money had ever made it into his personal control. He bought larger ticket items on his credit cards and then paid the credit cards from checks written on the LLC account. Vehicles were put in his name as needed and paid for with wires from the LLC. He took careful precautions to avoid any unneeded personal association with the money. He had slowly and carefully laundered a good portion of the cash, which had been converted into legal certificates of deposit that he no longer had to worry about explaining. Over time, he would sell the remaining few properties and make the same transfers into bank certificates of deposit which he kept in the name of his father's old company. He kept only enough cash on hand for a few years of living expenses and some emergency reserves. Smart investments in real estate had led to other gains that had also helped generate legitimate income.

All the clandestine travel and secret assassinations combined with the secretive and elaborate precautions he took to launder the profits had finally taken its toll on Cody. He was sick of his life and tired of all the secrets. He was tired of not being able to take the people in his life close to him into confidence about what he did and tired of lying about where he went and what he was doing. He was tired of being the paid killer of a crime network. He was oddly detached and ambivalent about the men he had killed. They were generally brutal thieves and drug runners who had crossed his client out of greed. There was no allegiance or loyalty toward the people from the syndicate who employed him other than the completion of the job they paid him to do.

Cody meticulously lived up to their agreements since he never wanted to have a contract put out on him for failure to deliver the expected results. Cody knew that there would not be any sympathy or understanding shown toward him if he were ever caught in the process of doing their jobs or didn't complete an assignment. He understood that he worked completely on his own with no cover or support network of any kind. He was careful in every way about the killings he did. He was a detailed planner, precise in his execution and careful to cover up any tracks he might make. He had never come close to getting caught or failing in his mission. As far as he knew, there was no reason to think that anybody suspected anything about his finances. He lived conservatively and without fanfare in a manner consistent with the way people would expect him to live. Until today, he had never taken anybody into confidence about the secrets of his life.

Dillon had listened intently to the long explanation with uncharacteristic silence and attention. Cody felt exhausted after talking unstopped for hours about how he got started, how he trained exhaustively with his Russian-made sniper rifle, trained in hand-to-hand combat skills with weapons and against weapons, studied explosives, lock picking, car stealing, and worked diligently on several different disguises that he had developed with matching passports and documents. He had risen to the top of his craft, and his services were in demand. When he had made it clear to his contact that he was no longer available for contracts, Carlos had reluctantly shaken his hand and wished him well after a minor low-pitched argument.

Thankfully, he knew nothing about his employers and they had no reason to pursue him or want him harmed for his refusal to take on more contracts. He knew he would never hear from them again and he had no reason to look back on his past. He was glad to finally make a clean break with them.

The sea was calm with gentle rolling waves that allowed the two friends to run at almost thirty knots on their way back into port. Dillon had adjusted the planers on the back of the boat so that they could run through the rolling waves at speed with minimal porpoising. Cody looked over to catch his friend staring at him in amazement with his silly grin. Moments later, Dillon reached into the T-top storage box and grabbed two of the Padróns. He handed them to Cody, who silently unwrapped, clipped, and ignited both cigars with the torch.

As he handed one of them back to Dillon, he quipped, "I wonder if your big woman will be there to meet us when we get back. And more importantly, do you think you could talk her into cleaning these fish for us? You need to take one for the team, Chief. You know we don't want to be spending the whole afternoon cleaning this boat and filleting these fish. You can't expect to wear me out telling me that about yourself and expect me to clean fish afterwards."

Cody cracked a small smile. He scanned the horizon as the buildings on shore peeked over the water line. The water was a deep blue, the sky was clear with the sun shining, the fish box was full, and the sea breeze was cooling as the boat skimmed over the gently rolling waves. There was no place he would rather be and nobody he would rather be with than his best friend. He knew his secret life was over and he felt a great sense of relief. He knew that nothing was changed between them and that his secret past was safe. He was on the path to regaining his old self back and it felt good. The world felt right again and he wondered why he had been gone so long.

CHAPTER III

Cody cursed under his breath when the drill bit slipped off the screw and the Phillips head bit jammed into the underside of the teak wood table that he had fabricated for the large Sea Ray yacht. He was completing a custom interior on the boat based on a design that the owner had come up with to accommodate his granddaughter. She had been involved in a serious car accident and was now confined to a wheelchair. The family was Canadian and planned to use the boat in the Islands later in the year, so Cody was under the gun to complete the renovation within the week. The granite tops, new plumbing fixtures for the revised bathroom, and hydraulic lift to lower her into the cabin had arrived while Cody had been down in the Keys with Dillon. Now he had to complete the extensive refit of the yacht's cabin in the next two weeks in order to have it ready for the family's planned trip. Cody had never met the owner; all of their dealings had been through the phone, email, and wire transfers of the deposit to Cody's account.

Cody had gotten the job through the boat's captain, Mike Timmons. Cody did not do a lot of work on yachts but Timmons had seen the refit of another boat he had done a few years ago and had been impressed. He had referred him to the owner of the boat he captained who had called Cody and sent him the plans that he had drawn up. The owner was a Montreal-based real estate developer by the name of Georges Perrier. He seemed reasonable and easy to deal with. He had immediately agreed to the fee that Cody had quoted him and had sent the wire with the deposit the next day without even waiting for the contract to show up. He had later returned the contract with no changes and a nice handwritten note attached. He had struck Cody as the type of person who would be good to work for.

Georges Perrier had a good friend who owned an elevator manufacturing company that had designed the lift and worked up the plans on the redesigned cabin as a favor to the man who Timmons referred to as G.P. Timmons had delivered the boat to the Westland Marina in Titusville and they had pulled it and placed it on jack stands in their yard for the duration of the refit. Timmons had told him that the kindly Canadian was heartsick about his granddaughter's accident and he was trying to help her through her depression with the refit on the boat to show her that she could still enjoy some of the things that she enjoyed prior to the accident. Evidently, the girl was distraught and inconsolable until her grandfather presented the possibility of the redesign of the boat and a possible boat trip down to the islands that she loved. From that point, Timmons said that his boss had been on a mission to make the boat accommodate the wheelchair-bound young lady.

Cody was sorry to hear about the girl's accident, but he was grateful for the work. If he was going to make it as a legitimate fabrication shop, he would have to take on work like this and do a good job of it under tight time schedules. Until now he had always resisted taking work that forced him into a tight schedule because that took the enjoyment out of it for him. Agreeing to this job was his way of confronting the reality of his new life and showing some of the flexibility that a small business owner had to show.

While Cody had been down in the Keys, the Richardson brothers had completed the demolition of the interior and carefully hauled out the scrap the way that he had asked them to.

The two brothers were not very bright, but they were honest and usually reliable. Cody had used them on different projects from time to time as he needed help on heavier work. They enjoyed working on boats and they appreciated working for him since they always needed something to do which paid well. They had readily agreed to tackle the job in spite of the heat and confined working environment.

After he tightened the last screw into the tabletop, he wiped the sweat off his brow and checked his watch. He packed up his tools and lifted the canvas bag up to the deck. He was finished with the work that had to be done before the lift could be fitted to the boat tomorrow by the elevator company. He had committed to Dillon that he would attend his cookout tonight and he had just enough time to wrap up his work for the day, clean up, and make it over to his friend's house in time for the seafood buffet he was preparing of all the lobster and fish they had caught on their trip to the Keys. The lift would take two days to install and then the granite would go in. After that he had the Richardson brothers scheduled to come back and help him finish all the punch-out work with a day to spare. He felt good about this job and wanted it to work out for the family who owned the boat as he stepped back and admired his work.

He looked over at the water as he laid the heavy tool bags into the back of the truck and noticed several dead fish and sea grass floating on the water; they were being blown up against the seawall where the travel lift piers jutted out into the seawall basin. When he scanned the marina basin and looked over into the overgrown acreage adjacent to the marina, he noticed an inordinate amount of torpedo grass floating all over the basin and numerous dead fish on the rocky shore around the undeveloped property owned by the marina. He made a mental note to ask the owners, Jennifer and Tom Jennings, about it when he saw them.

All the dead fish made it look like a red tide outbreak, but he had not read about it in the paper or seen anything on the local news on television. Tom and Jennifer were a brother and sister who had inherited the marina from their father when he had passed away a few years ago. They were simple but good people who worked hard and were trying to upgrade the property since they inherited it. They had always been good to Cody and they were well liked by everybody who used the marina.

After a quick shower at the marina and a change into some light-colored chinos and a white knit shirt that he pulled from the bag he had packed in his truck, he made fast work of the drive to Dillon's house while he downed a cold beer on the way over. As he pulled up to the house, he spotted Laura helping a tall, slender, busty woman unload some drinks from the backseat of a white convertible.

She called out to him and said, "Just in time, Cody. Can you help us carry these drinks to the backyard?" The slender woman stood almost six inches taller than the petite Laura and she pushed the designer sunglasses back on her head and smiled coyly at Cody as he walked up to the car. "Meet my friend Shirley, by the way."

Shirley offered her hand with the palm down and tossed her long hair over her shoulder while tilting her head in her best sexy pose. Cody gently clasped her hand around the fingers and remarked how nice it was to meet her.

She stared straight into his eyes when she said, "Dillon and Laura told me a lot about you. I was hoping to get a ride on that big Harley someday."

Cody released her hand and took the cases of beer out of Laura's hand. He smiled back at them. "I'll ride it over next time and take you out on it then." He looked over his shoulder as he walked away and said, "I'll get the rest of those in a minute."

He rounded the corner to the back of the house and set the drinks down next to the coolers and tried to protect himself from Dillon's bear hug. There were introductions all around to the neighbors who were helping Dillon monitor the seafood paella on the outdoor stand cooker. There were split lobster tails on the grill and some Bahamian-style mahi-mahi cooking with tomatoes, garlic, butter, and onion slices wrapped in foil on the edges of the grill.

Just as he was done with Dillon's introductions to all the neighbors, Shirley pulled up with a drink she had made for him. It was a tall Jack and Coke with a lime, just the way he liked it. For the rest of the evening, she never left his side. They made a lot of small talk and she surprised him by being a pleasant and charming companion for the evening. She had a pleasing smile, good sense of humor, and Cody knew he would be following up soon with that Harley ride. She stuck around through the cigar smoke and made it clear that she was interested. Before the night was over, they exchanged phone numbers and agreed to meet up again soon. Dillon kept looking over approvingly and was the perfect host the whole night. Cody knew that Laura would put Dillon up to calling for the feedback tomorrow.

On the hour-long drive back to his house that evening, Cody found himself thinking about the dead grass and fish on the shoreline around the marina again and wracked his brain trying to remember if he had ever seen that before. He made a note to find Tom Jennings at the marina tomorrow and ask him about it. He smiled to himself and enjoyed the memory of a nice evening with good people. He felt good about this change of direction in his life. Making the decision to stop the syndicate contract work made him feel like he belonged with regular people without constantly having his guard up about what he did for a living.

CHAPTER IV

Cody pulled up to the marina at mid-morning after a good workout at the academy where he trained for mixed martial arts. He was helping the staff train some of the up-and-coming fighters there get ready for an MMA tournament that was scheduled in a few weeks. Cody was an accomplished grappler. He had never tested beyond brown belt, but his jiu-jitsu skills were acknowledged to be among the best at the academy. At six foot three, he presented a real challenge for the light heavyweights at the academy because of his reach and surprising strength. His striking was fierce and he presented a real challenge to anybody of his size because of his surprising quickness and strength. He submitted several of the fighters that morning in some grueling grappling matches with arm bars and a heel lock. The staff there was asking him to help out in a few days with some sparring with a heavyweight fighter who had punished everybody else at the academy to the point that nobody wanted to spar with him anymore. Cody had the reach to match up with the kid and the power to keep him honest. Cody said he would think about it and get back to them at his next visit.

As he pulled up next to the big Sea Ray at the marina, he noted that the elevator installers had not arrived yet. He walked up the stairs to the boat, unlocked the makeshift door covering the opening down into the cabin, and strode over to the marina office to grab a cup of coffee. He looked again at the torpedo grass floating against the seawalls. It appeared that someone had scooped up the dead fish that he had seen yesterday. He walked through the heavy door leading to the customer lounge and made his way to the coffeepot. Usually there were several people hanging around watching TV and having coffee in the lounge. Cody helped himself to a paper cup of the steaming hot black brew and started walking out to the yard to await the elevator installers. Just as he made it to the door, Jennifer Jennings motioned through the glass window of her small office for him to enter. The little window unit air conditioner was already working hard against the August heat and he quickly slid into the tiny office to see her.

She said, "Your lift installers called me to let you know that they are running late. They said they would get here around 11:30 this morning."

Cody glanced down at his watch and said, "Thanks, Jennifer. Is Tom around?" He wanted to ask about the dead grass and fish.

"Didn't you hear? Tom is in the hospital now, for almost a week. He is not doing too well."

"What's going on with him?" asked Cody. "I hadn't heard anything about this. I just got back from my trip to the Keys for the past week."

The woman looked through the window out into the customer lounge area to make sure nobody was coming in and she lowered her voice to say, "He is having a breakdown, Cody. Things aren't going so well for us lately here at the marina and he is not taking it well."

"The place looks as full as it can be to me, Jen," he replied. "How can things not be going well? I don't think you guys could get another boat in here."

"You know Tom," she said as she wiped her thick glasses with a tissue. "He has always been talking about putting up those condos he dreamed about on the vacant land next to the marina. He took out a bank loan for all the costs to hire the engineers and architects to start the designs on the project, and now the bank is telling us that they won't extend the loan. He doesn't know any-thing about developing condos, Cody. We went to the City twice about getting the project approved and we got denied both times. Since the last time we got rejected, we got a notice from the bank that they aren't going to extend the loan again. Now he is afraid that we are going to lose this place. This marina has been in our family for over thirty years now. He is scared to death that the bank is going to take it from us. He can't handle the stress and he just had a nervous breakdown."

"What happened when he had the breakdown?" asked Cody in disbelief. He had known Tom for a long time and never knew him to be a weak or emotional person who would overreact to a tough situation.

"We had gotten a notice from the bank that said they weren't going to extend the loan, and he went to the bank to talk to Dexter Phillips over at First Commercial. After that guy chased us down trying to throw the money at us, the minute things get a little tough the bank panics and tells us we have to pay them back right away." She grabbed the notice off the top of her in-basket. "Tom got back from the meeting and started walking around the marina yard babbling to everybody about his condos and he just broke down and started crying uncontrollably on the long dock. It was terrible, Code. I have never seen him like that before. He is not the smartest guy and I knew that he was in way over his head with the plans for the condos, but he was so insistent. I didn't want to go against him when we finally got the bank to give us the loan. He chased Dexter around for a long time. Dexter turned us down at first, and I thought it was a dead dream, and then all of a sudden, Dexter shows up here in his flashy BMW and suit and says that he had a change of heart and that he would make us the loan. Next thing I know, Tom is having me sign papers for this big loan, and we use some of it for all this new equipment that we don't need, and all this money is going out the door for architects, engineering studies, civil engineers, surveyors, lawyers, and land planners. Everybody is lining up to get their check and they all want money in advance. Tom isn't real smart with money, Code. He wanted to show me that he could do something good for us by setting up the plan for these condos, but once we spent all this money on the designs and applications, we couldn't get the City to approve it." She sighed heavily and her voice started to break. "We don't make a lot of money after expenses here, Code. The property is valuable but we have had the same boats in here for a long time, and Tom never wants to raise the rents on the people that have been here forever with us. We don't have any way to pay the bank back."

Cody leaned back against the wall and looked at the gentle woman with the thick glasses as she blew her nose into a tissue and wiped a tear out of the side of her eye. "The worst thing is that I just want my brother back. I miss him and need him around here. I can't run this place by myself."

"What hospital is Tom at?" asked Cody.

"Coastal Memorial downtown," she said. "It would mean a lot to me if you go see him. He trusts you, Cody. He needs some friends now that can help him get back to his old self."

"I'll go this afternoon," he said. "You are going to get through this, Jen. The bank can't just take this place from you like that. We are going to get you guys some help and work this out. Just hang in there until we get Tom back up on his feet. I have to go now because while we have been talking the guys showed up with that lift for the Sea Ray. I'll go down to the hospital this afternoon and check in on Tom."

"He is heavily sedated. They have him on some sedatives most of the time to keep him numb. I hate seeing him that way but at least he isn't babbling and breaking down." She forced a brave smile and looked at him. "Thanks for caring, Cody. There aren't a lot of people that I can talk to about this."

"No problem, Jen." As he opened the door to her office, he looked back and asked, "What is up with all the dead grass and fish floating around in the basin? I haven't ever seen that before."

"We aren't sure, Code. There hasn't been any red tide or any spills in the marina. It just started happening a few months ago." She was still wiping her eyes and didn't want to look up. "Some of the guys at the marina think that it has something to do with the Russians that Tom is renting the vacant property out to. Come to think of it, it did start happening shortly after they started using the property."

"What are they doing with the property?" asked Cody.

"Tom just signed a long-term lease with them after the condo project failed at the second city council hearing. Supposedly they are keeping some equipment over there, but they only go over there at night so we don't know. They cut a trail into the back part of the property down by the shoreline. Every time Tom has gone over there he has never seen any equipment or anything else. All we know is that they pay on time just like they said they would and we sure need the money right now."

He saw the two installers looking around for him. "Gotta jump, Jen. I'll check on Tom later and let you know how it went tomorrow." Cody closed the door to the office and downed the last of the coffee while standing at the trash can. He tossed the cup in the can and strode out the door to the customer lounge across the yard to the big Sea Ray. He looked at the truck that the two installers had driven down and studied them through squinted eyes. They were big, beefy guys with pasty complexions. The license plate on the truck was Canadian and the truck had rusted-out rear quarter panels. "Must have been a long trip for you guys," he said.

One of the two men stuck a big paw out and said, "You must be Cody Houston. I am Hank and this is Bud. We are going to install this lift for Georges Perrier."

Cody took the big paw and gave it a firm shake, let go, and shook Bud's hand. "You guys need a hand getting this lift into the boat?" He was immediately questioning how the two of them were going to get the heavy lift from the truck into the boat without doing any damage.

"No, we are just installing the electric systems and the rack today. Tomorrow we have a boom truck coming and we will use it to hoist the lift into place. We need to install some reinforcement in the fiberglass at several points and we'll have to make some cuts in the bulkheads to install the reinforcing we'll need to anchor the frame properly."

"You guys normally install lifts like this so far from home?" Cody could tell right away that these two Canadians were craftsmen, and he couldn't believe that they could possibly be doing jobs this small all over North America.

"Nah," Bud piped up. "GP is a good friend of the owner of our company and he orders a lot of elevators for his buildings from us. I think our owner designed and built this lift for him as a personal favor and I don't even think he is charging him for it."

"This Georges, or GP as everybody calls him, must be some guy," said Cody. This had to rank up there with favor of the year if he wasn't charging for it. He was impressed with the pull that the boat owner had.

"Our boss's daughter is good friends with Georges' daughter," said Bud. "They have been out on this boat together many times. Georges and our boss have been friends for many years. Besides that, he orders a lot of elevators." Hank laughed. "Our boss picked us for this job to make sure that it goes right. We know we only have two days to get it done and it has to be done right by end of day tomorrow. It'll be our asses if it isn't."

Cody spent an hour reviewing the plans, working through the cuts in the bulkhead, the reinforcing they would put in, and the bolting pattern. After making sure that they had a good workable plan, he directed them to a decent restaurant for lunch and left the two big Canadians to themselves. He made his way across town and checked in at the front desk of the hospital to find out what room Tom Jennings was in. He found his friend heavily sedated and sleeping on his back with his mouth wide open. The TV mounted on the wall in the room was blaring. Tom was snoring loudly and Cody looked over at the other man in the room. There were tubes running out of both of his arms and he was passed out too. Good thing, Cody thought, because between the TV and the snoring, the racket in the room was almost like being in a jet backwash. He grabbed a piece of paper and a pen from the nightstand next to Tom's desk and left him a quick note. He jotted down his cell phone number and scribbled out a note telling Tom to call him when he woke up.

The hospital was freezing cold and smelled antiseptic. The nurses looked frazzled and always in a hurry with little sympathy for the people they were attending to. Cody could not think of anything he could say to Tom that could possibly give him any more motivation to get out of there than the hospital itself. It felt more like a place to get sick than to get healed. He called the marina and left a message with Jennie on his way out of the hospital to let her know that Tom was sleeping. Even though he hadn't spoken with her brother, he knew she would appreciate the effort. He looked at his watch as he hustled out the door of the hospital. He needed to get to his shop and begin the first application of polyurethane on the interior trim pieces so that he had them finished and ready to install in the Sea Ray when the lift install was finished. He smiled to himself as he thought about how he was beginning to feel all the usual pressure that people with normal lives experience.

Cody felt like he had been reborn. He felt sharp and alive again knowing that he had made a life change and was leaving the old bad news behind him. The simple stresses he felt now seemed minor in contrast with the normal challenges he normally dealt with in his work, but it felt good to let them become important and take over his consciousness the way they were.

CHAPTER V

The monotonous drone of the high-tech dance club music seemed out of place with the bright afternoon sun that beat down on the old house that was surrounded with a stand of giant live oaks on one side and an old abandoned citrus grove on the other. There was a collection of late-model European brand sports sedans parked all over the yard that sparkled in the bright sunlight. The girl had never been to this house before, but she had heard some of the other girls talking about it and knew that she was in for a rough gig with the crowd in this house. They paid well, though, if you did what they wanted. In her position that was what she needed right now.

She pulled her small car up next to a black Mercedes sedan with tinted windows and checked her makeup before she got out. Her shoulder-length brunette hair framed her pretty face that still looked fresh and young even though she felt old from working at the escort service. She was braless in a loose-fitting silk top with her large breasts swinging back and forth with each movement. Adjusting her short skirt, she clumped across the yard in spike heels, trying to look as sexy as she could manage with the strap from the small bag draped over her shoulder. She felt a twinge of fear in her stomach as she pushed the doorbell button and heard the buzzer sound over the thumping music. Half of her wanted to run across the yard, jump in her little car, grab her young baby, and drive home to Alabama as fast as she could. The other half of her knew that she couldn't live with the boredom that she would find once she got there. She stayed, waiting for the front door to open.

The longhaired man was shirtless; he pushed the screen door open with a sawed-off shotgun. "Who you here for?" he demanded in a thick accent. His arms, chest, and shoulders were covered in tattoos. He studied the girl carefully and scanned the yard to make sure that she was alone.

"They sent me for Dmitry." The girl took a step back on the porch.

"What your name," he said, leering at her breasts and legs.

"Karen," she said as she tried to look past the man inside the house.

The man turned sideways in the door and motioned for the girl to come inside. He gave her a crude goose on the backside as she brushed past him in the door. He yanked the bag off her shoulder and rifled it, leaving the lingerie hanging over the side of the bag. Satisfied that there was no weapon, he put his arm around her and walked her into the living room, where he proudly lifted up her skirt and said, "New pooosy for Dima." He laughed as the girl demurely tried to pull her skirt down and tear away from the man. He staggered over to the couch and pulled a semi-conscious girl off the couch and laid her on the floor to make room for him to flop down. The passed-out girl was naked except for her panties. Karen recognized her from the escort service that sent her there.

The stench of smoke from the water pipe and cigarettes was almost nauseating to the girl. She looked across the room at the giant man slumped down in the armchair. There was a beautiful blonde girl sitting on the arm of the leather chair passed out with her head on his shoulder with a dazed, emotionless expression on her face and a half-filled cocktail glass still in her hand. He had a bathrobe on with black socks still on his feet. The robe was open at the top, exposing tattoos that looked similar to those she had seen on the longhaired man's chest and back. His hair was closely cropped on the sides and crew cut on top. The coffee table in front of the couch was strewn with an assortment of drugs, paraphernalia, liquor and champagne bottles. This party had been going on for a while, from all appearances. Karen quickly understood that she was the second shift of the entertainment for this party. All the girls from the first shift looked like they were petering out, so these two were calling for reinforcements to keep the party going.

"Where's the other girl?" the man asked in a surprisingly low voice with just a trace of accent. She could barely hear above the music. The giant man looked her over from head to toe and motioned for her to come closer. He gently rubbed the back of his hand over her erect nipples and reached up her skirt to rub the insides of her thighs. He studied her face without saying a word and then nodded at the longhaired man.

The longhaired man crushed out his cigarette, rolled over on the couch, and fished out a wad of $100 bills. He peeled off four of them and slung them on the table without getting off the couch. "Call service." He grinned through a mouth full of bad teeth. "You tell them get other girl Tatiana over here now."

Karen gently pulled away from the large Russian and picked the cash up from the table. She tucked the money in her purse and pulled out her cell phone to call in to the escort service. She walked into the kitchen to escape the worst of the droning music noise. The older woman at the service cut her off as she always did. "Are Nikki and Angel okay?" she breathlessly asked. "They've been there for almost four hours. How many guys are there at that party with you?"

As Karen started to answer, a muscular, bald, tattooed man entered the kitchen and grabbed a bottle of water from the refrigerator. He leaned against the sink, staring at her from across the room while he guzzled the water from the plastic bottle.

"Karen, are you there? Are you there?" frantically asked the older woman. "What the hell is going on?"

The girl turned her back to the man and leaned slightly forward while she spoke in a hushed voice. "Everything's okay. Angel and Nikki look like they had too much to drink and they are both passed out. These guys keep asking me about some other girl that is supposed to be coming. Have you sent someone else out here with me? These guys give me the creeps, Liz. I am scared to death here; they have guns and drugs everywhere."

"Tatiana should be there in about fifteen minutes. They like her because she's Russian and they can talk with her. Try to get Nikki and Angel sobered up, sweetie. You girls look out for each other. Those guys are regulars but they can get a little rough sometimes."

"Okay, but call her and tell her to hurry. I don't know how many of these guys are here." Karen hung up the phone and looked at the bald man, who was still staring at her through his black-rimmed sunglasses.

"Do you have a bathroom where I can change into my outfit?" she asked him meekly, holding up the small bag that she had carried into the house.

The bald man growled in a gruff, low voice, "No Ingleesh," and pointed her in the direction of the living room. The girl walked back into the living room and found the bathroom in the hallway. She quickly changed into her outfit and packed her bag with the clothes she wore in. As she walked out of the room, the giant man in the bathrobe motioned for her to come over and sit on his lap while he talked on a phone.

She tried to walk as sexy as she could across the filthy room and sat on the unoccupied leg. The beautiful blonde who Karen knew as Angel had passed out. Karen took her glass and set it on the table next to the chair. The man took her hand and placed it on his chest while he talked in hushed tones in Russian. He moved Karen's hand up to show her where he wanted her to rub his temple. Karen gently rubbed both sides of the large man's head as he looked up at her and nodded his approval. The man looked like he was starting to get agitated at the other person on the phone. She was gradually watching his face turn red and his voice started getting louder. All of a sudden he roughly pushed both the girls off his lap and started yelling in Russian. He viciously threw the phone against the wall while waving his arms and spitting, yelling at the other Russians in the room. Before she knew it, there were six men in the front room of the house talking loudly and trying to calm down the big man.

In the middle of this madness, a petite girl walked through the back door of the kitchen and immediately walked up to the big man called Dmitry and started massaging his back and trying to calm him down. She talked with several of the other Russians in their language and went down the hall to the bathroom. Karen quickly moved down the hall and entered the bathroom before the small girl could close the door. She breathlessly asked, "Are you Tatiana?"

"Yes," she replied. "What's your name?"

"What's going on in there?" Karen asked, ignoring the other girl's question.

"They are having some kind of dispute with their Haitian partners," the petite Russian girl said. "It's better that you don't know too much or ask any questions." She looked up at the other girl and asked, "You've never been here before, have you?"

"No, and I heard these guys can get rough."

"A little, but I can keep them under control. I won't let them hurt us." She looked at herself in the mirror and smoothed out her low-cut top to reveal smallish but perky breasts. "What is your name?" she asked for the second time.

"Sorry," Karen said, blushing at her rudeness. "My name is

Karen and I am new to this business. I have only been out two other times and it was never to a place like this."

"Stay close to me. These guys are okay but they get messed up and they can be hard to handle."

They walked out together and joined the men in the large living room who were passing a bottle of vodka among themselves and talking in more muted tones. All the men were looking at the large-framed Dmitry who was still red-faced but no longer spitting while he talked. He grabbed Tatiana and she squealed as she wrapped her legs around his waist and arms around his neck while they walked over to the chair. He stepped over the passed-out brunette and sat down with Tatiana in his lap. They were talking rapidly in Russian and completely engrossed in each other. Karen walked over to the longhaired man who had paid her and locked her arm in his and began rubbing his shoulders. It was going to be a long night and she wanted to find someone she could feel comfortable with. At least the brute spoke some broken English. He flashed her a toothy grin as he led her down the hallway to one of the filthy bedrooms.

CHAPTER VI

The evening air felt cooling as the big motorcycle rumbled through the traffic. The pavement still radiated the heat from the strong sunshine of the day. As long as the bike stayed in motion and the fresh evening air washed over them, the ride was comfortable. With the heat from the engine combining with the heat pulsing up from the pavement at stoplights, the two riders felt some discomfort. Shirley was a trooper, though. She never said a word. She had jumped right on the bike with Cody without any hesitation and had refused the helmet that he had offered her.

Cody had called her to follow up on their introduction and had arranged for the date on the night that he was planning to test run the big Sea Ray owned by Georges Perrier. The work was completed on the big yacht and her captain, Mike Timmons, was scheduled to walk the boat with Cody tomorrow and sea trial her after the refit. Cody had permission to take her out for a preliminary checkout run and planned to do so with his new friend along. Timmons had no problem with Cody bringing Shirley along for a date or his plans to have dinner with her on the boat in the river. He was a well-known rascal himself and frequently had his stable of strumpets onboard for parties and cruises. As long as Cody cleaned up afterward, there would be no harm.

Shirley had been very pleased to hear from Cody and jumped at the chance for a ride on the motorcycle and dinner cruise out on the yacht. She led a mundane life of work as a pharmaceutical sales rep and she found herself surprisingly lonely after her divorce from a man who she had not loved for many years. Cody was a much-needed change of pace in her world and she had meticulously prepared herself for her date with new sexy lingerie, nail appointment, and a slight hairstyle change with some summer highlights to bring out her tanned complexion. She was a striking woman who turned heads but she rarely encountered men who interested her. She had watched Cody carefully at the dinner party and learned a lot about the man from her friend Laura by pumping her for as much information as she could get her friend to reveal. She had not stopped thinking about him since she had gotten to know him at Laura and Dillon's party. She liked his voice, his calm mannerism, and his eyes had the ability to knock her into a trance. She had always been attracted to taller men because of her own height and she loved feeling small standing next to him with his broad shoulders and muscular arms. Despite her better judgment, she intended to close escrow with him tonight and make this a night that they would both remember. Because of her lengthy unhappy marriage, the separation and divorce, and her lack of luck meeting guys she was attracted to, she had not been with a man in a long time and she was as ready as she could ever remember for that to happen. Cody met all of her criteria and she loved that he was setting up this elaborate date for the two of them to get to know each other better. This was a perfect opportunity to break her sexual drought.

Cody liked having the tall, slender woman on back of his bike. She had packed a small bag to bring with her that had some boat shoes and other personal items which they had stowed in the saddlebag of the bike. She had dressed appropriately for the bike ride and had brought along a few things to make herself comfortable on the boat as well. Cody had brought her a jacket for the ride back because he knew she would probably get cool when the evening finally siphoned off the Florida heat from the air. He wasn't sure how late the evening was going to last, but he was pretty certain that he was ready to make it last as late as she would allow it to after looking at her pretty smile when she swung her long leg over the bike. She had looked really sharp when she came out of the house in her spike boots, spaghetti strap top, and tight jeans. She had lightened her long strawberry blonde hair color since Cody had seen her last and it made her look very sexy with her tan complexion and bright red lipstick. Cody was trying to remember why he had resisted meeting this beautiful lady in the first place. He couldn't come up with any reasonable excuse as they pulled up in front of the big Sea Ray at the transient slips at the marina. During the ride she had wrapped her arms around his chest, held herself close to him, and Cody had reached back to rest his left arm on her knee. It felt like she had been a passenger on his bike for a million miles already.

Cody had the marina yard hands pull the boat off the boat stands in the yard that morning with the big travel lift transporter. They had slipped two hefty straps around the boat's hull and had slowly picked the boat up and moved it out to the end of the piers which jutted into the marina basin. The big Sea Ray strained the travel lift since it was at the edge of the equipment's load and size capacity. They had slowly lowered the yacht into the water again under Cody's supervision and he had fired up and checked out all the systems and engines that afternoon while docked in the marina. He had figured out the GPS, radar, depth finder, bow thrusters, electrical generator, air-conditioning, and the new hydraulic lift system that he had installed. They all worked flawlessly. He had gotten the stereo and satellite TV system going with ease and had spent some time running the big twin Caterpillar diesels at idle that afternoon to make sure that the cruise that night would go off without a hitch. He had familiarized himself with the bow thrusters on the boat and had slipped the lines to take the boat out for a slow lap around the marina basin to back the yacht into the slip that he had been instructed to take for the night by the marina dockmaster. After insuring that he could easily operate the boat and back it into the slip by himself without counting on anyone else for assistance, he knew that he was ready. He had transferred the evening's provisions from his truck onto the boat before he left that night so that he had the boat completely cleaned, stocked, and ready to go for the cruise.

Cody pulled the bike up to the back of the boat and swung his leg over the saddle. Shirley smiled at him coyly and said, "That was a lot of fun. I hadn't been on a motorcycle since college. I felt really safe with you, though. My old boyfriend used to scare the hell out of me."

"I'm glad you enjoyed the ride," he said. "You were a pleasure to have on back. Why don't you go on board and change into your shorts while I get everything together and ready to go."

Shirley stepped onto the board plank dock and down into the big boat. Cody noted with approval that she took her boots off before stepping on the boat deck and quickly changed at the helm behind the seat without having to go below deck. This was a savvy and easy to get along with lady who did not need a lot of hand holding or coddling. When she came out from behind the seat back in her shorts and boat shoes, Cody could not help admiring her long, tan, shapely legs.

"Nice wheels," he said jokingly.

She smiled sweetly at the compliment and said, "Can I pour you a drink?"

"You'll find everything down in the galley. I'll have to show you how to operate the lift in order to get down there."

Cody showed her how the lift operated and they rode the cab down together into the galley, where he found his bag and ducked into the restroom to change into his own shorts and boat shoes and silk shirt. She mixed a stiff drink and squeezed a quarter wedge of lime into it.

"Is that how you like it?" She held out the drink to him as he finished pulling on his shoes. "I want to make sure that I am making your drink the way you like it." The air conditioner had been doing its job and the galley was nice and cool. Her nipples were erect and pushing out of her shirt.

"That's perfect," he said as he sipped out of the insulated plastic tumbler. She had chosen the tumbler that said "Captain" on it for his drink. Her drink cup said "First Mate." She slid next to him and rubbed his back. "What do you want me to do now to help?" she asked as she looked up at him. Cody could feel the sexual attraction and fought off the desire to put his arms around her and kiss her the way she wanted him to. He knew he had her where he wanted her and he already knew how this evening was going to turn out. She was giving him all the signals and signs. He knew it was his responsibility to let her have some element of doubt about whether he found her attractive. In doing that he would further arouse her desire and make the eventual outcome more satisfying for her. He didn't just want to be a pushover for her obvious allure. She needed to know that he would dictate the pace of the evening and he would throw his move when he was ready. Until then, he wasn't playing his cards and she was going to have to wonder. Once he put his move on, there would be no doubt about what he was feeling and what he wanted.

"Let's fire this bad boy up and get this program moving." Cody grabbed her hand and gently led her over to the lift for the ride up to the helm station. He felt her substantial breasts against his arm. He smiled as he thought about the inquisition he was going to get from Dillon about how this evening turned out.

Cody cranked up the two big diesels and went to the bow to throw the line and pull the fenders. Shirley had already removed one of the two back lines off the cleat and was holding the other line waiting for her captain to get to the helm. Cody worked his way back to the helm after pushing off from the dock to give a better angle to ease out of the slip. He pushed the throttle on the port engine and gently goosed the yacht forward. The bow thrusters pulled the bow over, and he made a slick and effortless escape from the slip without any banging or drama. He pointed at the book of music and told her to pick something out. She picked out an Eagles concert DVD and he loaded it into the DVD player that played it on the ceiling-mounted TV next to the helm station and surround-sound system. The sound was crisp and clear and complemented the cruise nicely. As they exited the marina basin and turned into the main channel, Cody turned the sound up slightly to overcome the noise of the engines as he pushed the big boat up to a stately five knots. The evening air over the water felt moist and cool and provided a refreshing change to the hot summer Florida daytime heat that baked the mainland all day.

Shirley pulled herself close to Cody and he put his arm around her shoulders. "Thanks for putting this bike ride and cruise together. This is really nice. I haven't ever had a date like this before." She kissed his cheek and wrapped her arms around his waist. Cody casually kept his arm draped over her shoulder and calmly answered her questions about all the instruments and navigational electronics at the helm station. She looked intently at him while he rambled on about each piece of gear. He could tell that she was not listening to a word that he said and was just asking him questions to keep him talking. She was looking directly into his eyes and acting like she was fascinated with his simplified explanation about how GPS works while letting her mind wander into thinking about how she was hoping the evening would turn out. This big stubborn man was proving to be more of a challenge than she had anticipated and it was causing her to work harder to get the attention she wanted from him than she was used to. She kept wondering why she liked that about him so much and why it made her want him so much more.

After about a half hour of cruising down the Intracoastal, Cody pulled the big boat out of the channel over a deep grass flat that he knew would accommodate the draft of the Sea Ray. Shirley went down to the galley and started pulling together the food that Cody had stocked the galley with. She smiled when she noticed the chilled bottle of champagne Cody had put into the cooler and the fresh-cut flower that she knew he had gotten for her. She liked the thought that he had been thinking of her when he picked out the rose. She put the partially opened bloom up to her nose to inhale the sweet fragrance.

Cody busied himself turning the bow of the yacht into the current and then dropped the anchor. As he let the gentle current pull the line out of his hands to achieve the proper scope, he carefully wrapped the line around the bow cleat. Cody fished the boat's table cloth out of a storage locker and allowed it to settle onto the top of the table in front of the built-in seating at the transom.

They quickly laid out the little feast of brie cheese, fruit, baguette, and roasted chicken. Cody casually uncorked the champagne bottle and poured two flutes of the golden beverage. Shirley took hers from his hand and met his toast while looking directly into his steely blue eyes. He looked at her and leaned over to kiss her cheek. He whispered in her ear, "I'm glad you're here with me tonight." She beamed back at him, took a bite out of a strawberry, and put the rest of it into his mouth to share it. They both took sips of their champagne and washed down the fruit.

After relaxing through their meal, they wound up leaning back with their feet up with Shirley sitting between Cody's legs. They quietly talked and laughed for several hours in the moonlight.

They polished off the champagne and Cody fought off the urge to fire up a cigar. Cody liked this long-legged lady with the nice smile and good sense of humor. He didn't want to do anything like smoking a cigar that might set the mood back. He liked where things were going. Shirley excused herself to go downstairs and Cody heard the door open to the small head downstairs. He closed his eyes and sighed in contentment. The fresh breeze, moonlight, and champagne were making him very relaxed. He could smell a trace of the sweet perfume Shirley was wearing.

Cody briefly nodded off while Shirley was downstairs. He opened his eyes when he heard the lift gate open. He turned his head and saw Shirley walking naked toward him holding her rose in both hands. She had the look of a lady who knew exactly what she wanted.

An hour later they were locked in an embrace, looking into each other's eyes. They were spent and completely satisfied. Cody's clothes were strewn everywhere along with the pillows, towels, and leftover food and dishes. Shirley got up and mixed a cocktail for Cody and took a long sip before she gave it to him. She was completely comfortable being naked on the boat. Cody felt somewhat sheepish parading around with his tackle out. He snagged his shorts and pulled them on while Shirley mixed their drink. He kissed her cheek while taking the cocktail and told her he was going to start pulling the anchor to get them back to the marina. It was already midnight and they had about forty-five minutes of cruising to get back to their slip at the marina.

While Cody was pulling the anchor, Shirley got dressed and put on another music DVD and straightened up the table and plates without being asked. She brought Cody's shirt and shoes to the helm station and held them for him as he pulled them on. "All decent now," he said as he fired the big diesels up and turned on all the electronics.

She leaned up against him and sighed, "I don't want tonight to end," while looking up at him wistfully.

The big yacht cruised nicely through the night at an easy, comfortable speed. Cody wasn't in any hurry to end the night, either. After briefly probing into Cody's family history and not getting any real traction, Shirley started going into great detail about her own family. She told him all about her sisters and her brother, mother and father and beloved grandmother. Just as she was getting to her cousins, they approached the old abandoned sailboat that was resting on the outer edge of the Intracoastal channel, signaling that they were only a few hundred yards from the channel that split off to go to the marina. Cody heard the GPS alarm go off, announcing their arrival at the pre-programmed waypoint, and pulled the throttles back and killed the engines while he figured out how to turn the irritating alarm off. Shirley took the occasion to sneak a kiss in while Cody was bent over studying the GPS. Cody draped his arm over her shoulder and held her close to him as he stood up. When he looked over her shoulder he noticed a big speedboat with three Mercury outboard motors hanging off the back idling down the other side of the channel. Once the boat saw their big Sea Ray, they turned on their navigational lights. Cody looked over at the two black men standing side by side as they passed in the darkness. The two men did not look at Cody or at their boat. It seemed unusual to Cody. They were the only other boat that the two had seen on their way back to the marina. The boat slipped past into the darkness with its motors idling.

Cody cleared out the GPS settings and turned off the alarm and killed all the electronics except the depth finder since they would no longer be needed. He was about to fire the diesels back up when he overheard some animated conversation. He peered through the darkness onto the shoreline and saw the two men from the boat faced off with three men behind a pickup truck with a tank in the bed. The men were on the bank of the vacant property adjacent to the marina that Tom and Jenny Jennings owned. This was the property that Jenny had told him a group of Russians had leased. There were three close-shaven white men facing the two longhaired black men who were standing facing the back of the truck. They all appeared to be looking into a duffle bag resting on the open tailgate. Cody could hear the noise of the conversation but could not make sense of what was being said. Shirley stood by him and asked, "What are they doing?"

"I can't tell," said Cody. "Can you bring me those binoculars?"

He popped the caps off the lenses of the binoculars after Shirley handed him the case and peered at the men through the darkness. He could see that they all seemed very animated and were looking and pointing at the bag on the tailgate of the truck. After a few minutes of animated arguing, one of the black men grabbed the bag and handed it to the man standing next to him, who quickly started sorting through the contents. Although it wasn't clear to Cody from the distance, it appeared to be bundles of cash.

After several moments of frantic counting and looking at the contents of the bag, the two black men awkwardly backed away from the truck as if they did not want to turn their backs on the other three. Once the black men had disappeared into the darkness, the three remaining men focused their attention on the drum in the back of the truck. Two of the men got into the bed of the truck and held it as the third got into the cab and backed right down onto the shoreline with the water lapping at the rear wheels. The extended tailgate was well out over the waterline. The two men in the back were wrestling the drum to the edge of the tailgate. Once they got there, they tilted the drum down and began pouring the liquid into the Intracoastal Waterway.

Cody was at a loss to understand what he was seeing. He was far enough away that the men had not noticed the big yacht behind the sailboat hulk in the channel. He resisted the urge to fire the engines and continue the cruise back to the marina. He watched intently as the men finished pouring the liquid and then secured the drum in the bed of the truck lying on its side. Shirley had the good sense to remain quiet and not ask questions.

The two men in the bed of the truck were talking in a language that sounded like Russian to Cody. They vaulted down to the ground as the truck pulled out of the water and they climbed into the cab. The driver spun the tires and threw sand as he accelerated down the dirt access road leading down to the water.

Once the truck was no longer visible, Cody resumed the cruise and got ready for the questions from Shirley. He calmly explained that he had no idea what they had just seen. He asked her to not tell anybody about it in exchange for a promise that he would investigate it further and keep her informed as to what he found out. He had a very bad feeling that he had just witnessed something that neither he nor Shirley wanted to have any part of. He also thought about his friend Tom and had to question whether or not what he had just seen had anything to do with his breakdown.

Cody quietly and slowly backed the big yacht into the slip at the marina while Shirley put the finishing touches on the cleanup and stored all the gear in the right place. She was an efficient mate, thought Cody as he looked at her nice silhouette in the moonlight. They secured the boat, fired up the bike, and rolled through the night. The air was cool now and the moisture could be felt as they sliced the wind with the big bike's headlight boring through the darkness. It was after midnight and there was very little traffic to impede their progress. They got back to her tidy, attractive home and pulled up to the garage door. He swung the kickstand down and took Shirley's hand to help her off the bike. They quickly kissed and she slipped into the front door after making him promise to call her the next day.

Cody coasted the bike down the driveway and fired up the motor as the bike hit the street. Cody rumbled through the darkness and reflected on the night. He thought through the unusual events at the end of the evening while he sliced through the night with the light beam dancing on the pavement in front of him. He smiled when he thought about the time he spent with Shirley. Cody's recent love life had been marginally occupied with time spent with two different ladies whom he saw from time to time on a fairly casual basis. Among all the other changes in his life recently, Cody was beginning to think that he might have to make room for a girlfriend too and bounce the other two part-timers out of his life. He laughed to himself at the thought of it. He was sure that he was going to have a lot of questions to answer from Dillon tomorrow once Laura talked to Shirley. If he knew Laura, that would be pretty early in the day.

CHAPTER VII

Captain Mike Timmons was a pretty easygoing guy for the most part. When it came to his boat, though, he wanted it right. He had captained for numerous yacht owners all over Florida and the Northeast and he knew his stuff. He carefully eyed the lift and operated it several times to make sure that it worked smoothly even when it was hot from repetitive use. He looked over at Cody and said, "You have a rough evening last night? You look like the cat crapped in your mouth while you were sleeping."

"Don't you worry about me, Cap. I beat you here this morning, remember? Besides, when did you become qualified to talk about how anybody else looks?" Cody squinted at the boat captain in the sunlight. He did feel like crap. He never drank champagne and Jack Daniel's together and now he was reminded why.

"No need to get so bent out of shape, my man. I am just glad that you had a nice time on your little midnight sea trial. Some of the local spies here told me that you had a hot number on board last night. If I had known, I would have offered to drive the boat for you just so I could watch. How did such a butt-ugly sourpuss like you get a hot chick like that who likes boats and motorcycles? What did you have to pay for it? I know she didn't go out with you for free."

Cody stared at the captain with bloodshot eyes. He was half-way tempted to respond with both barrels, but the pain of the hangover and soreness from his full-body workout last night kept him from enjoying the exchange the way he normally might. He wanted this meeting over with. Timmons appeared to get the message.

"Okay, okay," he said. "I don't see anything here that needs attention. If something comes up you'll take care of it, won't you?"

"You know I will, Cap. You have a problem; I'll take care of it. You know, those elevator guys did not give me an invoice for the lift. They said that they were donating that to Georges without cost because of his long-term business relationship and friendship with the owner of that company. You can take that part of my bid off the invoice since they did not charge me."

Timmons pulled out the bid that Cody had prepared for him when they agreed upon the work. They looked it over, agreed on the deduction for the elevator, and shook hands. "I'll cut a check for you on the boat account and have it waiting for you at the marina office later on this afternoon. You better get home and get some sleep, bro. Looks like that girl wore you out, and she might want more tonight."

They shook hands at the dock and Cody shuffled off to the marina office to check in with Jenny, grab a cup of coffee, and find out how Tom was doing. He walked into the boat owner's lounge, grabbed the biggest clean cup on the counter, and poured it full of the steaming black brew. He popped two aspirins into his mouth and washed them down with a mouthful of the hot liquid. There were two boat owners Cody had seen around the marina over the last few days working on laptops and listening to the morning financial news.

Jake O'Leary was a retired stock broker from Kansas who knew everything going on in the marina. He was nice to everybody just for the purpose of finding out what their business was and what they were doing.

"That Sea Ray looks nice, Cody. You guys did a nice job on her. I looked it over the other day before you put her back in the water. Did she check out okay last night? Looked like you might be working her over pretty hard on your midnight cruise. Let me know if you need any help in the future." The two retirees looked at each other and giggled like little boys. It wasn't hard to figure out who Timmons's snitch was.

Cody looked over at the two and nodded thanks. He said he would get back with them if he ever got into something he needed help with, and he walked back to the small office at the back of the building.

Cody felt the cool blast of air-conditioning in Jenny's office as he opened the door to the cramped room. Jenny kept it cool in there and it felt refreshing. Cody felt like he had been sweating for the last twenty-four hours. He plopped down on the worn couch and sipped on the coffee. Jenny was talking on the radio to a boat owner who was trying to find the channel to get into the marina for transient dockage and fuel. Jenny gave the boat owner simple directions and then called her dockmaster on his yard radio to let him know the size of the vessel that was coming in so that he could ready a slip.

"Everybody in this marina is talking about you this morning, Cody. How the heck did you get so famous all of a sudden?" She winked at him as if she had not heard. "You lose your razor? You're looking a little rough."

"All the good people in this marina should try and develop their own lives," said Cody. "I feel bad for all of you if you have nothing better to do than sit around and talk about my boring life." He closed his eyes and leaned his head back as he spoke. "That Sea Ray is done, Jenny. The lift company is not charging the owner for the lift they installed, so I took that part of the cost off the invoice. Your ten percent yard fee on my bill is going to be a little bit less than I told you it would be because of that. Timmons is going to drop a check off this afternoon and I'll pick it up then. He seemed happy with the work."

"Good, Cody. Since this went so well, maybe you will try and get some more jobs like this. I would be happy to recommend you if you want me to." She looked at the tall man leaning his head back on her couch. "You feeling okay, Cody?"

Cody did not open his eyes or look at the woman. "How's Tom?" he asked, ignoring her question.

"No change," she said. "I am going to see him this afternoon. If I am not here when you come to pick up your check, my niece Karen from Alabama will be here and I'll make sure she knows where I put it." Jenny looked away and gazed out the window. "I don't know what I'm going to do with him, Cody." Her voice broke when she said, "He seems so lost in there. How do you get through to somebody when they are like this? I need my brother back."

Cody opened his eyes and looked at the woman who was trying not to let him know that she was crying. "We're going to get him back up on his feet, Jenny. Let the doctors get him stabilized and we'll get to the bottom of what's bothering him. It'll be all right soon. He's a tough customer, sweetie, and he's coming back sooner than you think."

"Thanks, Code. Are you going to try and see him again? I know it would do him good to see you. I think it might help bring him out of it because he respects you so much and he won't want you to see him in this state."

"You let me know when he's going to be awake and I'll stop by. It won't be today, though. I am going home for a nap and then I'll come back later this afternoon so that we can settle up on your yard fee." Cody walked over and gave the woman a quick kiss on the cheek and carried his coffee cup back to the sink in the customer lounge. The two men were deeply engrossed in analyzing a stock report on one of the laptops as he passed by on his way out to his truck.

Cody looked over at Timmons, who was overseeing the refueling of the boat and stocking of provisions on board in preparation for the arrival of the boat's owner later that day. Timmons waved and shouted across the yard at Cody. "I just talked with the owner and he said thanks for adjusting the invoice. He wants to meet you sometime if you get the chance. I'll have that check in the office around two this afternoon." Cody waved back and got in the truck. He made note that the aspirins must be starting to kick in since he was feeling a little better. He also swore that he would never drink champagne again.

As he was leaving the marina and driving back home, Cody reflected on all the developments in his life over the past several weeks. He had left behind his relationship with the Spanish mob and the contract work for a legitimate occupation; he had met Shirley and become smitten with her; and he felt himself being drawn into a messy situation with Tom and Jenny. He couldn't help but feel like there had to be some relationship to Tom's breakdown and the strange events that he had witnessed last night. Tom was a gentle and easygoing person and not the sort that would have enemies or be in league with bad actors like the ones he saw last night on Tom's property. The way the pieces were adding up in his mind did not fit with who he knew Tom to be. He could not sort out the relationship between Tom and the Russians. Cody wondered if the unusual amount of dead sea grasses he had noticed recently in the marina had anything to do with the Russians pouring a contaminate into the lagoon surrounding the marina basin. Cody made a note to devote more brain time to the subject when he was functioning better.

He pulled up into the driveway of the Mission architecture style home he owned with the large detached garage in the back of the property that served as his workshop and storage area for his motorcycle, dive gear, and the Shelby GT 500 that he used as his weekend car. The car was a 1969 model with the big block V-8 Cobra motor. The engine was 428 cubic inches of pure asphalt-throwing horsepower and torque. The car had been a hand-me-down from his father and, except for the mandatory odd occasion when he just couldn't stop himself from living the excitement of unleashing the powerful motor and letting the adrenaline flow from getting pushed back in his seat by the raw acceleration of the beast, Cody drove it very conservatively and carefully. The car was in immaculate condition and he kept it under a canvas cover in the back of the garage.

The house was simple but spacious with a large covered porch area off the rear and arched doorways throughout with a barrel tile roof. The flooring was all Saltillo tile except for the bedrooms. Large arched doorways and windows provided plenty of natural breeze combined with the large covered porches on both the front and back, which kept most of the windows shielded from the sun and kept the house comfortable in all but the hottest of Florida days. Cody punched the code into his electronic keypad to spring the automated deadbolt on the security system-armed doorway at the back of the house. He reached the refrigerator and pulled out a large plastic bottled water and guzzled half of it before setting it down on the countertop. He looked over at the blinking light on his answering machine and pushed the button on the recording device to play back his messages. He rarely got messages on his land line and it surprised him to see that there were three new messages from last night. The first of the messages turned out to be from Linda, a girl who was involved in a lesbian relationship with Paula, one of his neighbors. Paula had purchased the house three doors down about a year and a half ago and had been trying to persuade Linda to move into the house with her ever since she got settled.

Paula didn't know that Linda was occasionally showing up

to see Cody when the opportunity presented itself. The casual and non-committal relationship suited Cody perfectly. Linda was completely off the wall most of the time. A flighty artist who had no means of support other than the occasional sale of a piece of sculpture, she depended on Paula for financial help and was using her as a life raft to continue on with her artistic dreams without having the same intentions as Paula did for a committed, exclusive relationship. Cody didn't know anything or care anything about what type of relationship Linda was involved in or even if he was the only man in her life. All he knew was that she showed up from time to time and wanted man chowder, and he was generally inclined to serve it up for her. Up until now, there had been no expectations, no clingy demands, no hurt feelings, and no remorse on either side. Cody never asked any questions about her relationship with anybody else and he never answered any either. Linda usually showed up when she and Paula were having a disagreement or when Paula was out of town for some reason. From the message, last night must have been one of those times when she and Paula were fighting and Linda was looking to come by for her secret tryst.

Cody also maintained a similar relationship with an Australian flight attendant named Darlene, who showed up to stay a few days at a time when her layover worked out to give her some time in Florida. She worked international flights out of the Miami hub and drove up to spend a few days with him about once a month. Cody had met Darlene three years ago on one of his return flights from South America. She had no idea what he had been doing down there, and he had no intention of ever telling her. She had waited for him on the other side of the customs line to re-enter the country and they had shared a quick meal at the airport together while she prepared to catch her next flight. Just as he was leaving the airport to head back to his home, she had called his cell phone to tell him that the flight she was scheduled to work was being cancelled because of mechanical problems and that another crew was going to work the flight the next day. She explained to him that she unexpectedly had the next four days off until she was required to work again.

In what had turned out to be one of the smoothest executions of all time, Cody pulled out of the parking garage and through the concourse to pick her up just as she got down from the gate level, pulled into the airport hotel and got a room, and five minutes later was giving the poor girl from down under the proper "slap and tickle" that she needed. They spent the next four days wearing each other out, and from that point forward, Cody got the occasional email from her telling him when she would be back to visit again. They never spoke on the phone and never met other than when she showed up. It was strange but it worked for both of them when they were together, and they never questioned it. Cody was pretty sure that she was either married or had a significant other back home since she never invited him to visit or talked about her life there. It suited Cody fine, too. He never wanted to talk about his life, either.

These two part-time lovers had constituted the whole of Cody's love life for the past several years. He had not wanted to try to develop anything more meaningful with anybody else while he was entangled with the contract work for the Spaniards. He had not had a meaningful relationship with a woman in over ten years. He had just let his life spiral down into meaningless encounters with part-time lovers. That approach to living life had its advantages but also its limitations. The thought of a more significant relationship in his life seemed foreign to Cody, but he was beginning to think that he might be ready for it. Time would tell him.

The second message was from Dillon asking him to check in

and let him know how things went with Shirley. Cody was certain that Laura had put his friend up to calling him since he had not left the message on his cell phone, which he would have called if he wanted to talk right away.

The last message was the martial arts academy calling to ask if he could train with their heavyweight prospect in a sparring session tomorrow afternoon. Cody slammed down more of the water on his way to his bed for a much-needed nap. The last thing he wanted to think about right now was someone swinging at his head.

CHAPTER VII

The girl squirmed in her seat at the desk as she sat down from turning the air-conditioning up a notch. She was bent over and admiring the new tattoo that she had gotten last week on her ankle. The Russian guys she had been running around with had introduced her to a really cool artist who had given her the tat at a discount. Those guys had tattoos all over and really knew where to go. They scared her, but they paid well and they had turned out to be a pretty regular gig. She didn't see anybody else anymore, just them. She never knew who she was going to wind up with over there, but they had called her over almost every night for the last week and a half. She was too naïve to know that they would soon tire of her and the other girls on their list and quit calling as soon as they got to know the newest and freshest wave of recruits to the agency. Things were really turning out well for her since she left Alabama. That is until last night when the Russians had beaten up her friend Tatiana and she had found out that some of the things the Russians had planned were going to affect her aunt and uncle.

She looked at the clock and sighed. Her aunt told her that she could leave and shut down the office as soon as this guy Cody came in and picked up the check that was in the envelope on the desk. She had been instructed to take a check from him for the marina's commission on the check he was picking up and to release the customer's check to him. She was making the best of this boring chore by surfing the Internet looking for celebrity gossip that she could tell the other girls at the Russians' party tonight.

Her aunt had to go meet with the doctors taking care of her uncle at the hospital.

She heard the Harley rumble and watched out the small window as the tall man got off the bike and put his sunglasses up on the top of his head. He looked around briefly and strode into the office and almost caught her checking her makeup when he opened the door and came in. She was trying a little too hard to act indifferent and disinterested while she smacked her gum and stared at the computer screen.

"Can I help you?" she finally asked without looking away from the computer screen.

"Name is Cody Houston. I came to pick up a check for some work I did on the Perrier boat."

"Oh," the girl said. "I'll have to look and see if it is here."

She fumbled around briefly before she picked it up out of the top drawer, where she had placed it no more than ten minutes prior to this conversation.

Cody tried to break the ice. "You must be Karen, Jenny's niece from Alabama. How do you like it here so far? Are you going to be working at the marina?"

The girl made a face that looked like she had just tasted butt for the first time. "I would never work here. This place is too dirty and boring. I'm just here as a favor for a few hours while Aunt Jen goes to visit Uncle Tom at the hospital. If I wanted to work at some place like this, I could have stayed in Alabama."

She laid the check down on the desk and went back to the computer screen. Cody opened it up and pulled out his checkbook. He wrote out the check to the marina for their commission on the bill and folded the check up and put it into the checkbook. He noted with some satisfaction that this was the second check he had written on his business account in the last week. He had opened the account five years ago, and this was only the twentieth check he had written. He was starting to come out of the shadows of his own making. No telling where this new direction in life would eventually take him.

Cody thanked the young woman and was starting his bike up outside when she walked up behind him. He turned the tank-mounted switch to the off position and the motor stopped with a slight hissing sound. Metal popped from the sudden change in temperature as Cody looked back at her and said, "You like motorcycles?"

"They scare me," she said. "Yours is pretty, though."

Cody studied the girl in the short skirt and clunky shoes. She was attractive enough, but she seemed awkward and uncomfortable. She would not look directly at Cody. Every time he looked at her, she glanced away.

Cody turned the ignition back over and prepared to crank the motor again. He knew the girl wanted something, but he wasn't going to chase her around to find out what it was. "I'll see you around," he said as the motor cranked up again. He clunked the transmission into gear and was starting to pull out when she raised her hand as if to tell him to stop and said something that he couldn't understand. He pulled the clutch in and killed the motor again. "I couldn't make out what you said, sweetie."

"Are you going to try and help my aunt and uncle?" she asked. She suddenly looked very young and sweet. The hardened façade she had put up before was down now and she seemed vulnerable. "I need to know if I can trust you to tell you something important."

Cody surveyed the boats in the marina before he answered. "I don't know if I can help, but if I can, I will. What's on your mind?"

"I can't let any anybody see us talking," she said. "We need to go somewhere to talk. Have you got somewhere we can go?"

Cody briskly pulled out of the marina and onto the highway. The girl followed behind him in her small red sedan. The air-conditioning didn't work and the girl kept the windows down and let the hot, humid air blow her dark hair back as she followed the man on the big chrome bike. She stayed close behind and followed him to his house—conflicted between her sense of fear of the Russians and her sense of duty to her family. She had sized up this tall man who seemed pleasant but aloof. He hadn't leered at her like most men did. She felt a little uncomfortable with that because her sexuality was how she had learned to manage and control men. But she needed somebody who was smart and strong enough to understand and deal with what she needed to reveal about the Russians and what they were doing. The problem was compounded because of the *way* she found out. She had learned about some of their plans from Tatiana, the Russian girl from the escort service who talked to her at the Russians' parties. She had also overheard Dmitry speaking on his phone to a guy named Dexter from the bank and to the Haitians that the Russians dealt with. Dmitry had gotten drunk and beat Tatiana badly. When Karen took her home and helped her clean up, the slender Russian girl had revealed some of what she knew about the Russians' plans.

She did not know all the details, but she knew enough to figure out that the Russians were working with this guy Dexter from the bank to take over the marina from her aunt and uncle so that they could keep doing what they were doing with the Haitians. Karen was smart enough to not give Tatiana or the Russians any idea she knew the victims of their plan well enough to string together the random details that they had exposed her to. They also wouldn't think that a stupid little party whore would care enough to try to pull the random details together. There was no way she could tell her aunt and uncle what she knew directly without telling them how she found out. Letting her family know that she was working for an escort service was not an option. Not letting them know what she had found out was not an option either.

She followed Cody down the long driveway to the large detached garage in the back. She was impressed by the cleanliness of the neatly organized wood shop with the lumber up in racks hanging from the ceiling and all the wood working machines neatly arranged on a painted concrete floor. The large shop also housed a car cloaked in a cover and the space for the big motorcycle and a wall full of scuba diving equipment and tanks racked next to a compressor rig.

The girl struggled to match the tall man's strides across the pavement to the house. He stopped to pick up a plate of brownies that someone had left at the door and quickly read the note taped to the top of the plate. He could tell right away by the artistic handwriting that it was from Linda, who evidently wasn't going to give up easily on her search for Cody. *The girl must have some needs or is seriously pissed off at Paula*, Cody thought.

"Your girlfriend?" she asked.

"Just a friend who has been looking for me," he said without revealing anything.

Karen declined the brownie that Cody offered her and looked around the house. She noted how clean and orderly the home was. She slid onto the stool he motioned to as he reached into the refrigerator for a longneck bottle. "Cold beer?" he asked. She caught herself staring into his intense eyes when he turned to look at her. She turned her head to break the awkward moment and mumbled, "Sure." She rallied herself and drawled out, "You going to drink a beer while you eat that brownie?"

He pulled a stool out and turned it around while draping his arms over the chair back. "So, how long have you been down here?" He knew it was a lame attempt to make small talk, but he wanted to make her as comfortable as he could. He just wanted to get her started talking and whatever she had to say would come gushing out.

"Two months," she said. "I'm going to be leaving soon. I can't stay here in the middle of this any longer. I have to try and do something to help Uncle Tom and Aunt Jenny before I leave, though. What I am about to tell you has to stay confidential."

"It will," he said. "I can assure you of that much." She was really starting to get him interested in what she had to tell him by being so mysterious.

"I work as an escort at a local service and I have been going out a lot lately to see this group of Russians who all work for a guy named Dmitry. There is another girl, Tatiana, who goes with me sometimes. She is Russian and she knows them really well because she overhears them talking all the time when she is at their house. One of the guys beat her up last night when he got real drunk and I took her home and helped her get cleaned up and started talking to her. She told me that these were real bad guys who were involved in drugs and counterfeiting money. They are also trying to get my aunt and uncle's marina property by working through this guy at the bank who made them a loan that he knew they couldn't repay." Her voice wavered a little as she lost some of the indifference and toughness she tried hard to project.

"Do you know why these Russians want the marina?" he asked her.

"No," she replied after taking a sip of her beer. Cody noted that she still had chewing gum in her mouth.

Cody didn't understand the connection between the bank officer and the Russians. The scene he had witnessed the other night with the speedboat and the drum in the back of the truck didn't make sense either yet, but he was starting to see a pattern of dots that no longer seemed disconnected. He knew he was going to need some help to really understand what was happening and the reasons why. He was sure Karen was at the edge of her knowledge and understanding of the situation.

"What else did this girl tell you about these guys?" asked Cody. "Where do they live and where do they go? What do you think they want?"

"They live out in the country in an old citrus grove farmhouse south of town. Tatiana told me that they have dinner almost every night at this Lebanese restaurant down by the mall. That is about all I know. Are you going to help?" She looked at him as if disappointed that he didn't already know what to do.

"When are you leaving town?" he asked her.

"Just as soon as I can get some money up and clear out," she replied. "I don't want to see these guys anymore. They are crazy bad-asses and mean as hell. I think Tatiana's jaw was broken and she was all busted up when I left her last night. I just want to go back home to Alabama and forget all about this nightmare, but I can't leave until I think that someone is going to try and help my aunt and uncle." She started to cry and put the end of a long fingernail up the edge of her eye to catch the tear before it streaked her makeup. "I think that what is going on with these Russians has something to do with Uncle Tom's breakdown and that is why he is in the hospital."

Cody studied the young girl, who was openly crying now on the stool. "I am going to give you some money and I want you to clear out of town by tomorrow night. I don't want you to ever tell anybody that you told me anything about this and I want you to give me your phone and get a new cell phone number and never come back here again. I want you to call me on your cell number when you get a new number and tell me you are okay and out of town, but you must not tell Tatiana anything about me or tell her that you told me anything. Most of all, I don't want you to tell your aunt or uncle anything about this or that you know anything about me. You just need to tell them that you are going back home for some other reason, any other reason, and don't come back until I tell you it's okay. You got that?"

"Why do I have to give you my phone?" She sniffled.

"That is part of the deal. I don't know what I am going to do yet to try to help out, but if I do something I work alone and secretly. The only way I can do something is if absolutely no one knows that I am involved in any way. Never. You got that? You are going to need to forget all about this conversation and forget that you ever met me. Forget my name and forget my face."

"Are you going to go to the police?" she asked.

"Maybe, I don't know yet. I am going to have to learn more about what is going on and who is involved and then work up a plan." He offered her a napkin and said, "The hall bathroom is right down there. Make yourself up again and I am going to get you some cash to get out of town. Come back and start writing down the phone numbers that you need out of your cell phone."

Cody always kept some cash on hand in his house in a wall safe he had built into the wall framing of his master bedroom closet. As he pulled the door open and took out the canvas bag with the cash in it, he had to pull out the 9mm Glock pistol he kept in there with the cash. There were two fifteen-round clips in the bag with the pistol; he kept one loaded with rounds and rotated them every few months to keep the springs fresh. He was due to rotate the rounds from one clip to the other and he quickly did so with eerie efficiency. He felt the adrenaline of a new hunt coming on and it made him feel alive. He kept the pistol, the two clips, and a box of rounds out of the bag when he replaced it in the safe. He felt better having the little handgun out for faster access. He grabbed five thousand dollars in bundled hundreds and replaced the bag in the safe. He put the Glock, clips, and box of rounds in the nightstand next to his bed.

He walked back into the kitchen to find Karen writing down phone numbers on the pad. She said, "I do not understand why I need to give up this phone to you. All my friends know this number, and this is how everybody gets in touch with me."

"I am sorry that I have to do this, but it's the only way I can get involved," Cody replied. "I can't take the chance that you might change your mind and go back and see these guys and tell them that I know anything about this."

"I need all these numbers," she said. "I am going to be here all night writing this down."

Cody went over and looked at the names on the list to see if there were any Russian names or a number for Tatiana. He didn't see any yet. "Keep writing and put down the address of the house where the Russians stay." He walked over to the refrigerator and got another beer out. He pulled another one of the brownies out of the container and bit into it.

After what seemed like an eternity, she finished. He went over and took the list from her. There were about thirty names on the list and he reviewed each one with her to find out why she wanted that number. There were no Russian names and she had not copied down Tatiana's phone number. He took her phone and checked the directory. There was a number for Dmitry and a number for Tatiana. Since she had not copied them down he felt he could trust her. He wrote down the number for Tatiana and Dmitry from the phone directory together with her home number and tucked the list into his back pocket. He deleted their numbers and handed her back the phone and said, "You can keep this. I just needed to make sure that I could trust you not to contact anybody. Now that I have the list of all of your important phone numbers, you know that I can find you if you ever double-cross me."

"You don't want my phone, after all?"

"If I choose to get involved in this in some way, I need to know that you aren't going to run your mouth about me. You are the one possible weak link in this scenario. I need to make sure that you don't turn on me. If you do, you now know that I can find you."

"You are a suspicious dude."

"For good reason," he replied. "This is five thousand dollars. It will help you get started again when you get back home. Don't ever talk about me with anybody and don't ever contact me again. If I need something from you, I will call you. Leave by tomorrow night and don't ever come back until you hear from me that things here are resolved. Whatever you do, don't ever contact the Russians again and don't answer their calls or go see them if they call you. Just remember, if I go down, I'll tell them that I got information from you."

That last chilling statement had the desired effect on her. She looked at him without saying a word, took the money, and stuffed it in her purse. "I liked you a whole lot more before you said that," she said.

He looked directly at her eyes and said, "I am not going to do anything until I am certain that you are no longer in town. I don't always color between the lines and I need to know that I can do what I need to without being found out. I live here and plan on staying here. I can't operate if I have to worry about you running your mouth and this thing coming back to haunt me."

She could not hold his stare. She rummaged around in her purse and said, "You may be the right guy to tell about this after all. I thought you were just going to go to the police. Thanks for the money."

With that she stood up and clumped out the front door in her ridiculous shoes. He picked up the rest of his brownie and took a big bite. He was surprised how good it tasted with the beer.

Cody settled in on his favorite leather couch with his beer and brownie. He put his feet up on the coffee table and contemplated the facts. The Russians wanted the marina for their illegal activities. They were somehow strong-arming Tom through some connection they had at the bank to gain control of it. The Russians' link-up with the Haitians at night via their speedboats at the marina property as Cody had seen the other night. He could not explain the drum and the liquid they poured into the water.

Cody wondered why he was jumping at the chance to get involved in this. He had no idea what to do; he just knew that he had to learn more. Tom and Jenny were good friends and they were getting hurt by these thugs. That was motivation, certainly. He was feeling more than indignation about bad guys doing his friends wrong, though. He felt some excitement that he had been afraid he was not going to experience again. He knew right now that he was going to take these guys down. He might turn the matter over to the police after he found out for sure what was happening. Sure, that was probably where he was going to go with it, he thought to himself. That is, unless he could work up some plan to make these guys self-destruct without getting too involved or causing any trouble for himself. He would have to see where it went. First things first, he was going to have to learn more. Tomorrow he would visit with Tom and then go to the restaurant that Karen had mentioned to see who these guys were. Meanwhile he would pull up the address to their home on the Internet and map it out and pay it a little visit when he was sure that the Russians were at dinner. He would look at some satellite images of the place to see if he could figure out why they would be staying there.

He needed to do a light workout tonight, do some stretches, and go to bed early. He had agreed to meet at the martial arts academy tomorrow morning with the fighter they were training for a sparring session. Supposedly this guy was a brute and they were having trouble finding partners to spar with him. If he didn't lay off the beer and brownies and get some rest tonight, he was going to get embarrassed tomorrow.

He also needed to call Shirley and work up a new plan to see her again. The combination of his blood pumping over the danger that his friend was in, his upcoming sparring session, and the thoughts of last night with her were making him want to see her again real soon. He wondered if she might be interested in getting some Lebanese food tomorrow night. If what Karen told him about them eating there almost every night was true, Shirley would provide the perfect cover for him to observe them without looking at all suspicious.

He slid into the chair in front of his desk and fired up the computer in his home office. He quickly reviewed the email messages in his in box and saw none of particular importance. He jumped over to the Internet and pulled up the satellite photos of the address Karen had given him for the Russians. It was clearly an old grove property with several small sheds, barn, or shop buildings scattered throughout the back of the larger structure that had to be the house where they were living. He would have to drive the address to get a better feel for what might be going on there. He panned over to the marina and began traversing the channel that led to the marina basin. He carefully reviewed the vacant property next to the marina and the Intracoastal Waterway passing the marina basin. There was a plan forming in his head and he needed to gather more field intelligence to make sure it was feasible. He had learned that there was no substitute for direct observation in the field to make a plan come together without a hitch. Field recon was always tedious, but it was always the most important part of a successful project like the one he had in mind.

He had to build a high percentage blueprint with a contingency exit that would allow for an escape with limited possibility for being exposed, hurt, or captured. He was hatching the beginnings of a high-stakes plan of misdirection that would propel several powerful forces against each other with a good probability that it would lead to danger for him and the eventual demise of all the bad actors in this deceitful Florida drama.

He smiled with satisfaction at the thought of pitting his unique talents against the greed and violence of his adversaries. He planned to make sure that they never knew who they were confronting. Greedy and violent men were naturally distrustful of those they dealt with. It is the natural law that those who cannot be trusted have the least trust in others. Criminals were almost always the most security conscious and paranoid of all people. This was especially true in love and money; the two most basic of all lusts bring out men's purest and most powerful reaction. Unknown to anybody else late at night in his private space, he was contemplating a way to stimulate the outbreak of their natural brutality and bring their demise. He felt like a cat stalking prey in a cyber jungle; he couldn't wait to get his first look at his adversaries tomorrow night. He questioned what it was about himself that embraced a challenge of such intrigue and danger with so little regard for the precarious possibilities of being uncovered. The challenge brought a quickening of his pulse as he narrowed his piercing eyes while studying the computer screen. He focused on a small protrusion of the shoreline into a narrow part of the channel across from a channel marker. He had found where the first part of his perilous adventure would be hatched.

CHAPTER VIII

Good defense in a physical confrontation starts with the ability to move laterally when your opponent advances with his blows. Keeping your hands high to deflect and block the attacker's blows is the second strategy. Moving straight back with your hands down is the quickest way to get taken out. The third part of defending yourself is to be able to muster an effective counterattack when your opponent advances within the striking range. Effective counterattacking requires the combination of multiple rapid blows in a minimum of three punch sets. Effectively counterpunching forces your opponent to weigh the costs of mounting an attack.

The big deputy sheriff was repeatedly wading in with wild roundhouse punches thrown with bad intentions. He was a mountain of muscle and aggression—intent on ending this sparring session as soon as possible. The entire academy and several of the man's deputy sheriff buddies had turned out to watch this sparring match, and the observers were inadvertently ducking and grimacing as they saw the power of the big man's punches. He had at least two inches and forty-five pounds on Cody's six-foot, three-inch frame. Cody weighed 220 pounds of lean, muscular mass, with wide shoulders and a narrow waist and legs. At the fighters' mutual agreement, they had both passed on wearing the customary headgear that sparring partners usually used in these practice sessions. The fighters had agreed to restrict the match to kickboxing and Muay Thai strikes of knees and elbows. They wore heavier boxing type gloves rather than the fingerless lightweight striking gloves used in mixed martial arts fights to extend the training session. Men of their size could easily knock out an opponent with strikes to the chin or temple.

Cody cleanly avoided a wild roundhouse right by ducking down and to the left and came up with a double left hook to the midsection followed by a straight right to the face of his opponent for the third time in the first three minutes of the five-minute round. The big man shook off the punch with almost no visible effect except anger. Cody was amazed at the lack of response that the clean shots had on the big man. By using lateral motion and head movement, Cody had managed to prevent any direct blows to the face and head. The force of the blocked blows stung mightily, however, and Cody knew that any clean shot to his head or chin was likely to send him down because of the force the man mustered. This guy attacked with bad intentions and had the ability to shake off a direct punch with seemingly no effect on his balance.

Cody noted that the effort from the repeated full-force wild swings the man was taking were beginning to take a toll on the man's breathing. Cody watched him carefully to see where the opening might come for a more effective counterattack. The quicker repeat blows Cody had been landing seemed to have limited effect, and Cody had barely avoided being counterpunched in the exchanges. He needed to come up with a more effective counterstrike to slow the big man down. Cody lashed out with several wicked leg kicks that landed on the outside of the big man's left thigh. Cody tripped him up with a leg sweep that almost sent the man down before he recovered. As he got more tired from the aggregation of blows, swings, and leg kicks, his punches got wilder and he left himself open for counterattack. Cody moved in and absorbed several punishing blows on the gloves. Just as he anticipated, the big man leaned in with the punches and left himself wide open for the sudden uppercut that Cody sent in with a full shoulder turn. The quick punch snapped the man's head back and forced him to step back and recover just as the bell rang.

The second round was a continuation of the first, with Cody absorbing numerous blows on his gloves and forearms. He responded with numerous counterpunches, but with each ineffective assault, the crowd of deputies shouted their encouragement in boisterous support of their colleague. As the round came to a close, Cody started launching vicious front kicks into the man's midsection to keep him out of striking range. In the closing seconds of the round, the man advanced again with the intention of timing the kick to grab the leg and punch Cody's head. Cody saw it coming and moved slightly to the side and threw a spinning back kick that knocked the man backward against the ropes. Cody quickly followed up with some wicked blows to the body and a barrage on the head, shoulders, and chest that wilted the large man down to a knee just as the time in the round ended.

Cody decided to launch his attack early in the third round to try to take advantage of the wobbly legs his opponent was bound to still have from the punches at the end of the second round. The large gloves they were wearing prevented too much damage from being inflicted, but the combination of fatigue and the cumulative blows were showing on both the combatants. Cody went right after the big man and ducked several sloppy roundhouse punches. He caught the deputy sheriff leaning into him after the second wild punch, and delivered an uppercut that he launched from below his waist with a good shoulder turn. The punch landed flush on the big chin and Cody went into a frenzy of hooks and uppercuts while staying right on top of the man as he stumbled around. Cody backed the man into the ropes and started working the midsection to get the man to lower his hands and open up his head. Cody started teeing off on the man's upper body with full-force punches and saw his opponent take a knee. The referee stepped and discontinued the bout to the catcalls and whistles of the deputies who wanted to see their guy recover and take out this rangy stranger who had the audacity to not melt in fear of the vicious attack their comrade mustered.

Cody went over and checked on the man, who, despite the calls of his friends, was humbled and ready to stop the sparring session. He touched gloves with Cody and smiled at him with respect. The deputies started begrudgingly clapping for both the combatants, and several walked up to Cody and slapped him on the back as he walked into the dressing room. He stopped and looked at himself in the mirror. There was a slight mark under his left eye. Cody knew he had to quickly put some ice on it to stop any swelling or he was going to have a mark on his face that would require explanation tonight on his date with Shirley. He wasn't ready to reveal his martial arts background to his new lady yet. He asked one of the instructors for an ice pack as he stripped off the gloves. Just as he lifted the ice pack to his cheekbone, the big deputy came over and slapped him on the upper back.

"You throw about as hard as anybody I have ever sparred with. You are sneaky, fast, and have really good defense." He sat down on the bench next to Cody and looked at the ice pack. "Let me see that eye. I didn't think I hit you with a clean shot at all in the face the whole match."

Cody lowered the ice pack. "I knew if I got hit with any of those killer shots, it was going to be a short sparring session. I had to use every trick in my bag to keep you off of me. I don't see any marks on your face and I know that I hit you a couple of clean shots."

"I don't mark or cut easy." The big man chuckled. "Lucky for me because I usually take a few punches in these sessions. I've got my first real MMA fight coming up in a month and I am trying to improve my striking. You made me realize how far I have to go yet. I don't want to get embarrassed in front of all of these guys." He nodded at the group of deputies congregated at the entrance to the locker room in animated rehashing of the sparring session. One of them broke away from the group and walked over to them.

"Hey, Norman, we're going to get some lunch over at the diner. You coming with us? We all worked that murder case all night and we are starving to death. We didn't get any breakfast before we came here."

"Yeah, you guys go ahead and I'll meet you there." He looked over at Cody and said, "My name is Norman, by the way. Any chance that you would work with me a little to help me learn some of that defense and counterpunching you showed me out there today?"

Cody shook the big hand that was extended out to him and said, "Sure, man. Name is Cody. Don't get discouraged, Norm. You showed some good skills out there. With just a little fine-tuning we can get you where you need to be. I'd be happy to help you next week if we can work out a good time. The front desk has my number; you can get it from them when you want it."

The deputies were filing out of the locker room and Cody overheard them say something about Russians. He looked over at Norman and asked, "What was that murder case you were working on last night? I didn't hear anything about a murder on the local news this morning."

"Some cute little Russian girl named Tatiana. She was here illegally and we think she was working as an escort. We found her body dumped off a country road with a bullet in her skull. You want to go to lunch?"

80

"No thanks, Norm. I need to get to work and take care of some things. Call me about getting together next week." His mind was already racing about the implications of Tatiana's death. He hoped Karen had taken his advice and gotten out of town like she said she would.

CHAPTER IX

Cody looked admiringly as Shirley walked into the restaurant. Her smooth skin had a beautiful golden glow in a backless halter top. She had the killer combination of being a busty, tall, slender woman who moved lightly on her feet. She looked feminine in anything she wore, but tonight she dazzled in some loose-fitting, pleated cream-colored slacks and leopard print halter top. Every man in the room looked up to watch her approach Cody's table. Her best features were her elegant, long neck and beautiful arms and shoulders, which were on full display tonight. When she smiled at Cody as she approached, she melted him with her sparkling eyes, beautiful smile, and subtle perfume. Cody stood and bussed her on the cheek while holding her chair out for her. It was all he could do to keep from grabbing her, bending her over his knee, and laying a major lip lock on her. He wondered how she had gotten to him so quickly. It wasn't like him to fall so hard and quickly for a lady but this one had him by the nose already. He was going to have to work to keep from letting her know what she was doing to him for fear of scaring her off. It was nice to have someone push his button like this. It had been a while since he had felt this way about someone.

Cody made note of the fact that almost every one of the Russians sitting at the corner table in the back of the restaurant was still looking at them as he sat down in his own chair. Cody had been waiting on Shirley to arrive for about twenty minutes and had been reading the *Wall Street Journal* and periodically messing about with his cell phone as if attending to job-related emails or texts. He was actually carefully observing the group of Russians at the back corner table to learn what he could about the dynamics of the group. The large crew cut man who sat in the corner was clearly the leader to whom everybody deferred. Cody had been just about to confirm that it was him by dialing the cell phone number that he had gotten from Karen and loaded into the register of the disposable cell phone he had bought that afternoon. He wanted to confirm which one of these characters was Dmitry and he wanted to make sure that he had the right cell number for him in case he needed it in the future. He had replaced the little cell phone back into his suit jacket pocket as Shirley walked up to him. He would have to wait until she excused herself to the ladies room to confirm his suspicions.

"Don't you look so handsome in that suit? I didn't expect to see you so dressed up tonight." She glowed at him from across the table.

"I didn't want to let you down." He smiled.

"Mister, I have news for you. After the other night, I wouldn't care if you showed up here in your bathing suit and sandals. I have not stopped thinking about our last date since the moment you dropped me off. It sure is nice to see you again. Thanks for inviting me out like this. You really surprise me in that suit looking so professional and yummy like you do." She giggled like a little girl and smiled sweetly at him with her face slightly flushed.

"I am glad you could make it on such short notice, sweetie. I have been thinking about you, too. That was quite a date we had. You look absolutely good enough to eat, by the way. You are putting the sunshine to shame. I don't know if I am going to be able to keep my hands off of you." He returned her smile as he felt her foot coming between his feet under the table.

Cody had been studying the menu prior to her arrival and had talked with the waiter about several of the dishes so that he could provide a little direction when she ordered and preserve the illusion that he had some reason for bringing her here to begin with. He gave her a couple of suggestions after they ordered their wine from the waiter and she got up to go to the ladies room. Cody reached into his suit pocket and removed the little cell phone with Dmitry's number already in the register and ready to dial. He acted as though he was studying the menu while he pushed the send button and watched Dmitry as the call connected. The man casually looked down at the phone in front of him as he was pushing another forkful of food into his mouth. He set the fork down and pushed the ignore button without picking the device up. Cody heard the message begin to play in surprisingly clear English as he pushed the end call button on his little phone. He quickly turned the phone off and put it back into his jacket pocket in the event of a call back. This innocuous little maneuver confirmed that Karen was probably giving him good intelligence on the situation and it confirmed his suspicion about who the leader of this group of violent Russian misfits was and how to reach him if a situation required it.

Cody was studying the large group of tattooed men sitting at the table. Every one of them looked like a bad actor with little conscience. He quickly counted nine of the men sitting at the table. The restaurant owner personally doted on them continuously as though he were the only one who could service them the way they deserved to be treated. He was a short, balding Middle Eastern-looking gentleman with a slight paunch and thick glasses. Just as Shirley came back it was apparent that the group was leaving. Dmitry pulled out an impressive roll of cash and ripped off four bills and left them on the table as he shook hands and hugged the small man on his way out the door. All of the rest of the Russian posse thanked and nodded or waved at the smallish man, but none shook his hand or embraced him as Dmitry had.

The man clearly knew who paid his bills and made sure to pay homage to the leader of this motley crew of far eastern desperados. They filed out of the restaurant after their leader, and Cody looked over at Shirley and excused himself as if he had left something in the car.

Cody followed the group out and held his BlackBerry to his ear and walked purposefully past the group gathering around Dmitry just outside the restaurant to his innocuous-looking rented four-door sedan in the parking lot. He had parked it close to the exotic European sedans and sports cars scattered around the near side of the parking lot. He sat in the front seat looking at an empty notebook as if referring to some notes while continuing to hold the phone to his ear and acting like he was deep in a conversation. He watched in his rearview mirror as Dmitry stepped into a new silver BMW 7 Series sedan and he quickly wrote down the license plate number. He waited until the group had cleared the parking lot and re-entered the restaurant.

His work was done for the night and now he was going to attend to the fun part of the evening. Inside the restaurant, he smiled broadly at the beautiful lady sitting at his table when he caught her looking over her shoulder to see if he was coming back yet. She was casually talking to the restaurant owner, who had wasted no time in taking advantage of Cody's absence to make sure that this fine lady was well taken care of in his restaurant. He quickly introduced himself to Cody as he slid back into his seat. Cody firmly shook the small man's hand and thanked him for checking in on Shirley while he was gone. Funny how the need for checking on the service was mitigated once Cody returned as the small man whisked away into the kitchen. Cody was tempted to call the man back and use that to his advantage to make some off-hand inquiries about the Russians, but he reconsidered. He had learned enough for the evening and did not want to take any further chances of involving Shirley in what might become a dangerous play. Besides, he had something better to take care of at the immediate moment.

He and Shirley continued on through the meal holding hands as she told him all about her job as a pharmaceutical rep. She seemed to enjoy her work since it got her out and allowed her to meet a lot of people, but she despised the way the companies marketed their drugs through doctors and the corrupt way that doctors were compensated for prescribing the drugs for their patients. She was dismayed by the way money impacted the treatment of patients and how doctors could be influenced by it. Cody listened to her while trying to keep his mind from wandering forward. He could hardly keep from thinking about what he was going to do to this beautiful creature later in the evening. He was barely able to maintain his part of the conversation without embarrassing himself. He was glad when they finished the last of the dessert that they split and were able to head back to his house. Shirley gladly rode back with him in his rental sedan cuddled up against his side with his suit jacket wrapped around her in the large front seat. There would be time in the morning to return and get her car.

CHAPTER X

Florida had eight military installations at the start of World War II, and by the end of the war there were 172. There were twenty-two POW camps for German soldiers established in the state during the war. Florida played such a prominent role in the war effort in part due to the tenure of the elected congressmen and senators during the war and their ability to steer federal dollars into the state as a result of their seniority and involvement in important committees and the unique geography of the state with its miles of coastline and excellent suitability for flight operations. There was also an abundance of inexpensive, sparsely populated available land that was readily converted to military installations. The post-war population explosion in Florida was caused by a combination of the development of mosquito control, air-conditioning, and the return of all the service men and women who served in the military on bases in the state and returned after the war to make their lives here. For better or for worse, depending on a person's viewpoint on development, World War II cast an indelible mark on the state whose influence continues today.

During the war, many freighters supplied Europe with fuel from refineries along the U.S. Gulf Coast and the Caribbean. In the portion of the trip from Boca Raton to Cocoa, the freighters would run north in the powerful Gulf Stream current, which runs northward parallel near to the shore, and they would return running south between the shore and the Gulf Stream. This concentration of traffic in such a confined area created a hunting ground for German U-boats right off the coast of the U.S. The U.S. had an inadequate defense net protecting the coast from the fierce wolf packs of German U-boats that operated virtually unimpeded for much of the war. The Germans sank twenty-four ships off the Florida coastline with their deadly efficient crews and patient hunting techniques. As the war wore on, the U.S. learned to dim the lights facing the coast to prevent the backlighting of freighters against the coastline, making them less visible to the U-boat captains. Civilian patrols dubbed the "Mosquito Fleet" formed patrols of pleasure and charter boats that looked for subs and rescued survivors from torpedoed ships. FBI agents rounded up twenty-nine suspected enemy agents in West Palm Beach and Ft. Lauderdale in over fifty-five raids who were suspected of aiding the German U-boat effort.

In the end, the twenty-four sunken freighters remain on the seabed off the coast as silent witnesses to the atrocities of man in conflict against his own kind. Many valiant merchant marine sailors gave their all in a struggle to deliver the precious fuel so desperately needed by the European and African-theater Allied forces in the ground and air war against Hitler's mighty army and air forces. Today, the broken-down hulks of formerly great ships provide structure and habitat for an abundance of marine life in depths of thirty to 150 feet of water off the coast. They now provide some of the best sport diving and fishing locations off the abundant Florida coastline and are favored by both diving and fishing sportsmen who know their locations. A good boat with a bottom reader and a reliable GPS are all that is required to find them if a captain knows the coordinates. Most of the wrecks are within thirty miles of the shoreline. When the captain arrives on the location, they drop a buoy marking the spot and then initiate a cloverleaf search pattern around the buoy until the ship's hulk shows up on the bottom reader as relief against the bottom. Many of the wrecks provide up to thirty feet of relief against the bottom, which makes them easy to spot when the bottom reader sonar passes over them. Others have broken up over time and don't have the same amount of easily recognizable relief from the ocean floor. These wrecks require a little more effort and patience to locate in the big open ocean with no visible landmarks to guide a captain.

Dillon was making a large cloverleaf pattern around a bright orange buoy that Cody had thrown over when the navigation alarm went off. Tom was standing by with a yellow buoy to throw over when they actually got a read on the wreck. The *Jacques Crusteau* was running quietly, with its new four-stroke motors efficiently plowing the hull through the brilliant blue water. Florida had blessed them with a calm day on the seas. They had the French Canadian owner of the Sea Ray that Cody had worked for in Tom's marina, Georges Perrier, on board with them. Captain Timmons had set the meeting up and Cody had lured him into the fishing trip with the intention of introducing him to Tom so that he could talk about the marina. So far, Tom had been cordial enough to Georges and they seemed like they were hitting it off, but Cody could tell that Tom was reluctant to open up yet and talk about the marina condo project to Georges. Tom had been making a nice recovery from his breakdown since his release from the hospital but he still seemed vaguely distant. Cody chalked that up to embarrassment. No need to rush things, he thought. It was going to be a long day in a small boat, and if the subject didn't come up, he would force it later on. Cody had not told Georges that there was a purpose behind the introduction to Tom. Cody had easily been able to talk Dillon into hosting them on his boat. Any offer to go offshore fishing and diving found a receptive ear with Dillon. Cody had never known his friend to decline a proposal for diving or fishing if someone else would pay for the fuel.

"Here it is!" yelled Dillon.

Tom tossed the small buoy overboard and they all watched as the heavy weight stripped the line off the rotating buoy. It finally settled down and stopped rotating as the weight hit the bottom. "That marks the stern," remarked Dillon. "Now we are going up to the bow and throw a marker in there so that you can have a reference point." Dillon had carefully measured the line he put on the buoys so that there was very little extra scope, which caused the buoy to remain almost directly above the wreck. Any diver descending either of the two lines would see the wreck easily because they would be descending almost vertically onto the deck. Poor visibility and the ever-present current in these Atlantic waters dictated some precautions to make sure that the divers could find and get to the wreck they wanted to dive on. A hopeful scuba diver quickly finds out that the ocean is a big place with no reference point from the surface. Dillon carefully measured the current and dropped anchor to allow the current to push the vessel back over to the marker buoy over the bow of the boat.

They were planning to make a dive today on the *Laertes*, which was also known locally as the *Dutch Wreck*. She was an old freighter torpedoed by a German U-boat in about seventy feet of water twenty miles northeast of Port Canaveral about a mile inside the 8A reef. She was 400 feet in length and offered abundant spear fishing opportunities. Cody and Dillon geared up to make the first dive. They were anxious to find out what the water visibility would be. The sun had not made its way up over the horizon yet, so they arranged the gear using the cargo lights. Dillon gave Tom and Georges a detailed briefing on the boat and the navigation equipment, and the oxygen bottle he carried on board in case of a diving accident. Tom had been on the boat before and had gone through the same briefing each time he had been diving. Diving is a safe sport if done correctly and carefully. Good planning and thorough preparation with the ability to rely on those who are with you are critical. Both Georges and Tom listened carefully to the briefing and asked several good questions. Cody had the feeling that this was going to be a good day. After the two finished their briefing they turned their attention to Cody, who was working out the kinks in the spear fishing guns. He gave them both a quick rundown on the best way to stalk fish, the kind of fish they would likely encounter, minimum size limits on each of the species, and the types of fish not to spear.

There were also barracuda and sharks found on the wreck. While not normally a problem, the barracuda could be aggressive when they saw the wounded fish on the end of a spear. More than a few divers had lost their catch to a tug of war with a barracuda intent on stealing the speared fish. Cody explained the maximum bottom time given the depth of the dive, current, procedures for returning to the boat, and the standard briefing on the precautions necessary for safe diving on this wreck. Dillon and Cody planned on penetrating the wreck and exploring inside; they were asking Tom and Georges to maintain a clear view of the surface at all times to prevent them from getting trapped or lost within the confines of the wreck. Cody and Dillon had made numerous dives on all the local wrecks and knew them well. Dillon did the same for them on the operation of the boat. Tom was an experienced boater who could handle Dillon's boat easily if the need arose. He just needed a few pointers to refresh his memory on the navigation system. Tom seemed to be completely engaged and enjoying this trip. He was talking animatedly with Georges about making a wager over which team would spear the most and best fish. It was good to see him laughing and cutting up again and filled with his natural vigor.

Georges was not a highly experienced diver, but he seemed game for the experience. Tom was an experienced diver who had been out with Cody and Dillon many times before, and he appeared to relish the opportunity to lead the dive for Georges. He was enjoying being on the boat and out in his element where he was confident. This trip seemed to be doing him some good; he had been out of the hospital for over a week now and was doing better every day. Georges was very willing to let Tom take the lead for their dive and listened intently to him as Tom rehashed other dive experiences he had on other wrecks in the area. The two of them were getting along well. Georges was a gentleman and a pleasure to be around. He had a very easygoing and unassuming personality with a genuine interest in people that made him engaging and easy to talk with. At the same time, he was intently focused on what was going on around him and soaked up everything quickly. He was pleased to be able to experience this adventure with this group of new friends. He talked very little about himself but asked many questions about those around him. Cody made note of that and decided that it was a good quality for a man to have. It was even more endearing from a man as successful and wealthy as he obviously was.

Cody and Dillon descended the buoy line and landed on the bow of the boat and looked around the wreck. The visibility was about forty feet, which was normal this time of year at the depth of the *Laertes*. The old vessel lay upright in the sandy bottom covered in marine life of all kinds. The boat hulk offered habitat and shelter from the current for eels, crabs, and all kinds and different sizes of fish. They had descended through a school of amberjack that patrolled the wreck superstructure. The old wreck was literally alive with snapper and bait fish nervously darting in all directions. Cody settled down on the deck of the boat with his flippers and soaked up the view of the superstructure from the bow. Looking up to the surface he could see the torpedo-like outlines of the large barracuda motionlessly hovering over the wreck as if on military watch. The sound of the regulator releasing the air into his second stage mouthpiece and the bubbles escaping from his exhale and racing to the surface were the only sounds available to his ears. As Cody was beginning to reflect on the irony of the death of the ship and her crew now supporting so much marine life, he was interrupted from his private moment by Dillon's tap on his shoulder and animated motioning for Cody to follow him down to the ocean floor along the hull of the ship.

The two divers worked the deck of the boat and outside hull, spearing some nice hogfish, mangrove snapper, and a nice grouper. They never made the penetration into the hull that they planned to since they found all the game they wanted on the exterior of the wreck. As they made their safety stop at fifteen feet in depth for three minutes, Cody counted the fish on their two hoops. They had a total of nine fish between them. As they surfaced and stored their gear on the boat, Tom and Georges reviewed and measured the catch before throwing it in the iced hold on the deck of the boat.

Tom held up the smallest of the snapper that Dillon had shot, which barely made the legal minimum length, and remarked, "Jeez, Dil. Were you all by yourself when you shot this badass or did Cody help you?" He and Georges high-fived each other and snickered as they threw the last of the fish in the locker. It was good to see Tom dishing out a little grief. He seemed like a completely different person than the guy Cody had seen in the hospital a week and a half ago.

Dillon looked up from toweling himself off. "That small guy didn't go down easily, I'll have you know. He bit the hell out of my finger when I was trying to get him on my hoop. Little bastard. I am going to enjoy turning him into a sandwich." Dillon grinned at the pair as he pulled on his ridiculous-looking sombrero. "Is it time for a beer yet?" he joked. "All this plundering and carnage makes a man thirsty."

The two divers quickly geared up and backflipped into the deep blue water. They slipped down into the depth following the buoy line after teaming up on the surface. The two seemed to work well together and had done a thorough checkout of each other's gear before leaving the boat. Working as a team in a challenging environment always led to bonding among men that created good friendships. Tom was responding just the way Cody had hoped he would. He had his mind fully occupied with the dive and task at hand and was rising to the challenge of leading his new friend Georges on an adventure.

Cody handed Dillon bottled water from the ice chest and they both settled in for a relaxed wait while they watched the bubbles rising to the surface. With the two buoys marking the stern and bow of the ship, Dillon could confirm from the bubble trail that the two were on the wreck and working from the bow to the stern. Once they confirmed that the pair found the wreck, they stretched out in the morning sun and relaxed to a little music. The conversation lapsed into a time-worn, easy back-and-forth about the merits of older Buffett music versus his newer material. Dillon was passionately trying to convince Cody that the older songs, written when Buffett lived in Key West, were based on better material and were less commercial than his newer songs. Cody took his usual opinion that a person just needed to enjoy the songs they liked and leave it at that. Dillon could not sing a note, but he knew every word to almost every one of the older Buffett songs and would frequently be overcome with enthusiasm and sing along. After many years of enduring his friend's acoustic butchery, Cody had learned to accept it and good-naturedly refrained from comment since it served no purpose and never helped to stop the melodic torture.

The rest of the day turned into a pleasant and enjoyable dive and fishing trip. They trolled some rigged ballyhoo bait over the wreck of the *City of Vera Cruz* and caught several nice kingfish while waiting to off-gas from the first dive. The *Vera Cruz*, as it was locally known, was an old Mexican brigantine rigged steamship that had gone down in a late 1800s hurricane thirteen miles off Cape Canaveral with all but twelve of its passengers lost. The broken-down old 290-foot wooden hull did not offer much in the way of diving, but the remnants of the wreck provided enough bottom structure to hold bait fish and create a good fishing ground that frequently yielded dolphin and kingfish.

The second dive was made on the *Ocean Venue*, which was also locally known as the *Lead Wreck* due to its cargo of lead. The British freighter was torpedoed in 1942 by one of the deadly German U-boats in about seventy feet of water, and it did not disappoint this day, with about fifty feet of visibility and large schools of red snapper.

Both teams of divers shot some nice fish and Dillon netted a couple of unsuspecting lobsters migrating along the bottom to new habitat. They generally moved around at night, but these two were rambling along the bottom of the hull. They clearly had been interrupted in their movement by the sheer wall created by the ship's hull on the bottom and they were circling the wreck to continue on when Dillon spotted them. In nighttime migrations the crustaceans used their long antennae to reach back and maintain contact with the antennae of the lobster behind as if in some prison chain gang. Dillon had merely reached down with his net behind them as they were marching along and slammed the butt of his spear gun into the sandy bottom in front of them. They reacted instinctively by propelling themselves backward with their powerful tails right into Dillon's waiting net. It was almost too easy when they were in the open area.

Tom and Georges were in an animated discussion of the day's hunt while stripping off their dive gear. Dillon and Cody helped store the tanks and dive equipment while Tom and Georges rinsed and stored their gear in dive bags. All the fishing gear was secured with all four rods stored in the rod holders in the T-top rack. After checking the outriggers to make sure they were secured in the proper position, Dillon loaded in the home coordinates to take them back to the launching point and fired the motors. Forty-five minutes later they had made their way back to the dock and were unloading their catch for cleaning when Cody overheard Tom telling Georges about an upcoming encounter with the Russians.

"I get an ache in my stomach every time I know that I am going to have to deal with them. They will show up at close of business on Friday, just like they always do, with a stack of hundred-dollar bills. You would think that I would be happy to get some regular cash flow, but I hate dealing with them. I wish I had never leased them that land." Tom and Georges were standing side by side at the cleaning station while Tom skillfully filleted the fish.

Cody watched intently from the boat while the two were talking. A plan was taking place in his head that would require some swift action. He had to put a number of things in motion and be ready for Tom's meeting on Friday. Luckily, he still had some connections and could make things happen fast when he needed to. A thin smile spread across his face. Something primal was brewing in him and he knew that it had to play out. He would have to start out with a call to an old source for some special supplies.

CHAPTER XI

The hardest thing about a stakeout was the waiting. You never knew when you were completely wasting your time and when you really had the opportunity to accomplish the objective. This was the third night of a tedious stakeout and it was the final night that it could be pulled off without having to reset and wait for the next month. Tiny insects that the locals referred to as "no-see-ums" relentlessly pestered Cody as he lay across the deck of the grounded sailboat. They had a stinging bite and seemed immune to the spray that Cody had applied to himself. They seemed to easily bite through the black dive skin and dive hood he wore. On top of the relentless attack from the no-see-ums, the old sailboat was grounded in the channel at a list, which gave Cody visual cover but made the long hours of stakeout uncomfortable because of the constant battle to maintain his position. Gravity was a tireless opponent.

Cody had an inflatable kayak tied up to the old wreck with specialized gear he had obtained from his Miami-based special supplier—someone his old employer had connected him with. Ralph Davis was an old Vietnam era chopper pilot who had never quite found his way after returning from the war. He lived down in the Florida Keys just outside of Miami in a shack on the water by a marina. He operated an old de Havilland seaplane that he was able to taxi right up to the dock in front of his rundown shanty of a home. The plane looked like a relic and was in serious need of some new paint, but it was meticulously, personally maintained by Ralph, who had become an expert mechanic on the old Sea Otter. He was constantly sought out for advice on repairs and maintenance of the old birds by legions of other bush pilots who were still flying them. They had become famous in the back country of the northern lakes in Canada by guides who used them to run charters and fishing tours in the wilderness. They were the transportation lifeline of the back country and had proven themselves over the decades as worthy battlers of the elements and harsh weather of that part of the planet. They were the equal of the rugged, hardy men who flew them.

Ralph Davis had converted his hard-earned military flying prowess into an independent life of flying tourists around the backwaters of the Florida Keys. He had flown thousands of hours over the jungles and rivers of Vietnam as a hard-charging helicopter pilot transporting troops over the hostile terrain. He had come back as a disillusioned captain with a reputation for fearless flying and an outstanding track record of bravery and a reputation as a skilled pilot. His wounded choppers had made it back time and again from hot landings to pick up stranded soldiers. He gained a reputation for fearless mojo under fire and his reputation attracted the best crewmembers as co-pilots and gunners. When he returned from combat after two tours, he struggled to make the transition to civilian life, and his life had slowly spiraled down into a semi-legitimate lifestyle in the Keys, servicing the tourist industry but also running a few drugs and turning into a source for illegal products from a variety of Caribbean-based suppliers.

Along the way he had bought the old de Havilland Sea Otter and created a niche for himself among the colorful Key West characters who serviced the tourist industry. He enjoyed many beers and more than his share of the always available tourist ladies down in Key West. You could usually find him hanging out at Captain Tony's or somewhere in the off-Duval street pubs. He generally started the night out alone but usually wound up in the company of some unsuspecting tourist lass before the night was over. After all the years of heavy drinking, he had forevermore lost his driver's license, so he had to transport himself on a three-wheeled trike with a flowered basket on the back and a small billboard advertising his air charter service. Many a local had seen Ralph pedaling home across town late at night with an inebriated tourist girl sitting in the back of his trike as he slowly made his way back home to carry on with the party.

He had officially lost his pilot's license, too, at the same time that they took his driver's license. But they couldn't take his plane and they couldn't stop the tourists from wanting rides in it. So he existed, like so many other inhabitants of the Keys, off the grid. He gave cash plane rides from his house in a seaplane to tourists referred to him from a network of other "pirates" as they called themselves. He supplemented his living with the sourcing business he got from Cody and others from time to time. The sourcing was a high-profit endeavor but it wasn't very steady. Cody had proven to be a reliable and reasonable repeat customer. He seemed to need a Russian weapon or some other supply at least several times a year and he was always good for the final payment on delivery without complaint. Ralph was always grateful for the extra income because that gave him the money he needed to keep his plane in tip-top shape. Parts for the old de Havilland were expensive and hard to come by. He was always on the lookout for something he might need and bought parts whenever he saw them come up for sale, whether he needed them or not.

Ralph had quickly learned that just about any illegal weapon, drug, device, electronics, or information that was wanted by somebody could be obtained somewhere in the Caribbean. He was part sourcing agent and part transportation service for the goods that he obtained. He became a turnkey source for the Spanish crime syndicate that had employed Cody and for a few others, as well. Cody's contact with the syndicate had put him onto Ralph as a source. He had proven reliable and honest in his dealings with Cody, and Cody had confidence that he would deliver what he said he could. Cody never knew where Ralph went to obtain the items he needed, but he had never been able to stump the old captain with a request for items he couldn't find.

The pilot never landed on land these days. His illegal pilot status forced him to stick to water landings on lakes, rivers, and protected ocean harbors and inlets. He became a master at slipping in and out under the radar of the authorities by flying low. He literally flew nap-of-the-earth over the Everglades through all the remote passageways that he knew to have limited surveillance by the FAA. Whenever Cody met him, he had to find some remote dock or waterfront restaurant located in uncontrolled airspace. The old pilot was always right on time for his prearranged meetings. He would appear suddenly out of nowhere and skim the surface of the water right up to the location of the party he was going to meet and then gracefully plow the old bird into the water, flawlessly coasting right up to the meeting place. He was always within two or three minutes either way of the predetermined meeting time. He treated every mission with military precision, and the old discipline which had served him so well in combat came back to take control on every mission. Cody had met him at an old fish house dock on a remote lake where they had met previously and gave him the list of items he needed for this mission. The pilot had reviewed the list carefully, asked a few questions, and then quoted a price for the goods. As always, Cody paid half cash up front and held back the final half for delivery. Two days later, Cody had gotten a cryptic call from the captain's satellite phone with a meeting time at the same location for later that day. Cody had met him at their meeting place, carefully looked at the goods, made the exchange, and within a few minutes of the landing, he had pushed the old bird off the dock and was watching the pilot lift off from the glass-smooth water with his shopping list of items in hand.

Cody had used the two days that the old pilot needed to find his needed supplies to work out the other details of his trap. He had gone back to the abandoned sailboat outside the channel where he and Shirley had seen the speedboat meet the Russians on the edge of the marina property leased by the Russians. Cody had rigged up a steel cable along the bottom of the channel lashed to the navigation piling on the far side of the channel from the land. He had rigged a pulley and rope to a palm tree trunk on land with sandbags suspended from the tree. The sandbags were suspended by a small hydraulic latch that Cody could activate from across the channel on the sailboat by pushing a button on a remote control. The latch would open and the sandbags would swing down and pull the cable taut across the channel at water surface height. The system was set up so that Cody would be able to quickly detach everything and load the kayak up and disappear with all evidence except the cable, which would be lying unseen on the bottom of the channel. Cody would come back later and recover that.

The plan was simple in concept but would require precise execution to safely pull it off. Cody presumed that the Haitians and Russians regularly used the back marina property for exchanges just as he had witnessed the night he had been with Shirley in the channel. He intended to catch the boat as it crossed over the cable and trip the latch. The cable would come up around the bottom of the boat and catch in the area between the transom and lower units of the boat's big outboard motors as the vessel moved forward. Cody had rigged the cable with some small diameter rope stringers that would trail out of the cable from the current in the channel. Cody knew that the first response to the sensation of the boat being snagged would cause the boat captain to reverse the engines. That would cause the rope stringers to be pulled into the propellers and foul them. While the boaters were busy unraveling the mess caused by the stringers, Cody had a surprise planned for them.

The supplies that Ralph had gotten for Cody included three small pneumatic pistols with one-cc cannule darts—commonly used for tranquilization of wild animals at close range. Cody had gotten a supply of liquid ketamine, which was developed as an animal tranquilizer and caused an immediate, acute catatonic state in humans when intravenously injected. If injected intra-muscularly, it had a similar effect but it took longer to deactivate muscular control. The cannule darts used the momentum of the flying dart to inject the liquid into the recipient once the dart impacted the flesh. Under normal circumstances, an injection anywhere in the neck area would cause almost immediate loss of muscle control. Cody was anticipating only two men on the boat, but he brought a third dart gun for backup.

The pistols were all single shot .22 caliber weapons with ex-tension tubes attached for accuracy in shooting the dart cannules. One cc of ketamine was a minimum dose; Cody was erring on the side of caution to prevent a possible death or injury to the recipi-ents. He was trusting in the plan he had set up to achieve a very close range shot into the necks of the targets; this would rapidly cause them to lose muscle control without losing consciousness. As a backup, he had a Mossberg twelve-gauge pistol grip shotgun which was deadly at close range and sure to get maximum re-spect from anybody it was pointed at. He brought that only as a backup to the tranquilizers. He hoped he would not need it. He had rehearsed the plan in his head over and over as he always did.

Three nights in a row of waiting for four hours on the old sailboat was beginning to try Cody's patience. He looked at his watch for the hundredth time that night. It was shortly before midnight and approaching the time that Cody had observed the last meeting. Just as he was beginning to replay the memory tape of his night with Shirley that night, he heard the sound of idling outboard motors and saw the navigation lights of a boat slowly coming down the channel toward the marina. As the boat rounded the bend, Cody recognized it as the speedboat he had seen before. It was manned by the same two black men. Cody smiled to himself. His pulse accelerated slightly as he reviewed the plan again in his head. Cody scanned the shoreline carefully to see if there was any sign of the Russians. Just as he was scanning the shoreline, he saw the headlights of a vehicle through the vegetation as the front-end headlights bounced up and down while the truck made its way down the rutted path to the water's edge. The meeting was happening tonight, and the game was on.

Cody watched as the Haitians pulled the bow of the boat up to the shallow water. The more slender of the two slid down the side of the bow and gently lowered himself into the water. The driver stayed on the boat, gently nudging the throttles to keep the bow up against the shallows. He was an impressive-looking, well-muscled specimen with long dreadlocks, which made Cody rethink the strategy of using only one cc of the ketamine. Luckily, he had an extra dart. From the size of this guy, Cody was thinking that he might need it. Cody knew that the only way to remain anonymous in this endeavor was to make sure that nobody got seriously hurt so that the police did not get involved.

As the truck approached the shore and the slender black man standing in the shallow water, the driver turned the lights off and took a sudden hard left. The driver reversed and then backed the truck up close to the shoreline. A tattooed Russian man got out wearing a wife-beater tee shirt and they exchanged a brief one-arm hug with a handshake. There was an air of familiarity between the two, but there was still a wary caution. Gauging by the way the boat driver and the truck driver were maintaining their distance, there was familiarity but not absolute trust between the two groups. A few brief words were exchanged and then the Russian returned to the truck and walked back to the Haitian with a duffle bag. The Haitian shone a small flashlight inside. He counted the contents and then waved at the boat driver, who bent down and picked up a package, handing it down to his partner, who had waded back into the water close to the cockpit of the boat.

The Russian stabbed a knife into the package and placed some of the powder into a vial, which he held up to the flashlight. He swirled the tube around and then re-checked it. He shook his head and slapped the Haitian man on the back. After that he set the bag down on the shore and he and the Haitian waded out and took two more packages from the boat driver. The Haitian bent down and helped him quickly re-tape the opened package. The two men had obviously done this exchange before based on the practiced way they went through their ritual. The slender black man grabbed the duffle bag and waded out to the waiting boat. He vaulted over the side after handing the duffle to the driver.

The Russian carefully placed the three packages in the back of the truck bed and closed the tailgate as the Haitian boat slowly backed out of the shallows. The Russian climbed into the cab, and the truck started slowly making its way out the rough path it had come in on. The driver turned on the high beams and Cody could track it through the vegetation. He noted that the truck made it to the road just as the Haitians backed into the channel and were starting to make forward progress back toward the awaiting cable trap.

Cody heard the men talking in their native Creole as they headed to their positions around the helm station. The larger man was driving the boat, and the more slender man turned on an overhead light and opened up the duffle bag for the driver to inspect. Cody carefully watched through his binoculars as the man zipped up the bag and tossed it into the small cabin below deck. Cody felt his pulse accelerate and his breathing noticeably pick up; he began to reference the position of the boat to the location of the palm tree and imaginary line he visualized from the piling marking the channel to the palm tree. His location on the old sailboat was forward of the cable line by approximately fifty yards. He had vectored the reference points in his head for the past three nights as to where he thought the reference point would be from his location when the bow of the boat crossed over the cable line. He studied the slowly idling boat as it approached the reference point and he quickly went through the whole plan in his head one last time as he slipped on the dive gloves and secured the Velcro straps on the backs of his hands.

He glanced down at the kayak and saw that all the gear and weapons were laid out perfectly and strapped down against the top front, just as he had worked out, with easy access from his sitting position with his right hand. The elastic straps holding them to the kayak were sufficient to keep them from slipping off but not so resistant that they would present a problem for Cody in getting them to easily release the weapon as needed. He had carefully laid out the three pistols with barrel extension, the Mossberg twelve-gauge pump pistol handle shotgun, and a two-foot length of #5 smooth rebar. In addition, Cody kept a nine-millimeter Glock pistol in a shoulder holster in the bottom of the kayak that he intended to slip on once he got under way, and a large dive knife in a sheath strapped to the inside of his left leg at the calf muscle. The other supplies he needed were in a small fanny pack that he would put on before he left the sailboat.

As the slender man reached over to kill the overhead light, the two Haitians felt the rear of the boat bump up as if they had just run over something. Immediately, their progress slowed and then stopped. The two looked at each other as the driver worked the throttles and then pushed them into neutral. He cursed and then reversed the motors. The slender man turned the overhead light on again and started rummaging for a flashlight. The driver killed the motors and they both went to the back of the boat and leaned over the transom to see what was happening.

Once Cody heard the engines stop, he knew his plan had worked. The reversing of the propellers had sucked in the tag lines floating off the back of the cable and had fouled the propellers. It would take them at least several minutes to get the props spinning freely again, during which time they would be completely preoccupied. Cody took one last look at the two men bent over the transom and silently slid down the deck of the sailboat into the waiting kayak. He smoothly slipped on the fanny pack and the holstered Glock pistol, and slipped the trolling motor assembly into the water.

The trolling motor was designed for a much bigger boat and it powerfully and silently pulled the kayak through the water toward the bow of the boat. Cody knew that with the overhead light on, their ability to see him in the darkness was impaired. Even if they did look up and scan the water around the boat, there was only a small window when they might see him crossing to the channel in their sight line. Once he got to the bow of the boat, he carefully steered around it to line up parallel with the boat and slowed down. The inflatable kayak was a fairly stable platform, but Cody needed to make sure that he kept it in position so that he could rapidly stand, aim, and fire. To do that, he had to grab the rub rail around the edge of the hull of the big speedboat.

Cody listened as the two men cursed in the steamy night. They seemed to be arguing between themselves as they hacked away at the lines that had fouled the propellers. Cody knew that he had very little room for error with this plan. He had not anticipated that both men would be bent over the transom; he had thought that he would be able to take out one man bent over with a clean neck shot and then rise up and shoot the other man, who would probably be by the helm station pulling out a weapon after he heard the first shot.

Cody pulled the kayak silently forward another five feet and then pulled out all three pistols; he put two in his left hand and the third in his shooting hand and stood up again. He calmly took dead aim at the groin of the larger man and pulled off the shot. The sharp crack of the weapon and then the sudden painful shriek of the man as the dart cannule splattered into his sensitive groin area broke the calmness of the night. His companion was shocked by the sudden noise and the thrashing of his companion as he struggled to reach around and find what was causing the burning pain between his legs.

Cody calmly dropped the first pistol into the bottom of the kayak and replaced it in his shooting hand with another pistol and aimed it at the second man, who stood up and faced the attacker. Once he saw the hooded man pointing a weapon at him, he raised his hands over his head and uttered something unintelligible. Cody calmly squeezed off another shot that landed in the neck of the slender man. The impact of the shot caused him to fall into the first man, who was already beginning to feel the paralyzing effects of the ketamine. The highly vascular groin area was rapidly circulating the drug into his system and he was almost immobilized already.

The slender Haitian dropped to his knees and plucked the dart out of his neck. Cody cursed and lunged forward past the man to grab his companion and keep him from falling overboard. Preoccupied pulling the heavy brute back into the boat, Cody did not observe the smaller man stagger forward and lurch toward the cabin. Cody caught him by the dreadlocks just as he was reaching inside and slammed him to the deck facedown. He reached inside his fanny pack and pulled out the wire ties he had brought for handcuffing the men. He quickly put the two heavy-duty wire ties around the man's hands and pulled them tight with his hands behind his back. Cody did the same for the larger man and collected both the darts. He reached inside the cabin and grabbed the duffle bag he had seen them get from the Russians and grabbed a handgun and rifle. He pulled the clips out of the weapons and racked both of the slides to eject the rounds already loaded and tossed the clips and rounds in the water together with the keys from the ignition of the boat.

After pausing to look around one last time, Cody lowered himself into the water and waded over to the kayak. He tossed the duffle bag onto the inflatable boat and pulled the small craft up to the shore to keep it from floating off. He ran over to the cable and pulled the knife out of the sheath on his leg, then cleanly cut the line attached to the cable and heard the sandbags thud when they hit the ground at the base of the tree. The weight of the cable would pull it down to the bottom of the channel. Cody ran over to the palm tree and began lugging the heavy bags one at a time over to the water to slice them open with his knife and empty the sand into the water. Then he quickly gathered the empty bags and the rigging and pushed the kayak back out into the river.

The kayak willingly planed out from the strong trolling motor thrust at about five miles per hour. Cody had rounded the bend in the river before he heard any stirring in the speedboat behind him. One of the two was calling to the other to see if he was okay. Cody ran about two hundred yards past the bend in the kayak at full throttle and then pulled the little craft up on shore. He pulled the plugs out of the air filler and heard the air hissing out of the small craft as he hoisted the front of it into the back of his truck. Cody gathered the gear and put the rigging in the bed of the truck with the kayak and recovered the Mossberg, pistols, fanny pack, rebar, and binoculars, stuffing them in a long duffle. He grabbed the two duffle bags and put them on the floorboard behind the passenger side front seat. The small kayak was partially deflated now and Cody stepped up into the bed and yanked the trolling motor off its mount and pulled it forward. He jumped down and walked around to the back end of the kayak and folded it into the bed of the truck so that it would not be visible if he were seen leaving the area.

Cody drove slowly over the sandy terrain in four-wheel drive low gear and most of the way out to the road without headlights. He turned them on as he accelerated onto the road and glanced behind the truck to make sure no one was following. He looked down at the cell phone he had left in the cab to check the time. It was 12:35 AM. He noticed that there were messages, but he had no interest in listening to them now.

The trick to not being noticed was to neither drive too fast or too conservatively. He looked back to make sure the kayak was continuing to deflate and was concealed in the truck bed. As he drove through town, he regularly checked his rearview mirror.

After hitting the last of the stoplights in town before turning off for his house, Cody checked his rearview mirror one more time and breathed a sigh of relief. The operation had gone amazingly well, and it appeared that no one had any way of linking him to the scene. He was anxious to pull the duffle bag out of the truck and go through the contents, but he resisted the temptation until he was secure in his house. He was suddenly feeling tired from the adrenaline rush. He also felt a sense of relief and satisfaction that his plan had worked out as well as it had. Chuckling, he remembered the split-second decision he had made to shoot the first Haitian in the groin. That had not been the original plan, but it seemed to work out well enough. Luckily, he had been able to keep him from going in the water. It would have been difficult to keep him from drowning in his semi-paralyzed state, and it could have cost valuable time. Cody was fairly certain that neither of the men had been able to see him. He had kept the dive hood and gloves on at all times and had never given either man an opportunity to look directly at him. Sometimes adjustments are necessary; combat is always a fluid situation.

He pulled into the driveway to his home and noticed a car coming down the street behind him in his rearview mirror. Cody found it odd that a car would be on the street at that hour. He pulled into the garage and turned the lights out on his truck. He reached behind the seat and pulled out the nine-millimeter pistol, quickly pushed the button to close the garage door, and stood on the bumper of the truck, looking out one of the garage door windows. He saw a new model four-door sedan that he did not recognize pull part of the way into the driveway and stop. After several seconds, the car rolled forward toward the house and stopped. Cody felt his heart rate pick up as he tried to make some sense out of this development. He was not accustomed to visitors at this hour and he didn't recognize the car. In light of the activities of the night, he couldn't just rule out the possibility that he had been tracked here. He was beginning to retrace every step from the time that he hit the road when a petite blonde woman opened the car door and partially stood up, looking at the garage.

"Cody?" she called in a sweet Australian accent. She stared at the garage for signs of motion.

Cody smiled to himself when he recognized the woman as Darlene, his flight attendant lover. The phone messages he had seen and not listened to must have been from her letting him know that she was on her way for a visit. Cody was too tired to get into a long-winded discussion about how he couldn't see her anymore because of Shirley. He may have been feeling tired, but the excitement of the mission and the danger had him worked up. The bad news he was going to have to deliver to her would have to wait until tomorrow morning, he decided.

She smiled broadly when she saw him emerge from the garage and start walking across the yard to her car.

"You silly bloke," she said, jumping into his arms and kissing his face. "I knew that was you when I saw you driving down the road. I've only been here a dozen times tonight looking for you. Since when did you quit answering your phone, you prat? What's a girl got to do to get some action around here, anyway? Who did you think I was, some bloke looking for his girlfriend with a gun in his hand? Where have you been anyway, diving?"

Darlene started moving to look into the bed of the truck. Cody grabbed her hand and picked her up again and said, "I am glad you are here. Why don't we go in and make me a cocktail and run us a bath. I've got to get out of this dive skin and into some clean clothes. I smell like low tide."

"You won't be needing any clothes at all for what I am here for," she said shamelessly.

Cody locked up the truck and the garage and turned the alarm on before closing the door and walking into the house. He wanted to get in that duffle bag and see what his score had netted him. This surprise visit was not what he had planned on, but he was just going to have to make the best of it. He slapped Darlene on the bottom when he walked into the kitchen, where she was making his drink, and she let out a mock shriek and giggled. Plan B wasn't going to be so bad, he thought. All the excitement of the night had him feeling tired but strangely ready for more action. Cody had a feeling that his little friend was not going to be disappointed tonight. Duty called and the soldier was ready for action.

CHAPTER XII

Darlene took the news calmly when Cody told her that he had a new woman in his life and wouldn't be able to see her any longer. She smiled knowingly and admitted that she was not free to see Cody in Australia either and that she understood. She had made him a huge breakfast of pancakes, eggs, and bacon that he was trying to ignore while they had the first honest discussion of their long-running but superficial relationship. She had slipped her arms around his neck and given him one last kiss before she collected her things and left the house without ceremony. Cody had promised to contact her if things ever changed in his life. Somehow he knew he would never see her again as she drove away with him standing on the porch.

With that done, he wolfed down his breakfast and limped over to the garage to input the security code to open the door. Between the three nights of stakeout, the brief fight with the two Haitians, and the full-throttle sex with his surprise visitor repeatedly last night, his body felt like it had just survived a car wreck. The sweet lady did have an appetite; he smiled to himself. She was classy enough not to make any snide comment about how Cody could have told her about his other woman *before* their romp last night. She knew that she had shown up without invitation and practically thrown herself at him. Turnabout was fair play since she was unavailable to him for anything other than an occasional fling. Cody felt some small sense of betrayal toward Shirley, but he knew they were a bit early to be proclaiming exclusivity and making forever plans. Besides, the nice lady had come around when his blood was up and he couldn't come up with a reasonable way to send her off that night without arousing suspicion. His conscience knew it was weak, but it was done now and that rationalization would have to serve.

The duffle bag had contained exactly what Cody had hoped it would. It was filled with bundles of hundred-dollar bills. Counterfeit money was randomly mixed in with real money and it was high-quality printing. Counterfeiters frequently bleached dollar bills and reprinted the linen paper as a one-hundred-dollar bill. It was difficult for them to match the intricate designs in the border, though. It took some studying on Cody's part to pick out the counterfeit money from the real bills. He snatched two of the counterfeit bills from the stash and tucked them into his money clip.

The afternoon rains had paused for the time being and steam was rising off the pavement as he pulled into the marina. He parked next to the office entrance and walked inside the big metal building. As he pushed the door open to the office, he saw both Tom and Jenny staring at him in relief. "It's just you, Cody. We are expecting one of those Russian fuckers to come around and give us our rent money. Makes me sick to my stomach when I have to meet with them," said Tom, glaring at Cody.

"You look like you are doing better, Tom." Cody smiled. "You've got your fire back at least."

"We are sick of having those guys around here, Cody," said Jenny. "Did you hear that they found a speedboat floating around in the Intracoastal with no one on it last night?"

"Yeah, man. The Coasties came and towed the boat away this morning and brought it in here for storage. No sign of foul play or anything. Just a boat floating in the water with nobody on it. Nobody can figure out what happened." Tom looked over as Cody walked through the aisles of merchandise and tried to find something that cost more than a hundred dollars to purchase that wouldn't look suspicious or out of line.

He spotted a box of remanufactured propellers and started rummaging through it. Tom came over and asked what he was looking for, and Cody casually replied, "A friend of mine asked me to keep an eye out for a propeller for him." He studied the tags on several of the propellers and picked out a large stainless steel prop that fit a Yamaha outboard shaft. He picked it up and studied the blades for dings and checked the interior grommet. He noted that the price was right and replaced all the propellers but that one in the box. He walked over to the cooler and picked up a twelve-pack of beer and laid it on the counter next to the propeller and looked over at Tom.

His friend stood up and examined the propeller and said, "Who you buying this for? This is for a big block Yamaha outboard shaft. Are you sure this is what you want?"

Cody replied, "It's for a friend of mine who guides down in the Keys. Last time we went out with him, he dredged his prop pretty bad getting to a place I told him was safe to go to and I just feel like I owe him a new prop."

That seemed to satisfy Tom and he rang up the purchase and took the two hundred-dollar bills that Cody offered him without suspicion. Cody noted that he placed them in a Ziplock deposit bag rather than in the register. It looked like Jenny was already getting the nightly deposit ready. Cody picked up the items off the counter after putting the change in his money clip and started to walk out. He turned around and looked at Tom and asked, "If you don't mind if I have one or two of these beers in the customer lounge, I'd be happy to hang around out there until that Russian dude comes with your rent money. Give you a little backup."

Jenny emphatically shook her head up and down to signal her support of the idea behind her brother as Tom bravely dismissed the idea as unnecessary. "Naw, man. I got it. No need for you to worry about me." He walked over and slapped Cody on the back. "We are fine. Don't worry."

Cody was glad to see his friend get his spirit back. He was just pulling one of the beers out for the drive home when he saw the red BMW 7 Series sedan pull into the parking spot next to his truck. A slender, longhaired man with dark sunglasses got out without looking at Cody carrying an envelope. Cody waited a few minutes sitting in the back of his truck bed with the tailgate down, appearing to search for emails in his phone until the Russian re-emerged and left without comment or making eye contact.

Cody went back into the marina to check on Jenny and Tom. They were busy stuffing money into a deposit bag and closing out the register. Tom looked at Cody and said, "That guy didn't say a word, Code. He may not have known how to speak English. He just handed us these bills and walked out."

Jenny spoke up. "We are closing up now, Cody. Is there anything else you need?"

Cody looked over at his friends and said, "No. I hadn't left yet and when I saw the guy come in I just wanted to make sure everything was okay. He sure didn't stay long. You taking that to the bank tonight?"

"Yeah. We deposit every night," replied Tom without looking up. He was busy counting the bills and making notes.

"You guys take it easy." Cody opened the door and walked out of the office.

His plan had worked to perfection as long as the bank picked up on the two fake bills he had given them to buy the propeller. That would send the authorities running to Tom and Jenny and then eventually lead them to the Russians as they tracked down where the fake hundred-dollar bills came from. Tom and Jenny would probably also mention his name to the authorities, but he was prepared for that.

He sat down behind the wheel and took a long pull on the cold beer before heading back home. He was going to sleep well tonight. He had some sirloin marinating in rock salt and olive oil, waiting for the hardwood grilling he was going to put on it tonight. Shirley was coming over for some of the promised feast and makeup time. After a long week of boredom, insect bites, the unexpected visit, and the brief jumping of the Haitians on the boat, he was ready for a little relaxation and downtime with this new lady in his life. Next week's routine of getting back to working in his shop on some furniture projects was suddenly very appealing. His mind wandered onto the subject of where he had left his long Brazilian *espetos* he used as skewers for meat when he grilled over his hardwood pit grill. There was nothing like the prospect of carbonizing some flesh over an open fire in the company of an attractive lady to bring out his primal instincts. Shirley was probably in for more than she knew tonight. He drained the last of the beer and tossed the can in the community recycling bin as he pulled out of the marina.

CHAPTER XIII

Dexter Long was talking in hushed tones in his office with the door shut. He had been calling around to a number of community leaders in town to try to raise money for his father-in-law, who had decided to run for City Council later in the year. He was calling his bank loan customers and leaning on them for political contributions for the campaign he wanted to mount. Dexter couldn't believe they weren't falling all over themselves to support him and donate. His initial requests for contributions were being coolly received and he was having to resort to ever more coercive tactics. He found himself getting frustrated with the process.

He was the executive vice president of the bank and head of commercial loans. He had rapidly vaulted to that position despite having no banking experience because he had married the daughter of the founder and principal shareholder of the bank. Dexter had been a poor student in college and had focused more of his time and energy in being the lead singer of a rock-and-roll cover band during his college years. He had a knack for mimicking the man-chick screeching of the popular bands of the time, and the band had developed a small but devoted following on the local campus club scene, which had produced some modest celebrity for him in certain campus student circles. Just as the band had begun to disintegrate due to the eventual graduation and maturity of some of the members, he had gotten his groupie girlfriend pregnant. So, after seven years of college, during which he had accumulated very few college credits, he lied to everybody in his family and told them that he was graduating as the announcement of the pregnancy was made. Out of sheer survival instinct, he had quickly gotten his long locks cut and adapted a more conventional look and demeanor to take advantage of the opportunity given to him by his future father-in-law to come to work at the community bank of which he was the chairman. In the hustle to get everything settled with minimal family embarrassment over the pregnancy, Dexter found himself employed and married in a rapid-fire sequence of events in which the review of his college credentials was overlooked by the human resources department of the bank. He had the in-law pedigree and did not need a business or accounting degree, as was commonly expected of others who entered the commercial lending field. Fortunately for Dexter, human resources overlooked the normal drug test, too.

His astute father-in-law had surrounded him with capable support staff who evaluated each situation and made the actual presentations to the board for loan approvals. As his father-in-law began to realize what a limited mind his son-in-law possessed, they relegated Dexter to a glad-handing and public relations role within the bank. He rarely spoke up in the meetings that he chaired, and everybody quickly came to know him as the empty suit that he was. His wife had rapidly lost her respect and love for him, also. She wondered how she could have been so devoted and crazy about such an ignorant and incapable man. She knew how everybody in the company ridiculed him behind his back and she suspected that he was having numerous affairs with the unmarried girls who worked at the bank. She had gotten to the point where she was beyond caring. She knew better than to talk to her father about it because he would have no sympathy. She was just waiting for the time when he would commit some irreversible mistake and she would have the cover she needed to drop him and get divorced. She was immensely unhappy married to him but put on a good public face to save herself the embarrassment and recriminations of her father about such a poor choice. At home, she worked hard to make her idiot husband miserable by privately ridiculing him at every opportunity.

Dexter frequently reminisced about his days as the lead singer of his band in college. He was still a rock-and-roll star in his own mind. It irked him when people who knew him from that time did not show him the proper respect and failed to bring up how talented and good-looking he was. He was also an excellent on-stage showman with terrific moves when he was singing. That was something he had worked on in front of a mirror for countless hours. He was certain that if he had been surrounded with more talented musicians, the band could have gone places. If any of those guys could have written any original material for him, he could have gotten them a record contract purely on his own good looks and talent. His band mates had all been too busy chasing girls and sparking up fatties to ever spend any time getting creative. It was a high RPM and low IQ band. Dexter himself had thought of it as his duty to bed every girl he could get away with during those years. It was his right as the lead singer; all the other guys just got the girls he couldn't get to. In those days his motto was "Burn some weed and then give 'em the seed." Things were simple in his life back then; the groupie girls wanted him and he liked taking it from them. It was like shooting fish in a barrel.

He still thought in terms of rock-and-roll lyrics. Frequently, when he did say something at the bank meetings, it was some rock-and-roll cliché right out of a Journey song that was completely out of place and disconnected with the flow of the discussion. He always concluded every meeting by saying, "It's a long way to the top in rock-and-roll." The harder he tried to say something meaningful, the more he resorted to the rock-and-roll lyrics always bouncing around in his head. At one board meeting, he had been called upon by his father-in-law to give an impromptu report on the loan portfolio, and he had gotten so out of sorts that he had been unable to say anything other than a series of unrelated snippets of vapid lyrics from the song catalog in his head. His comments devolved into an incomprehensible jumble of weak clichés that caused alarm among the board members and further led to his isolation within the organization.

That suited Dexter fine. He cared almost nothing about his life. Internally, all he could think about was getting together some money, losing the paunch he had gained at his desk job, growing his hair out again, and leaving his hateful wife and this loser job behind. He had himself convinced that with some funding he could put together some real musicians who would complement his enormous talent, and he could break into the real rock-and-roll action. He could hire some writers to put together some original music for the group and then he would underwrite the costs of putting together an album. With a little momentum like that, he was certain that his natural talent would take them to the top. He was convinced that he would have gotten a real break if his first band hadn't been such a bunch of weed-smoking losers. They had never respected what a talent they were working with and didn't take advantage of their opportunity to crash into the larger scene that could have been theirs.

Once Dexter knew that the gig at the bank was coming to a close, he became receptive to the overtures that the Russians had made to him about trying to help them gain ownership of the marina. That stupid Tom Jennings had swallowed the bait just like he thought he would and had borrowed more money than he could repay from the marina operations. A few strategic contributions to city councilmen and Dexter had secretly been able to derail the marina applications for the condo project, which had put the loan in default. All the executives had initially congratulated him for pulling together his first significant piece of new business in his eight years at the bank. After the condo project had derailed, they lost enthusiasm for the project. Now that the Jennings were having money problems and were facing difficulty keeping up with the payments, the bank staff was anxious to rid themselves of the loan and get it paid off. It had further alienated Dexter from the rest of his coworkers. They had no idea how he was using the situation to personally gain. He had casually suggested that he knew someone who might want to buy the defaulted note, and the bank management had lunged at the chance to sell it at a discount. Dexter had used a few well-timed comments to suggest that the Jennings might be in more serious trouble than they actually were.

As was the case with most marinas, the development value of the property greatly exceeded what the marina operations could support in loan payments. Dexter had put together some fake information for the analysts at the bank to get the loan approved. The Russians wanted to buy the defaulted note secured by a mortgage on the marina property and eventually foreclose the Jennings out for a fraction of what the marina was worth. Once the loan defaulted, the bank would sell the note for less than the face value, and the Russians would be able to essentially buy the marina for a fraction of the appraised value. All Dexter had to do was sell a defaulted note to the Russians, and they would pay him a handsome bonus, which he would use as his "walking away money" to fund the expenses of the new band and the recording costs of their first album. He couldn't wait to tell his bitchy wife to kiss his ass and leave town. He would have no problem lining up the new groupie girls who would completely make him forget her once he got his record deal.

The deal was close now; he had gotten the bank to agree to sell the note after the condo deal was disapproved by the City and the Russians were working on pulling together the cash to buy the note. The Russians had promised to have this deal worked out within a few weeks. All Dexter had to do was keep things together for a few more days at work and he would be checking out of this life and getting back to his rock-and-roll adventure. He leaned back in his chair and propped his feet up on the desk. Closing his eyes, he visualized his new life and began to mentally grind out some on-stage gyrations that he was sure would send the audience into a frenzy. As he drifted off and engaged in some of his familiar fantasies, he was jolted upright into his chair by the raspy sound of his father-in-law over the phone intercom system.

"Dex, what is this I am hearing about with your marina client?"

The abrupt sound of his father-in-law had caused Dexter's heart to begin racing. He had nearly fallen out of his chair at the interruption. "What is the problem, Hubert? No one has told me anything," he replied, using his best professional banker voice and demeanor.

"They found some counterfeit bills in their deposit the other night and turned them over to the Secret Service for investigation. I just got a call from Special Agent John Bond, who wants to come out and make some inquiries. He is arriving tomorrow at ten. See to it that you are available to meet with him and tell him what you know. Are these marina people in more trouble than you have told us about, Dex? Lord knows, you have done little enough in this company since you started here. Please don't tell me that the one big account you managed to put together is not just unable to pay but is counterfeiting also. I can tell you that it would be a major disappointment for me if that turns out to be true after the recommendation you gave them to us in loan committee when we did that deal. Not being able to meet the terms of their deal with us because they couldn't get their project approved is one thing, but counterfeiting money is quite another." The chill in the older man's voice was unmistakable.

"I will make sure that I am here with all the files for that meeting, Hubert. I don't know anything about any counterfeiting, but I promise I'll get to the bottom of it. By the way, the fund-raising is going real well, Hubert. I think we'll have several thousand dollars for you by the end of the week." He always felt like he was a little child running around seeking his father-in-law's approval.

"Several thousand, eh? That is chump change, Dex. I can raise that in one phone call. Just see to it that you don't embarrass us tomorrow with this agent. Try to act like you know what you are doing for once."

Leaning back in his chair, Dexter quickly ran through the probable scenarios. He knew that Tom and Jenny were not in the counterfeiting business; they weren't smart enough to pull something like that off. He was concerned, though, that they might have taken some counterfeit cash from the Russians, and the attention from the investigation might unravel his deal with them before he could cash out. He knew they were actively counterfeiting. They had approached him first about laundering some of their money before they came up with the marina plan. He had been smart enough not to knowingly get involved with any of the counterfeited bills when they first approached him because he knew it was too risky. He was going to have to call Dmitry as soon as he could to find out what he knew and to warn him.

Suddenly, he felt sick to his stomach. The possibility of his plan unraveling began to climb, and he began to think about the unpleasant realities that it might create for his life. He suddenly felt the need to seek some stress relief. He would go spark up a fatty in the parking lot of the music store and call out his little sometime groupie girlfriend to come out and play with him in the parking lot. A little doobie at lunch helped him relax and forget about the grief and stress he got at work and home. Since he never got any attention at home, he relied on his little strumpet at the music store to take care of his needs during her lunch hour. She willingly obliged him since he promised her that he would take her out of there when he got his band going again. In the meantime, the hundred-dollar bills he slipped her occasionally to keep him supplied with marijuana helped her remain motivated to help him out when he called. Lately, he had been calling her more often, and she was beginning to whine about wanting more and more money. One more part of his life that was not working as well as it used to. Hopefully, he would be able to still put his plan together and get out of town soon with some cash. He had no intention of taking her with him either way.

Dexter was busily texting the girl to let her know he was coming as he walked by the tall, dark-haired man in the pickup truck who was waiting in the parking lot. He paid no mind and pulled out of the parking lot; the truck eased into traffic behind him as he made his way down to the music store for his rendezvous with his parking lot lover. He didn't see the truck across the street observing him when the girl came trotting out in her short skirt to let herself into his BMW. He had parked in the shade of a tree in the back of the parking lot which he used as their little getaway spot.

Cody smiled when he saw the smoke drifting out of the door of the car when it opened. The windows were tinted, preventing him from seeing inside the car with his binoculars. When the car jerkily started moving up and down, Cody had no need to see anything further. He smiled a thin smile and put down the binoculars. He had just found the opening he had been seeking.

CHAPTER XIV

Krav Maga is a self-defense system developed by the Israeli Special Forces. Cody watched as the muscular black deputy instructed several interested martial artists on how to disarm an attacker holding a gun to the head. He went through the same motion repeatedly in slow motion, showing the other deputies how to use the edge of the hand to quickly wave the pistol away to an angle so that the discharge would miss the skull while simultaneously moving the head away from the discharge vector. The next step was a reversal of the positions and controlling the hand that held the weapon. Cody approvingly noted to himself that the deputy seemed to completely understand the nuances of the move and did an excellent job of repeatedly demonstrating the move with good technique. Cody had been trained in the system himself during his tenure in the service and was an expert in portions of the system. He had trained numerous others in the techniques during his days of service in the Navy SEAL teams. SEALs trained constantly and took responsibility for training themselves within their teams to even more advanced levels. All SEAL combat swimmers were diligently trained in numerous martial arts fighting styles, including Krav Maga techniques. Cody liked the system; it was designed to quickly and efficiently disable an adversary with brutal and simple techniques that were effective in real-world situations. As in all martial arts, building muscle memory with repetitive practice of the techniques was critical to successful execution in a stressful combat situation.

After their last sparring session, Cody had agreed to train with his new friend Norman and help improve his striking and defense. Norman had seen Cody when he walked into the gym and had acknowledged him when Cody waved him off from leaving the Krav Maga training. Cody had reflected on their sparring session and had decided that the big deputy needed to work on his footwork and balance to improve his defense and response time. That along with the discipline to keep his hands up higher would make it much more difficult to successfully attack him.

Norman ducked out of the training and ambled up to Cody while wiping himself off with a towel. He had obviously been training for some time already and had worked up a sweat. He stuck out a meaty hand in the upright position and clapped Cody on the back with his other as they did a brief one-armed embrace—the tradition among martial artists when greeting one another.

"A little Krav Maga training, eh?" said Cody.

"Yeah, Anthony studied it in the service, and he is always showing us different moves that we can use on the job. He just joined the force about six months ago, but he is doing real well. He is the one that agreed to be my sparring partner for this session. Thanks for helping me out with this, by the way. My fight is in two weeks and I need to learn some of that striking and defense of yours. I have never had anybody knock me down in a fight, and you did it twice, dude. You got to teach me some of that."

"Well, let's get started, then. I figure we are going to need at least a couple of sessions, though. Today I want to work exclusively on your balance and defense. We are going to need Anthony, but not for fighting. You are going to go three rounds with him without hitting him back. You are going to do nothing but work on your balance, lateral movement, and defense with your hands."

"Man, how am I going to keep him off of me without being able to hit him back? He is a mauler. I have a tough enough time handling him when I am striking him back." The big deputy shook his head.

"How many times did you land a clean shot on me when you and I sparred?" asked Cody.

"Not one clean shot." He chuckled.

"Well then, if I give you the tools I know, then you should be able to make it through three rounds without taking too much punishment. You will still be able to use your feet, just not your hands. Remember to use that front kick and side kick to the upper thigh to keep him off of you. That is all part of your defense. You will both be wearing headgear and heavy gloves. He won't be able to damage you too much even if he does hit you."

Cody worked with the big deputy in the ring on his lateral movement and balance. Cody repeatedly threw three-quarter speed punches at the man and coached him on how to laterally move his head and keep his balance. He changed his stance to more of a crouching position with his hands held up higher and his feet slightly closer together. They went over and over the idea of moving laterally rather than backward to avoid punches. Cody instructed him on how to avoid the deadly uppercut that he had used to end their sparring session. After forty-five minutes, the deputy took a break and was taking some water when Anthony broke up his training session and walked over to the ring.

After a little friendly back-and-forth chin music between the two deputies as they got into their headgear and gloves, they entered the ring with Cody acting as referee and coach. The two deputies circled each other with Norman moving counterclockwise against the other man's right hand. After several clumsy lateral lunges to avoid the vicious blows from Anthony, Norman seemed to gain confidence in his new defensive tactics. He began to lash out with leg kicks into the midsection and some side kicks into the thigh of his attacker. The thigh kicks began to slow down the aggression just as Cody had told him it would. As the first five-minute round came to a close, Norman got caught with a barrage of punches and was pushed up against the ropes. Just as Cody was about to step in and intervene, Norman managed to evade a powerful right cross to his head and gained position that allowed him to spin his attacker and escape the assault.

Cody blew the whistle to end the round and began the coaching. "At the end of the round there, you let your hands down. When your arms get fatigued, you have got to force yourself to keep your hands up and maintain your discipline."

The man looked intently into the steely blue eyes of the trainer and nodded slightly. He remembered the way that Cody had handled him in their sparring session and he knew that he was getting good advice.

Cody demonstrated the more crouching style he wanted the deputy to adopt and the closer feet positioning he felt would improve the man's balance. He wanted Norman to move with smaller, quicker steps. "Try to keep from overreacting to his punches. Move only enough to slip the punch and keep yourself in position to counterattack. You are doing well on your lateral movement; keep yourself centered over your feet."

Both deputies moved in at Cody's whistle and began their focused dance in the center of the ring. Cody shouted encouragement to his disciple and watched as he smoothly began to cause Anthony's vicious punches to barely miss. The two deputies began their verbal exchange and Cody watched carefully as Norman skillfully evaded a barrage of hard punches thrown by his adversary, laterally sidestepping, ducking, blocking, and then kneeing his opponent in the stomach three consecutive times while holding his head down. The knees to the midsection had a devastating effect on the unprepared man. He dropped to his knees and keeled over, unable to catch his breath. Cody rushed over to rotate him onto his back and to pull his arms down to his sides to free the man's breathing.

After allowing the deputy to recover from the wicked knees to the midsection, they helped him stand up and moved him to a chair outside the ring. He shook his head in embarrassment and reached up with a gloved hand in congratulations to Norman. "You got me good, man. I have never been put down like that before. I don't think I am going to be able to breathe right for the next week."

Once seated on the floor around the deputy, Norman lay down on his back with his hands above his head in exhaustion. Gradually, the other deputies migrated over and joined in the conversation, and a free-flowing exchange began recounting the sparring session. There were a few laughs and some gentle barbs poking fun at the two men as the other deputies needled the two combatants.

Cody silently enjoyed the back-and-forth exchange. The men all looked like a tight bunch who knew each other extremely well. The incessant ribbing and kidding seemed to be well tolerated by everybody with no hard feelings shown. There were almost no limits in the exchanges. Girlfriends, wives, conduct on the job, and anything that could lead to some kind of slight or insult all seemed to be fair game for this crowd.

Cody picked a minute when the back-and-forth died down and announced to Norman, "Just curious what a good citizen does when he witnesses a recurring crime."

"What do you mean, Cody? You got a bad neighbor?" Norman rolled over on his side and propped up his head with his hand.

"Nah, nothing like that. I was working this job over off Thirty-third Street and spent a few days watching some guy in a big red BMW sedan smoking weed in the parking lot of that music store over there. He had girls going in and out of the car and it looked like he might be doing the nasty with them in the backseat. It happened at lunchtime twice out of the three days I was working there." Cody tried hard to look like it didn't really matter to him one way or the other if the deputies were listening or not.

The revelation caused an immediate response from the crowd of deputies. Everybody turned and looked at a heavyset brute who was stretching on the floor. "You hear that, Daytime Watch Commander Phillips? You got a prominent taxpayer violating the moral code of this fine community. Burning doobies and spilling man juice with working girls in the backseat of his luxury imported vehicle right under your nose in the music store parking lot." Several of the deputies slapped hands and hooted at the mere prospect of arresting someone prominent in a compromising situation. Norman lay back down on the floor with his hands above his head, smiling.

Funny how cops always feigned sanctimony, thought Cody. They were exposed to so much in their jobs that nothing ever surprised them. Acting like something like this was a big deal to them was part of their coping mechanism. Cody knew that the prospect of busting someone important in the community would get them excited.

"We'll see about that." The heavyset man winked at one of the deputies. "Nothing I hate worse than some rich citizen thinking he can do what he wants in public while us stupid fuckin' cops drive right by. I'll put Dukes on it tomorrow and maybe we'll just start eating lunch at that sub shop across the street until we catch him. We'll take my undercover car so that he doesn't get spooked off." Phillips looked at Cody. "Do you know who it is?"

"I don't have a clue," Cody lied. "Must be someone important to be driving a car like that, though."

"That makes it even better." Norman confirmed what Cody already knew about cops. "Nothing we like better than knocking the slats out of some fat cat's ass. Might have to accidently bump his head when we put him in the backseat."

Cody smiled to himself. The bait had been taken as hoped. Dexter was about to have a long conversation with someone wearing a name tag, and it wasn't going to go well for him. With just a little nudge in the right direction, these cops were going to use Dexter's weakness to collapse his cozy little life into a bad dream. He shook hands with the deputies and slapped Norman on the back and then strode out of the gym. He needed to get back to his real business now that he had set up the trap. Hopefully Dexter would repeat his pattern before the deputies tired of the chase.

CHAPTER XV

Special Agent John Bond graciously accepted the coffee from the attractive young lady who handed it to him with a big smile. He was tall, good-looking, and well-dressed at all times. The other agents referred to him as Ralph—as in clothing designer Ralph Lauren. He was a clothes horse who incessantly shopped for designer suits at outlet centers. His tall and lean build looked good in the clothes, and he got pleasure from always looking his best. The girls noticed how well-dressed and groomed he was, and he enjoyed getting the second looks and glance backs from them. He used a sideways glance to observe the attractive brunette glancing back at him as she left the conference room. Banks always had nice-looking, pleasant women working for them, he thought. Certainly better than the old warhorses in his office. Probably best for him that there weren't any lookers at his office or he would be tempted to cross the line. There was little understanding or acceptance for hanky-panky in government employment.

Just as he sat down and started to pull the file out of his brief-case to prepare for the meeting, the brunette opened the door and stuck her head back into the room to say, "I forgot to tell you that you can keep that cup, if you like. I'd be happy to wash it for you and put it into a box." She smiled so sweetly that he had no idea how to say no to her offer.

"Well, thanks. That's real nice of you. Our meeting probably won't take long. I'll look you up when we finish." He gave her his best pleasant smile. Too bad he wasn't going to be around for lunchtime, he thought to himself. He would have to consider that if he came back here.

Just as the woman was trying to explain where she sat so he could "look her up" when he was done, Dexter Long came bustling into the room with an armload of files. "Hey, Janet," he said. "How about getting me a cup of Joe?"

"Of course," she said, without looking away from the agent. She quietly eased the door shut as Dexter stuck his hand out and briskly walked up to the Secret Service agent. "Dex Long," he said. "I thought you would be from the FBI. I didn't know you Secret Service guys did anything other than protect the president."

"The Secret Service has jurisdiction over matters affecting the U.S. currency, including counterfeiting." He looked at the paunchy banker with the pasty, fleshy face. "We are mostly known for providing security for the president and vice president, but we have more agents working on currency matters than we do on security details."

Dexter looked at the card he had picked up from the receptionist. "So you are Special Agent John Bond from the Atlanta office, eh?" He grinned. "Bond, John Bond, is it?"

The agent smiled weakly at the worn-out joke he had heard so many times before and responded with what had become his standard answer, "Yes, shaken and not stirred," in his best British accent.

"Well, I am an old rock-and-roll guy myself," said Dexter. He was just starting the standard recount of his glory days as lead singer in his old band when Janet came back in with the coffee.

"Dex, you are not going to abuse the special agent with all that worn-out nonsense about being a rock-and-roll star, are you?" She smiled so sweetly it was impossible for Dexter to take too much offense at the open slight. All the people at the bank had heard the ridiculous talk about his band so much that they tried hard to save others from the absurdity of it when they could.

"Yeah, Janet. Thanks for the coffee. You can take the midnight train going nowhere now," he said with some exasperation.

"Let's talk about the Westland Marina account," offered Bond. He wanted to get this dialogue started so that he could check out the outlet mall in Orlando before he caught his flight back to Atlanta. He had heard that there were several designer stores with good selection and great prices. He was due to add some new suits to his wardrobe. At last count, eighty-five suits just weren't enough to keep him dressed the way he wanted. He knew he had a problem, but a guy just couldn't get enough good suits the way he saw it. He could have worse problems, he thought to himself. Like this idiot Dexter, who was still obviously living his rock-and-roll college life.

"Well, Westland is a fairly new account for us that obviously has a counterfeiting operation behind them," said Dexter. "If I had known what a bunch of crooks they were, I would never have made them the loan." He made his best serious banker face and then continued. "What do you want us to do so that we can shut them down and get this bad operation stopped, Special Agent?"

"Is this the only incident of counterfeit money showing up in their deposits?"

Dexter looked at Janet, who had stayed in the room without being invited to stay. "We haven't had any other suspicious activity with them, have we?"

Janet looked directly at him and said, "You know we would have alerted you if we had." She shook her head slightly and said to Bond, "The people who own that marina have been in business there for many, many years. I grew up in this town and we all knew their parents, and now the brother and sister who run the place since the parents died. I would personally be real surprised if they were doing anything wrong. They may not be our best customers here at the bank, but that doesn't mean they are counterfeiters."

"It's usually not the business where the bills got deposited that is actually behind the counterfeiting," said the agent. "Usually they are just passing along the currency that they accumulate in the conduct of their business. Most businesses are not equipped to catch real good counterfeiting. It may not even be one of their direct customers."

"I will go get the bills and the deposit information from that particular deposit. We retained it just the way your office told us to." Janet excused herself from the room and silently closed the door again.

"Has the client been alerted to the fact that you found these bills in their deposit?" asked Bond.

"No, we haven't talked to them about it. They are a distressed borrower with us and we aren't on the best of terms anymore. We are asking them to repay a loan that they can't repay right now, and they are upset with us." Dexter fidgeted during the explanation. He was hoping that the agent would be more suspicious about the marina. Arresting them for counterfeiting would have provided a tidy conclusion to this little drama and would have put the bank under more pressure to sell the loan to the Russians. It didn't help that Janet was piping in with her two cents about what good people they were. He felt a tightening in his stomach as the stress built up again. He was probably going to have to go to the music store for lunch again. He made a mental note to text his little friend after this meeting so that she didn't make other plans. She developed an attitude if he waited too late to let her know he was coming. Like she had something better to do for lunch than take care of him.

"You have a rent roll for the customers at the marina and other information about how they operate the business in your loan files, don't you?" asked the agent as he adjusted the cuff links on his shirtsleeves. "Why don't you tell me a little about their cash flow cycle? What are their sources of revenue and how do most of their customers pay them? What would their primary sources of cash income be from, and who would those customers be? What services would they receive cash for, and would those specific customers be the same as the customers who kept their boats at the marina?"

Dexter felt a rush of nervousness at the detail of the questions. He was completely unprepared for this type of inquisition. He noticed a small smile spreading on Janet's face. "You can get on back to your other responsibilities now, Janet," he said to avoid being embarrassed further in front of bank staff.

"Of course," she said. "Let me know if there is anything else that you need." She smiled broadly at the agent and let herself out of the conference door.

"Thanks, Janet," said the agent as he caught her glance.

Dexter's mind was racing as he considered the questions posed by the agent. He had no earthly clue how to respond to the questions. He felt his stomach turn as the probability of being exposed as the fraud that he was began to increase substantially. For some reason, he didn't want the agent to know how little he really knew about his client and the banking business in general. As usual, he reverted back to the vapid rock-and-roll lyrics that always rattled around in his head.

"This marina, well, you gotta understand. She dealt me a queen, she gave me a king. She was wheelin' and dealin' and doing her thing." He smiled weakly at the agent, who maintained an emotionless expression.

Dexter rattled on. "I have been trying to make everybody here at the bank realize. You know, you got to roll with the punches to get to what's real. I had no way of knowing the place would show up on the potential counterfeiting list."

"How well did you know these people before you made them the loan?"

"How well can you know any customer? My philosophy is you look at things and then that is the way lady luck dances. Roll the bones." Dexter leaned back in his chair and sniffed. He was back in his comfort zone now. He deluded himself into thinking he made perfect sense and was sounding profound with his rock-and-roll blather. This Secret Service guy seemed to be getting him perfectly. Most people were jealous of him because he was so smooth in the way he talked. He felt relieved that his natural cool persona had re-emerged.

Agent Bond sat expressionless, looking at the fool in front of him. This was a new low in his experience of dealing with bankers. At best, he might actually get directions to the place from this idiot. Anything else of any substance seemed doubtful at this point. He would have to work this out on his own.

"Well then," he said. "Maybe you could give me some directions to this place so I could talk to these people myself. I'll just get out of your hair for now and follow up on this with you from my office based on the monitoring you guys do on the account."

CHAPTER XVI

Cody pulled into his driveway and turned the bright lights on in his truck out of habit so that the perimeter of their light shone over the heavily vegetated back and side yard that surrounded his detached combination shop and garage building. As the over-sized double garage door opened, from his peripheral vision, he caught sight of an unusual profile on the top step leading up the side door into the house. He turned his head and peered into the edge of the light and saw that it was another plate of brownies or cookies with a note attached to it. He cursed softly under his breath as he carefully pulled the truck into the garage and eased it forward until the fishing float suspended from the ceiling tapped the windshield.

He entered the security code into the keypad at the side of the garage door and strode across the yard as the door shut. He pulled the note away from the tape and opened it. The artistic flair to the short, printed note allowed him to immediately identify it as Linda's. This crazy loon was starting to lose it, Cody thought. He needed to call her and stop this craziness. Lucky for him, he hadn't followed up on his impulse to bring Shirley back with him to his house tonight. He was battling with himself over whether he was ready to try to spend the whole night with her or not. He knew he needed to try, but he was not good at sleeping with other people after so many years of being alone. After sharing a nice meal at a quaint little lakefront Italian restaurant, they had shared a glass of wine on her back porch and talked quietly together after dinner. She was the first girl he felt like completely opening up to. For some reason, she could get more out of him than anybody else ever had. He had never had a problem being secretive about himself, but with her, he had found himself dangerously close to divulging information about himself that could lead to other, more uncomfortable questions.

Cody had gently excused himself for the night when the questions became a little too penetrating. The woman was like a heat-seeking missile trying to uncover everything about his life. She was especially curious about his past love life and lack of significant others in recent years. If she had come home with him and seen that plate of brownies, he never could have come up with a story that could have satisfied her. It would have thrown everything he had told her into doubt about his past life. He couldn't let that happen. He needed to completely end it with Linda so that there could never be any kind of incident like that happening in the future. He couldn't allow himself to lose Shirley over something as casual as he had with Linda. He had no interest in seeing her again, anyway. Shirley was occupying all the available shelf space in his mind these days.

This spastic bunny boiler did make up a good batch of brownies, though, thought Cody as he peeled off the wrap and bit into one of them. For some reason, they made him crave a cold beer. Ever since he had tried that strange combination, he had to have a beer anytime he had a brownie now. Kind of like mustard on French fries. It sounded weird until you tried it and then it seemed kind of natural.

Cody made his way over to the refrigerator to pull out a beer with a mouthful of brownie. He looked over at the phone and saw the light blinking rapidly on his answering machine. He felt himself getting angry. He disliked getting messages on his home phone line because it felt invasive. His home was his private space and he only wanted to let certain people in at times of his choosing. The fact that anybody could call and leave him a message felt like a trespass. It was never a problem when he didn't get many messages. All of a sudden lately there were too many callers and too much activity at his house. He made a mental note to get the line disconnected.

He was certain that Linda had been calling all night leaving her increasingly vitriolic messages because she hadn't been able to find him. She would get mad at Paula and then immediately jump into bed with someone else out of revenge. She seemed to think that Cody was on short notice standby for any of her romantic wanderings. She always acted frustrated anytime he wasn't immediately available for her pleasure when she was on the outs with Paula.

He harshly punched the play button and then twisted the cap off of a cold Yuengling bottle. As expected, the first message from 8:30 PM was Linda cooing into the answering machine, sweetly letting him know that she was available to play when he got home and that she had dropped off a plate of brownies on his porch. That was followed up with a hang-up message that had to be her and then another message from 10:30 that night that made Cody turn cold and stop in his tracks.

There is a sound of true fear in a person's voice that can't be imitated. Cody heard that sound in her voice. The message was halting and almost incoherent. Cody heard her blurt out, "They have taken me hostage and won't let me go. Help me, Cody."

Just as she was about to try to explain more, a man's voice interrupted and said with a slight Russian accent, "We have your girlfriend and we will kill her if you don't call us on her cell phone tonight. You have something that is ours and we want it back."

Cody's mind was racing as he replayed the messages and immediately began to size up the implications and the options. Just as he sat down on a stool to ponder this event, the phone rang loudly in front of him. He let it ring to allow the answering machine to take the call. He wasn't ready to show any cards in this poker game yet. He heard the machine beep and begin recording. There was a long pause and then he heard Paula's halting voice say, "Cody? Are you there? Please pick up; I need to speak to you."

He reached over and picked the phone up. Before he could even say hello, Paula urgently blurted, "Have you seen Linda tonight?"

"She has been here but I haven't seen her."

"I need to talk to you. I am coming over." She hung up without waiting for a reply.

Paula was a slightly plump, matronly looking woman. She was frantically in love with Linda and tolerated her ridiculous, high-strung, artistic emotionalism. Her eyes were puffy and red from obvious crying. Within minutes of hanging up the phone, she was knocking on Cody's front door. Cody let her in and offered her a cup of the tea that he kept on hand for the occasional visits he got from the two ladies.

She graciously accepted the steaming brew and sat down on a stool, facing Cody in the kitchen. "I see that she made you some of her brownies," she said, looking down at the plate on the countertop.

"She left them for me here tonight. I found them when I got home." Cody returned Paula's stare. "What's on your mind?"

"I know about you and Linda. I am not stupid, you know."

"I would never think of you as stupid," replied Cody. "It has not been anything serious. She comes over here when you guys are fighting sometimes."

"I know that she was over here earlier tonight. She stayed here about an hour. Was she with you then?"

"I didn't get home until almost midnight. I had a date with Shirley tonight. How do you know she was here? Are you stalking her?" Cody wanted to push back and put her on the defensive a bit. Both these women were starting to get on his nerves. He was tired of the accusatory tone in Paula's voice.

"She carries a phone that I provide her. She doesn't know that it has a GPS connection and I can track where she is over the Internet. I don't want her to know I can track her like this; so please don't tell her, Cody. We have enough problems as it is. I know she comes to you. You probably never approached her. She has told me before that she was attracted to you." She started to cry and dabbed the tear away from the corner of her eye with a fingernail. "I know how she is. She needs attention all the time."

"Do you know where she is now?"

"Someplace out southwest of town. I wrote down the address and printed a map because I was going to drive by there after this. She has been there for a couple of hours already. I didn't know she knew anybody out there."

"Let me see the map," said Cody.

"It's out in the car. I'll go and get it. You aren't going to tell her about the GPS, are you?"

"Go get it and let me see it," he snapped back. He was tired of this drama and needed a little time to think about things. He did not want Paula going out there and getting involved. He had to figure out a way to get Linda back before Paula started asking too many questions.

Paula returned with the map and handed it to Cody. "Why do you want to see it? Are you going to keep seeing her?" Her voice quivered.

Cody looked at her and put his arm around the woman. "I don't have any interest in her, Paula. I assure you of that. I am involved with Shirley and very happy with what I have with her. In the past Linda has come over here and things have happened. I can tell you that is over with and I won't let it happen again. She cares about you, Paula, but she gets wild when you guys fight. She doesn't handle it very well."

Paula sniffled and shook her head. "I know what you are saying is right, Code. She and I have to figure out a way to not argue so much."

"You need to go home and get some rest, Paula. You shouldn't be driving right now. You are upset and you have been drinking. I am going to drive past there tonight and check this out. I will call you in the morning and tell you what I see. It is probably nothing."

"I just can't figure out how she got out there if she was here without you and her car is still at my house."

"I can't answer that," Cody lied. "Let me go check it out and I will try and get a read on it for you."

"Will you call me if you find her?" she asked pathetically.

"I will call you if she comes back over here. I will send her home to you." Cody walked her to the door. "Promise me you won't get on the road tonight. You have no business driving. Don't be so hard on yourself about fighting with her. She is not the easiest person to get along with. You and I both know that. Everything is going to be okay in the morning."

She kissed him on the cheek as she stepped out the door. "Thanks, I feel better now." She walked down the stairs and waved back as Cody shut the door.

Cody took the map over to the kitchen and laid it down next to his beer. He already knew exactly where the address was. He went into his home office and pulled the map out that he had printed of the address that the escort Karen had given him when telling him about the Russians.

Cody laid the two maps down side by side and confirmed his suspicion. It was the same location. At least he knew for sure who he was dealing with and where they were keeping her.

He cursed under his breath. He wanted another pull on his beer, but he walked over to the sink and poured the rest of it out. He needed to be sharp. He had a feeling that there was not going to be much sleep for him tonight. He picked up his phone and scrolled down to Linda's number and dialed.

CHAPTER XVII

The Shelby had a rolling lope to the engine at low rpms which was caused by the high lift camshaft that Cody had installed in the motor, creating more high rpm horsepower. As the rpms increased the motor smoothed out and the horsepower steeply ramped up. The stock 428 Cobra motor installed in the GT 500 model that Cody owned produced almost 400 horsepower stock and was a rocket ship in the relatively light car without any modifications. There were only 1,534 of the fastback model versions produced in 1969, and only forty-three of which had the Gulf Stream aqua paint and white interior that his had. A gold stripe ran the length of the sides of the car in the middle of the panels and identified it as a Shelby. The GT-350 version featured the small block Ford V-8, and Cody's GT-500 featured the big block Ford V-8 power plant. Cody had installed the high lift camshaft, larger carburetor jets and pumps, and header exhaust system which improved the motor's breathing significantly and upped the horsepower by another seventy according to the dyno testing equipment he had put the motor on.

Cody had driven the car through the quarter-mile strip in under twelve seconds on several occasions, and the suspension and shock absorber upgrades he had installed on the car to set it up for the modern oversized radial tires had dramatically improved the high-speed handling and cornering over the original capabilities. The car came standard with racing harnesses for the two front Recaro bucket seats and an interior roll bar. The 1969 model was the first year when the front bucket seats featured headrests for the driver and front seat passenger. There were few cars on the road that could keep the old Shelby in view for long over an open road if Cody was intent on losing them.

The Hurst four-speed shifter worked smoothly and allowed rapid shifting through the gears. The car ached to be taken through its paces and it was difficult to drive without surpassing the speed limit or over accelerating in traffic. Cody had never been a fan of extremely loud cars, however, and tonight he was thankful that he had kept a moderate amount of muffler on the twin exhaust to keep the noise down at slower speeds. At higher engine rpm, there wasn't any muffling the beast in the motor. It had a nasty growl that no muffler could suppress when the 735cfm four-barrel Holley carburetor was opened up and pumping the fuel through the big V-8.

He slowly rolled the car to a stop in a hidden but accessible area off the road that would provide for quick access without danger of high-centering the low-slung car as he re-entered the roadway. The car had never had much clearance; adding the header exhaust system decreased that even further. Cody carefully turned the car around so that the nose pointed out toward the road. He had no idea how tonight was going to turn out and what kind of departure he was going to have to make, but he wanted to have the car ready for a hasty exit. He had been careful to check the oil level and tire pressure when he filled the car with gas. He kept the old beast ready for action at all times; it would not let him down if he called on it tonight for performance in an extended chase.

Cody had carefully studied the Google satellite photos of the area online and had familiarized himself with the surrounding geography. He had reviewed the roads, the buildings on the property, and the surrounding homes. He had a primary escape route in mind, a bailout, double back, and a secondary route firmly in his head as he parked the shiny car. He couldn't help but admire it as he walked away. He hoped nothing would happen to the old beast during tonight's events. Cody never executed operations without planning and preparation for all the conceivable contingencies. Tonight's operation was going down without the normal amount of study, planning, and preparation that Cody would typically invest. It made him feel uncomfortable, but he welcomed the opportunity to finally strike back. Passivity was not his style.

Cody had called the cell phone from his house as instructed and had a terse, intense conversation with the Russian on the other end of the line. Cody assumed that it was Dmitry himself who had spoken with him. The conversation had ended with Cody agreeing to return what he had taken from them in exchange for the return of Linda unharmed. Cody had delayed the handoff and transfer until two days following. He had insisted that the proposed turnover happen in the county courthouse at two in the afternoon. Anybody coming into the courthouse would have to be scanned for weapons, and the number of police officers in the immediate vicinity at any given time would foreclose any idea of retribution from the Russians. Cody had no intention of waiting for two days to make the exchange, however. He intended to liberate Linda tonight to keep from elevating Paula's knowledge of his involvement in the events that led to Linda's capture. He knew that Linda would not want Paula to know that she was abducted from Cody's house, so he was sure that he could get her to agree to a story that they would tell Paula. Of course, Paula would know she was lying but wouldn't call Linda out on it because she wouldn't want Linda to know how much she knew about what she did and how she knew about it. As long as the lies between the two held up, neither would know the complete truth, and Cody's involvement in this conspiracy would remain a secret. As soon as he found out how the Russians linked him to the theft and found him out, he would be able to contain any further leakage about his actions.

In order to end the conflict with the Russians before his profile got elevated any higher, he was prepared to return the cash he had taken from the Haitians. It had served its purpose for him already, anyway. He was confident that the two counterfeit bills he had circulated would cause the authorities to come after them. Setting up the meeting for two days later would put the Russians at ease and make them less attentive tonight.

The Kevlar vest he wore on the outside of his black long-sleeve jersey was making him sweat as he made his way through the overgrown woods to the back of the property where he planned to observe the goings on and create some kind of plan to free Linda. He was carrying a Mossberg pistol grip shotgun and a Vietnam war era refurbished M-16 that had a fully automatic fire mode, which he planned to stash on his way in at a place where he would be able to easily recover it. He had several extra magazines for the M-16 and extra shells for the twelve-gauge Mossberg pump. The Mossberg was devastating at close quarters and it doubled as a sturdy and dangerous club for hand-to-hand combat. He would bring it in with him to the house and leave the M-16 stashed in the event he needed it to pick off pursuers at longer range.

The knapsack on his back carried a nine-millimeter Glock pistol with three extra fifteen-round combat clips. Cody carried it in a holster with the three extra full clips attached in pouches on the vest. Also inside the knapsack was a pair of binoculars and a deadly looking hunting knife that he kept razor sharp. Cody knelt down beside a tree and extracted the pistol, knife, and extra clips and shells. The vest was set up with pouches, clips, and pockets for carrying the extra gear and a built-in sheath for the knife. He laid out the extra magazines for the M-16 to the side and began systematically storing the gear. He shoved a clip into the bottom of the Glock handle and racked the slide to chamber a round. Then he slipped the pistol into the holster on his side and made sure that the clips in his vest were all turned the right way for maximum efficiency in pulling them from the pouch to slapping them into the bottom of the weapon. Smiling, he confirmed that they were already stored correctly; old habits died hard. He tested the knife sheath to confirm that the knife was locked into it. He had brought some large plastic wire ties used by air-conditioning contractors to suspend ductwork in attics to use as restraints. Several folded terry cloth towels and the wire ties came out of the knapsack and were put into one of the cargo pockets of his black fatigue pants.

After loading five shells into the Mossberg, Cody pulled out the blackface and began smearing it around his eyes. The thin black ski mask material slid easily over his head, and the thin black stretch gloves cloaked him in black. All the weapons and gear were blacked out to prevent the twinkle of shiny objects. After he re-stored the M-16 magazines into the knapsack and attached the sling to the M-16 for ease in carrying the weapon when running, he was ready to approach the house.

He surveyed the home with the binoculars attempting to catch sight of activity in the lit rooms. Unfortunately, at his angle, he was not able to see anything that was meaningful or helpful. He tossed the binoculars into the knapsack and cinched the top before stealthily moving across the yard with the Mossberg in his left hand and the duffle bag containing the Russians' cash in his right hand.

Cody planned to circle the house to fully recon the situation and find a point of entry. There were several lit rooms and he wanted to look into them and try to catch a glimpse of Linda or confirm her location. Based on what he could overhear, there was some club music playing and talking going on in at least one area of the house. There did not seem to be anybody watching the outside of the home or any dogs to worry about.

The bottom of the windows of the home were just about chest height on Cody. He slunk to the side of the closest window and peered into the darkness with his hands covering the sides of his head to block out any ambient light. He listened for sounds and heard none. He carefully pushed on each window to see if they were unlocked. He repeated this process going counterclockwise around the house until he got to an illuminated smaller window with frosted glass that clearly had to be a bathroom window, partially open for ventilation. Cody listened for several moments for anybody moving about in the small room. After not hearing anything, he looked inside the bottom side of the window to make sure nobody was inside. The room was vacant. He pulled the screen out of the windowsill and pushed the window open. He was just tall enough to launch himself into the opening up to his waist, which allowed him to bend over and crab his way onto the toilet without making too much noise.

He stood up and turned off the light. After performing a quick check on all the weapons and ammunition, Cody grabbed the Mossberg in his left hand at the midpoint of the weapon to allow him to use the butt of the handle as a striking weapon. He listened carefully for footsteps and then eased the door open while lying down. He looked both ways down the hall and saw a man sitting in a tired old dining room table chair reading a magazine. The chair was strategically placed in front of a door. This had to be where they were keeping Linda.

Cody estimated the distance to the man at about twelve feet. He visualized the three strides it would take to get there and the foot movements needed to stand up. He choreographed them in his head and visualized the man's reaction when seeing him approach. The man would naturally respond by backing to his left and reaching for a weapon. Cody had no opportunity for a stealth approach in such close quarters. He would be immediately exposed as soon as he stepped into the hallway. The only hope that he had was speed and efficiency. He had to knock the man out with one strike to the head and then quickly tie him up and muffle him to keep him from alerting the others. Thankfully the droning beat of the ridiculous music would help cover the inevitable commotion. With luck, Cody would be able to free Linda and they could escape undetected.

Cody elevated to a crouched position and smoothly stepped out on his right foot as choreographed in his head. Just as he was taking his second step, the man looked up and saw him. He reached down to grab the weapon at his side, and Cody made the third stride forward while raising the Mossberg with both hands. The Russian was trying to jack the slide back on the pistol when Cody drove the butt of the heavy twelve-gauge into the man's temple, instantly knocking him out cold. Cody did not hesitate for one second, immediately slipping a long plastic wire tie out of his cargo pocket and cinching it tight around the man's wrists behind his back. Cody worked efficiently and smoothly to drag the unconscious man out from in front of the door and cinched another plastic tie around his legs and through the other tie holding his hands. It was virtually impossible to move or even crawl when restrained this way. If nobody checked on him, it might literally take him fifteen minutes to make his way into the other part of the home.

Cody rifled the man's pockets and fished out two sets of keys. The first set contained a car key. The other set appeared to be two of the same keys on a key ring. He slipped one into the door knob lock and it easily opened the new exterior lockset they had installed. Cody grabbed his gear and the duffle bag and slipped into the room in a crouched stance with the Mossberg at the ready. He kneeled as he made out a figure huddled on a bed in the back corner. After scanning the room again to insure that they were alone, he flipped on the light switch in the room and locked the door from the inside. He put his finger to his lips and whispered loudly.

"It's Cody, Linda."

She released a shuddering sob and threw her arms around him as he approached the bed. She clung tightly to him and he had to pull her arms from around his neck.

"We have to go now, sweetie. No time to waste. We are going to knock the screen out of that window and run through the woods to a car I have waiting and get out of here." He looked down at her feet. "Where are your shoes?"

"They took them," she said meekly.

"Damn," he grunted. He was going to have to carry her through the woods. She would be able to make it through the yard with no shoes but not through the woods.

He flung the duffle with the money in it on the bed and jerked open the balky window. He pulled the tabs on the screen and let the flimsy frame fall to the ground.

Without warning he swept Linda up in his arms and stuck her feet out of the window and began rotating her so that her stomach lay on the bottom of the opening. It seemed like an eternity since he entered the home, and he knew his time was running short.

After lowering her as gently as he could to the ground, he pointed to the tree where he had stashed the M-16 and told her to run toward it. She backed away slowly and stared at him as he slipped one leg in and then the other. He easily slipped to his side and swung down the few inches to the ground.

"Move!" he barked at the woman ferociously. He needed to snap her out of her stupor. She appeared to be drugged and was reacting very slowly. Cody snagged her left arm and draped her across his shoulders in a fireman's carry with her head on his backside.

As the two approached the tree, Cody slowed down his pace to stand the woman up on her own feet and grab the M-16. He shoved the duffle bag into her hand and told her to hang on to it. Slinging the weapon over his shoulder, he roughly positioned the woman over his other shoulder and put the Mossberg back in his left hand as they entered the woods. He needed to get them into the woods deeply enough so that they would not be automatically seen by pursuers. He was already breathing hard from the adrenaline and effort of carrying Linda.

The weight of the woman, the weapons, the bulletproof vest, and the extra ammunition amounted to over 150 pounds of weight he was carrying in a bulky, unbalanced configuration. He was quickly blowing hard as he made his way into the woods in the darkness. The weight of the woman on his shoulder was causing stress and discomfort in his upper back and shoulder as she bounced up and down with his steps.

Cody steeled himself to the effort and focused on moving as smoothly as possible down the dark path. He was pumping air into his lungs at maximum pace now and his chest was heaving with the effort. Just as he stopped and bent over to swap shoulders, he heard someone yelling orders in Russian. Cody turned around with the woman on his shoulder to see bright floodlights illuminate the back of the house. He cursed and leaned forward with his load when he heard the door to the house slam repeatedly.

Linda was trying to talk to him, and he heard cars starting up and roaring out of the front yard. He had considered disabling the vehicles prior to entering the house, but had dismissed it as too time-consuming and risky. His legs were burning and his heart felt like it was going to beat itself right out of his chest;

the stress of the woman's weight was beginning to take its toll on his other shoulder. The early morning darkness was beginning to recede, and the earliest stages of sunrise were beginning to lighten skies in the distant horizon. Through the thick overgrowth, he could see the dim light shining off his Shelby, which caused a flicker of hope and gave him encouragement. He heard a spray of bullets in the woods from behind. It came from an automatic weapon and he knew that he had pursuers on foot as well as in cars. The cars were evidently driving the road in the immediate area in their search.

Cody took the weapon discharge to be a sign that someone had seen him. He heard intense yelling and the crashing of men charging through the thick overgrowth converging on his location. His pace had slowed as his muscles played out. There was only so much air his lungs could push and only so much oxygen that could be extracted from that air to fuel his body. He was heaving and sweating profusely as he approached the car on the right side. He had left the doors unlocked, and he stuffed Linda unceremoniously into the passenger seat and flung the knapsack and shotgun into the rear seat, then clumsily fished the keys out of his pocket. Leaning over the roof of the Shelby, he fired a burst of rounds into the woods from the M-16 to try to delay his pursuers by giving them something to think about.

Linda was groggily sitting up in her seat and looking at him with wide, uncertain eyes as he shoved the weapon over the console and slid into the driver seat. He depressed the clutch and the mighty engine roared to life with the flick of the key. Cody slapped the gear shift into first gear and smoothly engaged the clutch while the engine roared its eagerness. He was careful not to allow too much power to the rear tires. He wanted acceleration, not spinning tires. The grass and gravel surface would cause a loss of traction and possibly be difficult to control. It took all his discipline to not over-accelerate the car. A burst of gunfire blasted out the rear windshield of the Shelby, and Cody felt a round blow through the bucket seat and hit the vest he was wearing with limited force. He glanced over at Linda, who was struggling to fasten the overhead harness. She appeared unhurt. Cody felt the last of the four tires hit the pavement and steadily pushed down the accelerator after he jerked the gearshift into second gear. The old motor literally roared like a lion in the jungle as it pumped out power to the rear wheels. The front of the car lifted up and the exhaust barked when he slipped the gearshift into third gear just a few hundred rpms below the engine redline.

Linda was slumped down, trying to remain awake. She did not seem fully aware of what was happening, but she kept trying to keep her hand on Cody's arm. Every time he shifted gears, her hand would fall off and she would put it back on to keep some connection. Cody looked in the rearview mirror and saw a line of headlights in the distance. The chase was on and Cody knew he had two choices. The first was outrunning the line of cars, and the second was pulling over out of sight and doubling back when the cars passed him. He had found a place on his review of the satellite photos online that was fast approaching after the upcoming bend that would provide the necessary cover.

He was breathing more easily now but still blowing hard. He continued to sweat profusely but did not turn on the air-conditioning. As he pulled off the road he lowered the window and turned off the headlights while he pulled the car behind some bushes to hide it. Fishing out a napkin from the center console, he wiped his brow. He readied the M-16 in his lap and waited for the cars to pass. The line of cars sped past them with all the drivers focused on the curve they were negotiating at high speed. Not one hit their brakes as they sped through the early morning darkness. Four large BMW sedans sped by accelerating hard as they finished the turn in pursuit of their prey.

Cody eased the Shelby back on the road without headlights and eased up the road for several minutes before switching on the lights and accelerating hard again. He rolled up the window and turned on the air-conditioning. He maintained a good, smooth, rapid pace without being obviously on the run. Rolling up the windows eliminated the wind tunnel effect being created by the missing rear windshield. He switched on the driving lights and sped past the area that he had staged the car when breaking into the house. The exhaust rumbled behind them as the car sped through the heavy morning air. The sun was slowly making its way over the horizon and brightening the sky to the east. He checked on Linda and found her passed out. They must have heavily drugged her, thought Cody.

Cody took a deep breath and tried to regulate his still ragged breathing. He wiped the sweat off his face with the back of his hand and pushed the sleeves of his wet black jersey up to the elbows. He glanced in the rearview mirror for headlights and checked out the shattered rear windshield. Several prominent shards were sticking up from the bottom and the rear seat was full of broken glass.

Just as he refocused on the road ahead, he noticed the brilliant blue glare of halogen headlights commonly found on European luxury cars. The car had its bright lights on and Cody gauged that it was moving fast based on the back-and-forth movements of the headlights. As they approached each other, Cody saw that the car was slowing down and moving over into his lane to apparently block his passage and force him to slow down. Cody reached into the holster on his vest and took out the Glock. His mind was beginning to race with the different possibilities and options.

He looked over at Linda and barked, "Get down in your seat and stay down until I tell you different."

She looked over at him groggily and said, "What's happening?" as she leaned down in her seat. "I need some water," she said hoarsely.

Cody stared at the car as he approached, trying to make out the type of car and who was in it. He had slowed down to about twenty miles per hour to avoid the possibility of a head-on collision. The other car was barely rolling and Cody kept his bright lights on as it moved over into its own lane. He stared over at the other car until he passed the front headlights and then realized that it was the same silver 7 Series BMW he had seen Dmitry get into at the restaurant the night he had taken Shirley to observe them. He saw the driver and immediately recognized the crew cut hair and saw a pistol aiming at him through the rolled-down window. He quickly romped on the throttle and felt the big block Ford motor start breaking the tires loose, causing the rear end of the Shelby to graze the side of the big BMW and jostle the occupants. From the brief glance that he got, Cody thought there appeared to be a brunette woman in the passenger seat next to Dmitry. Cody heard two shots go off but did not feel or hear either of them strike the car. The Shelby's power drift must have knocked his aim off enough to force him to miss the car entirely.

Cody snapped the shifter into second gear with the accelerator fully depressed in a power shift that caused the tires to bark and the rear end to crawl sideways again. He calmly steered into the minor drift, and the tires regained their traction. The big block was pumping out the power and propelling the car like a rocket down the road in an almost uncontrollable explosion of torque and horsepower. When the tires broke loose they literally threw up pieces of the road asphalt against the rear quarter panels of the car. Cody looked in the rearview mirror and saw muzzle flashes of what appeared to be five rounds from the pistol in rapid succession. Of the five shots, Cody heard and felt one round hit the back of the car but noticed no damage. Cody mentally counted the rounds fired. There had been two and then at least four and possibly five. The clip in the pistol had at least six rounds fired of either nine to sixteen rounds depending on the weapon and the type of clip. He thought it likely that his attacker had only one clip since it was unlikely that he had taken the time to prepare for a response the way Cody had prepared for the attack. An undisciplined adversary probably would not keep extra clips on hand the way a militarily trained fighter would or someone who anticipated gunfire exchange due to his attack. The bigger question would be how many rounds were in the clip.

In the brief chase, it had been apparent to Cody that he had the advantage in car speed. He wondered if he could bait his adversary into expending his ammunition so that he could engage him in a way to disable but not kill him in hand-to-hand combat. He backed down on the throttle of the Shelby and monitored the rearview mirror. The halogen lights of his attackers' car became brighter and closer. The driver was reckless and forceful. He lacked the finesse of a driver trained to take the straightest line possible through a curve, smoothly accelerating out of turns and decelerating into turns. Police are trained to drive steadily in pursuits and are able to post better times with more control by smoothing out their driving. Dmitry clearly had not been exposed to that concept; he was all over the road with sudden, harsh movements of the vehicle that left him barely in control. He was driving emotionally and taking his car to the limits of its capabilities by thrashing it through its paces.

Cody kept a short length of rebar next to his seat on the floor of the Shelby. Rebar was a potentially deadly but easily hidden weapon. It could be used as a blunt knife in stabbing ribs or the solar plexus or as a heavy and deadly club to the head, shins, or arms of an attacker. He kept a short length of it in all his vehicles because it was not considered a weapon by police but yet was more deadly than any knife in the hands of someone trained to use it. As he was driving he felt for it next to the rail of the seat track. He pulled it out and laid it next to his thigh on the seat. Just as he glanced in his rearview mirror, he saw another muzzle flash from his pursuer. The car had gained substantially on him, and one of the rounds grazed the top of the Shelby. His attacker had fired at least eight and possibly nine rounds now. He would soon find out if his instincts were correct about the Russians' supply of ammunition.

Cody braked hard and threw the Shelby into a 180-degree turn while slamming the gear shifter into first. At the expense of his tread and some new flat spots on his tires, he was able to quickly reverse directions and accelerate into a head-on collision course with his pursuer. He maintained a course directly bearing down the Russians and slid down in his seat, knowing that he would be drawing any remaining fire from his attacker. His windshield shattered with the impact of the bullet smashing into it, and Cody positioned his head so that he had a view through some of the remaining clear glass. He veered at the last second and passed the big BMW sedan on its right side while looking at the driver. He could see the bloodshot eyes of the driver staring at him with intense hatred. He could also see the barrel of the automatic pistol exposed from the slide being locked back. It meant that the last shot from the clip had been fired and the weapon had ejected the last of the spent shells from the chamber. Unless Dmitry had another clip, he was out of ammunition and the gun was now worthless to him.

Cody locked up the brakes of the Shelby and threw the door open. He stepped out of his car with the rebar extending upward from his hand and hidden from sight behind his forearm. Over a distance of fifty feet, he was staring at his adversary through the broken car windshield. He could confirm that the man did not seem to be looking for a replacement clip for the weapon. Carefully maintaining his position for easy access back into his car in the event Dmitry decided to spin his car around and try to run him over, Cody loosened the clasps on the front of his vest and gestured with his left hand for the Russian to step out of the car. Cody was torn between leaving the vest on for protection and taking it off for increased mobility. Not knowing for sure yet whether the Russian might have another gun or a replacement clip, he decided to keep it on.

Dmitry's expression was a wide, sinister-looking smile mixed with the eagerness of anticipation of righting a terrible wrong done to him. He couldn't believe the good fortune being presented to him here. This crazy American was challenging him to a fight. The guy was clearly not in his right mind and did not know what he was getting into. Dmitry's sheer size kept most adversaries from challenging him; most others stayed away because of his well-earned reputation for cruelty and violence. He rarely had the opportunity to engage in conflict anymore.

Cody saw again the enormous stature of the man in front of him as Dmitry got out of the car. He saw the large knife in the Russian's hand and allowed the rebar to drop down into a striking position into the palm of his own hand. The two advanced slowly toward each other and began a slow, clockwise circling when they were within a few feet. The Russian grinned an evil smile and spoke in a low, controlled voice.

"So you want Dmitry, eh? You think you can take me, cowboy? You make bad mistake."

The two circled each other deliberately, steadily moving closer. Cody stared intently at his adversary's eyes, looking for signs of pending movements. Almost always, attacks were telegraphed by eye movements and facial expressions. He made no response to the verbal taunts.

Suddenly, Dmitry stepped forward and wildly swung the blade at Cody's upper body and then swept the knife back at him with a backhanded movement when Cody sidestepped the first attack and ducked underneath the backhand assault. Cody was surprised at the agility and quickness of the big man's attack. He quickly feinted a swing with the rebar and evaluated his adversary's response. Dmitry leaned back and to the side to avoid the possibility of an advance from Cody, but he did not move his feet to maintain balance for a counterattack.

Cody planned his move and shaded his position slightly to the left of his attacker's centerline. He was certain that Dmitry would try another advance almost immediately, and he was not disappointed. As Dmitry closed in with another lunge, Cody stepped to his left and turned his back while crouching low. As he turned his body, his eye lined up a bead on the Russian's right shin, and he cocked the rebar for a full-force blow on the sensitive and fragile exposed front part of the bone. The Russian's knife swept over Cody's body, and the heavy rebar club cracked him on the shin while Cody completed his turn and put his entire body and the centrifugal force of the spin into the strike.

The blow created a dull thud on the bone that immediately caused the man to crumple to the ground in intense pain. The bone was shattered on impact. Cody stepped in and smashed the hand that held the knife with another blow of the rebar and then kicked the knife out of reach as the Russian was reaching down to feel his battered shin bone. Cody grabbed him by the head with both hands and drove his knee into his face with all the force that he could muster. The knee strike crunched his nose and caused blood to spurt from both nostrils. The Russian reached up weakly in an attempt to stop additional attacks while falling backward. He numbly reached up and felt his nose and dabbed at the blood gushing down his face.

Dmitry looked up at Cody and wiped the sweat off of his face. He was breathing heavily and grunting with pain and fear—surprised at how quickly he had been disabled and embarrassed by the position he was in. He now knew that this was going to end badly for him and there was nothing he could do to protect himself. He looked at the road to see if any of his posse was driving up to his aid. That was his only chance.

Cody snorted at the man's desperate glance at the road. "There is nobody coming to help you, Dmitry. It's just you and me here." He made a fist and slightly shook it at him for emphasis. "You are about to meet the hammer, and it's going to administer some justice. Justice for all the people you intimidated, killed, and hurt in your little reign of terror. When I am through with you, you aren't going to be so anxious to intimidate and hurt people. You are going to know what it's like to be brutalized. You are a bastard and a coward. The least you can do is take your beating like a man."

The conflict had been devoid of any conversation between the two combatants until Cody spoke. Dmitry spat blood into the ground and grimaced in pain as he maneuvered to his knees and tried to find a comfortable position. He looked up at the lean man towering over him. He weakly gathered a fistful of dirt to throw into his attacker's face when the inevitable attack happened.

Dmitry looked back down at the ground as he heard the sound of his voice weakly gasping out the words "If you stop now I won't have you killed. If you do anything else to me, you better kill me now because I won't stop until you are dead."

Cody watched the big man attempt to regain his wits and struggle to rise to his feet again.

Just as the Russian was getting his good leg under him, Cody stepped in and began repeatedly, viciously punching the Russian's ribs and face alternately with full-force swings until he felt a rib crack. The Russian instinctively covered his ribcage with his arms, and Cody delivered a sharp blow with his fist to the temple, which knocked the big man unconscious. He folded up and crumpled to the ground in a heap. Cody covered the mans forehead with his palm, pushed his head to the ground, and began using his fist to pummel the man's face with straight, heavy blows. He made sure to work over the broken nose and cheekbones. He was making a statement to these violent thugs. They weren't the only ones who were capable of punishing violence and brutality. Dmitry was going to survive this beating but was going to remember it forever. He was going to be broken up and in recovery for a long time. More importantly, he was going to be weakened in the eyes of his mob and would lose standing and respect among them.

Their leader was going to need months of recuperation to recover from the beating he was taking at Cody's hand today. Crippled like this, he might not be able to hold onto his status within the gang as its leader because others would seize the opportunity to displace him during his weakness. His reputation would be seriously damaged no matter what. That, in and of itself, would present problems for Dmitry in maintaining his role as the leader of this band of miscreant thugs and would make the gang less effective in any response because they would have leadership issues. In the near term, having him incapacitated would mean that the other Russians would need time to regroup and would delay any counterattack on him or his property. Returning the money to them might make them reconsider how badly they wanted to wage war on Cody; they had what they wanted back. If Dmitry did not re-emerge as the leader after recuperating, the others might not think the attack on Dmitry warranted a retaliatory response.

As Cody walked over to pick up the knife, he heard one of the

BMW car doors open. He instantly looked up to see Tom and Jenny's niece Karen staring at him from behind the door with one leg still in the car. She looked at Dmitry for a second in disbelief as he lay on the ground. Then she suddenly slammed the car door and came running at Cody with her face completely contorted. She slammed into him and buried her face in his chest and started sobbing loudly.

"Thank God! Oh, thank God!"

"What the hell are you doing here?" demanded Cody. He was suddenly able to answer the question in his mind of how the Russians had linked him to the theft.

"They came to Alabama and kidnapped me. They made me tell them about you." She stared upward at Cody and tried to shake him by the bulletproof vest for emphasis. "They were threatening to kill me. You have to believe me; I wouldn't have told them anything, but I thought they would kill me like they did Tatiana."

Cody was suddenly too tired to discuss it further. "You got anything in that car that you need to take out of here?" he asked.

"They took my purse and everything in it," she replied. "I haven't had a change of clothes in almost three days."

Cody shook his right hand slightly as they approached the Shelby. There was a slight pain in the knuckle from the repeated blows to Dmitry's head and face. He opened and closed his fist several times before he reached for the driver's side door handle. He looked over the roof of the car at Karen, who was staring at him hopefully. She was not sure yet that she was being invited to go with him.

"Careful with Linda in the front seat there; she is drugged and not very responsive yet. There is glass in the backseat. Make sure you wipe the seat off before you sit down."

CHAPTER XVIII

Cody was exhausted when he shut the door behind Linda and Paula. Paula had been so relieved to see Linda again that she hadn't even flinched at the story they had concocted. Linda was still groggy but was beginning to regain her faculties. She had let Cody do the talking; it was a strange situation. Linda and Cody were lying to Paula, and Paula knew it but wouldn't say anything to dispute it because she was involved in her own deception with Linda. Cody and Paula were deceiving Linda by not telling her that Paula knew what was going on between her and Cody. Cody was involved in a double deception with each lie dependent on the other lie holding up. Strange circumstance; the vanity of the two women would backstop the deceptions.

Paula had been more than happy to take Linda back home and care for her. Linda had been more than happy to be taken care of again. Cody was spared from having to tell Linda that their tryst was off. It was unlikely that Linda would be coming back for any more after what happened to her tonight. Cody was too tired to think about it further.

He snagged another brownie and a beer and walked out to the garage, where he had stashed Karen while he dealt with Paula and Linda. He opened the door and found her sitting on top of his motorcycle. She looked up, leaned back slightly, and crossed her arms.

"Is it safe for me to come out yet? Y'all sure took your sweet time. I was about to ride this thing out of here and head back to Alabama." She swung her leg over the gas tank and slid off the bike. She was trying hard to act unfazed.

"It's time for us to chat a bit," responded Cody. "Let's go into the house." He wolfed down the last of his brownie and took a pull on his beer. His lungs still felt ragged from the exertion of the night. He was walking with a limp from some unspecific tweak to his right knee. His lower back hurt, his feet were sore from the pounding they had taken carrying Linda over his back, and the soreness in his knee was causing him to favor that leg on each step, which caused an uneven gait. His hands hurt from the pounding he had inflicted on the Russian. He felt a calmness and relaxation from exhaustion and success in liberating Linda without completely compromising his identity. He needed sleep and a hot bath. He could smell himself as he moved through the heavy morning air.

"You still drinking beers with brownies?" she asked. "That is the weirdest combination I have ever heard of." She looked at him with her forehead wrinkled. She watched him limp in exhaustion toward the house. She had watched him destroy an enormous, armed man who was considerable larger than he was without even flinching or hesitating.

She studied his back, arms, and shoulders as he walked in front of her and noticed the strength in his wide upper body. It was not normally all that noticeable, but now that he had just a tank top undershirt on, she could see the power in his body. She felt herself getting excited remembering the fight and watching him act so calmly while in such a dangerous situation. She felt herself getting turned on and wondered if he needed her to give him a massage. She had been certain that he would have no chance in a fight against the Russian. Now that she had seen it, she knew that the Russian had been the one who never stood a chance. The brutality of the beating that he had administered had been unlike anything she had ever seen. She had never known a man who deserved it more than Dmitry, though. Thankfully, he had delivered it and freed both her and Linda.

They walked across the lawn together and Cody disposed of the empty bottle in his recycling bin on the way into the house. He was exhausted to the point of not being able to function. He knew he needed to coach Karen on what to say and what to do, but he needed to rest first. He reached for the phone as he entered the house and called for a cab.

Karen stared at him. "You calling that for me?" she asked with disappointment in her voice. "You sure you don't need me to give you a massage and help you work some of those kinks out? I am really good at it."

"Another time," he said hoarsely. "Right now I need to get a hot bath and some rest." He was not sure that he could have satisfied any lady right now. The invitation had stirred a reaction in his loins, though, and he found himself thinking of Shirley. He was sure that at least some of the messages on his recorder that were causing his light to blink were from her. He had been neglecting her lately and he needed to make things right or she might begin to question what was going on with him. He didn't need her getting suspicious for the wrong reason.

Cody sat on a stool in the kitchen munching on a sandwich and deflecting Karen's questions until he heard the cab drive up. He walked outside and handed the driver forty dollars. "Take her to the Island Inn and only to the Island Inn. Don't take her anywhere else or let her stop on the way," he instructed the driver.

He looked at Karen and said, "I am calling the owner of that hotel and will let him know you are coming. He will give you a room. Get some sleep and don't talk to anybody or call anybody. When I get up I will come to you and we will talk. In the meantime, don't let anybody else in."

Karen tried to protest but he put his finger to her lips. "Not right now. Just do what I say." He gave her a steely look and she immediately sat down in the backseat of the cab and closed the door with a pouty expression.

The cab pulled out of the driveway and Cody walked into the house and grabbed the cordless phone to call directory assistance for the hotel number. He walked into the bathroom and started a steamy bath running. Despite the sandwich and brownies he had knocked back, he felt famished and still needed to eat. The exhaustion was catching up with him, though, and he was not sure that he could.

After he hung up with the hotel desk clerk to book the room on his credit card for Karen, he typed out a quick text to send to Shirley's cell phone. He kept it simple and direct. He just asked her to see him for dinner later that night at the place of her choosing. He offered no explanation; he would work up his story later when he could think straight.

The hot bath felt good as it swallowed him up. He saw his phone vibrate with the return text from Shirley, which ended with a smiley face. "My house at 7" was all it said. He smiled and leaned back. Damn, he liked this girl. No big fuss, she would wait until tonight for the explanation and she would be happy to be with him again. Perfect, he thought, sinking down deeper into the bath to let it work its magic on his sore muscles and joints. Long soak in the tub, sleep until mid-afternoon, visit with Karen to reinforce the story line and the need for secrecy, and then off to see Shirley tonight.

CHAPTER XIX

Cody closed the garage door using the keypad mounted on the side of the garage door. The Harley loped at idle outside, slowly warming its big two-cylinder motor for the upcoming ride. Cody had carefully checked all the security system components before he activated them. He had not activated the system in some time. He checked the glass break, motion detectors, and break-in monitors that were looped throughout the house and the garage. A network of motion detector controlled security cameras were staged around the exterior of the house. The central system was wired to the Internet and sent a text to Cody's cell phone in the event any of the sensors were tripped. Any motion detected activated the recording of the digital cameras strategically staged around the exterior and the entrances.

Several keypads to activate the system were staged around the house. Cody entered the house and punched in the code to activate the system and checked to make sure that the unit gave the correct response. He listened for the beeping and let himself out the door again.

He swung a leg over the bike and slowly made his way out into the street. He felt refreshed from the sleep and was looking forward to the bike ride. He needed it after inspecting the Shelby. He had covered the Shelby with the canvas cover he had custom made after inspecting for damage. The car had been his father's. He felt sickened looking at it with the bullet holes and shattered windshields. None of the mechanical systems or fuel tank had been hit, however. The car was repairable. He would have to trailer it out to Arizona to a specialized Shelby salvage yard to get the repair parts for the job. The front seats had taken several rounds, and the back trunk area had taken numerous hits. He loved the car and would make repairing it an immediate priority.

After asking the front desk clerk of the hotel to alert Karen that he was coming, he strode across the parking lot to the room where she was staying. She opened the door wearing a robe with her hair still wet from a shower and smiled broadly. Cody brushed past her on his way in, sat down in a desk chair, and put his feet up on the bed. Karen sat down on the end of the bed facing him with her hand draped over his legs.

"Feeling better?" she asked. "I know I am. I washed those nasty clothes I was in and just finished my bath. This old motel is pretty nice. Jacuzzi tub with jets. Maybe you should take those clothes off and get in. Let little Karen fix those sore muscles for you. I can't blame you for not wanting me earlier because I was so dirty. Now I am all clean and I know you want it." She smiled coyly and tilted her head. The front of her robe was revealingly open with her substantial breasts on display as she leaned back on her hands from the edge of the bed.

Cody felt a very cold internal reaction to this obvious manipulation. Karen felt uncomfortable with her inability to control him with the one tool she knew how to use with men to get what she wanted. The more vulnerable she felt, the more determined she was to regain some sense of control over him. She did not know the noble side of men; she had probably been the victim of sexual advances from an early age and had learned to control men using her sexual charms out of sheer survival. When Cody rebuffed her earlier, it made her uncomfortable to be so out of control of her situation again.

Several possible response possibilities flooded through his mind as Cody instinctively sized up this vulnerability and insecurity in her. He opted for a gentle approach. He was saddened that such a young and attractive woman had gotten so skewed and cynical in her outlook toward men. He leaned back in his chair and sighed heavily.

"That is a nice offer, Karen. I can tell you any other time I would be tempted to take you up on it. The truth is, I have just started seeing a new lady in my life and I am all about her right now. There is just nothing left for anybody else at the moment. I am going over to see her after I leave you and plan on staying with her tonight. As much as I know I would enjoy being with you, I wouldn't feel right about doing that to her."

"Damn," she snorted. "What romance novel did you fall out of?" She suddenly stood up and stomped into the bathroom. "Rescuing women, saving yourself for your girlfriend because you love only her, beating up the bad guys. You sure you don't want to get in my pants? I'll bet your junk doesn't even work and you just don't want to admit it. This is probably all some kind of big act you like to put on to make yourself feel like the good guy." She was clearly getting irritated that her old reliable tactic wasn't producing results. She felt scared and weak, which made her angry.

"Sit back down here and talk to me. I need to know the whole story about what happened and what you know about these guys. Did you learn anything else about them since we talked last at my house?" His voice carried a cutting, harsh tone. He was through mollycoddling her; if she was going to start acting bitchy toward him, then he would heat the torch up.

Like a teenage girl being forced to change clothes, she slumped down on the bed, lay down on her stomach, and started crying. "I just want to get back home to Alabama and forget all this crazy bullshit. I want to go get my baby boy from his dad and start all over again. I want to go to nurse's school and get a real job and have a real life." She started sobbing with huge shuddering spasms and loud wails. She sniffed and wiped genuine tears from her face and lifted her head off of the bed.

For the first time, Cody really related to this girl and felt an urge to help her. They were both going through the same thing, after all. They both were transitioning from the old self to the new self in search of self-respect and peace of mind. At some point the internal view of oneself has to reconcile with how one sustains one's own existence. It can be warped and manipulated for a season, but in the end, the two have to converge on a common point. The reconciling can be painful when the two lines are widely divergent. Cody knew this better than anybody. He understood the internal struggle the girl was having with her own life and the painful internal collision of values.

Through a painful download of sobbing and sometimes incoherent babbling, the girl told him how she had been taken from a public parking lot in a quick daylight abduction by three Russian men and hauled back to Florida for an intense inquisition. She had been forced to tell them about what she had told Cody and expose him as the probable thief of their money. She had not known it, but once she became a regular at their house, they had copied down her basic personal information from her driver's license in her purse and done a minor background check to make sure she wasn't with the police. When she stopped showing up, she immediately became suspicious in their eyes, and they set out to find her once they suffered the loss of the counterfeit drug money. She hadn't been hard to find in the small Alabama town she came from. Fortunately, they had never thought to ask how Karen had found Cody or known him. It seemed that just knowing who it was and going after him satisfied their lust for revenge. They still hadn't connected her to her uncle and aunt at the marina.

When they had come for Cody, Linda was unfortunate enough to be waiting at his house. Cody wasn't there; they took what they thought was someone close to Cody as the next best thing and automatically presumed Linda was Cody's girlfriend. Both Linda and Karen had been caught up in their net because they had a connection to Cody. Cody had wronged them and taken from them; they would take from Cody and hurt those important to him in retribution. These were bad actors with no fear and no conscience. They seemed to act with impunity and feared no consequence. That made them dangerous. He knew he needed to close the curtain on these guys right away before his cover got blown further and he was exposed. Now he was acting out of self-preservation and continuation of this new life for himself that he was building; that made him a little dangerous, too.

He needed to check in with Tom and Jenny at the marina to find out if they had been contacted by either the bank or anybody else to the counterfeit money he had run through their cash register. He had just enough time to casually talk with them to get that download before they closed. His back and knee still felt sore from the escape last night. He adjusted the way he sat in the chair and looked at Karen thoughtfully. She had shifted over to her side now with her head propped up on her arm and was looking back at him and wiping some tears away from her cheek.

"You left me there for a minute," she said softly. "I was just babbling away and you drifted off on me."

"There are a lot of things in motion right now that I can't explain to you, Karen. I need you to stay here out of sight for a few days more, though. I am going to have to bring everything crashing down on these guys in the next few days or my cover is going to be blown. I may need your help to do it. At the very least, I need you to stay out of the way and not put yourself in danger again. I don't think those guys are going to look for you here. I think if you stay out of sight here, you will be okay." He smiled at her gently.

"I can help you with a lot of things in your life if you hang in here with me and stay out of sight. I may need you to go to the cops for me on an anonymous basis," he continued. "I want to see you get into nursing school too and get going in your life with something better for yourself than what you have been doing. I can see that you are a good girl who just took a wrong turn. We can get you going on a better path and your life will be a lot better. A lot safer, too. If you are really ready to do it, I can help you get there."

She started crying again. "I know. I think about my son and what he would think if he knew what his mamma was doing. I got to get him back and make something out of my life. I have been lazy and stupid. People back home are looking for me, though. Can't I call them to let them know I am okay?" She looked at him uncertainly with moist eyes glistening and sniffed.

Cody reached over and grabbed a tissue from the box and handed it to her. "Just a few days, sweetie. Let me get my bearings here and cook up my plan. I will come back here tomorrow morning and we will talk again when I know a little more. In the meantime, here is some money for your food and other things you need." He peeled two hundred-dollar bills off his money clip and handed them to her. He wanted to give her enough to be comfortable but not so much that she could run away with it.

He tenderly wiped away a tear on her cheek and gently brushed the hair out of her eyes while he squatted down in front of her. "Don't leave the hotel and have all your food brought to you. Use the hotel toiletries for now and don't let anyone else in here for any reason. Tomorrow when I come back I will bring you a few things to make you more comfortable as well as a few clothes for you to change into. I will jot down my cell phone number so you can call me if you need anything. I am going to pay for this room for another two nights before I leave. Hopefully, we don't need it." He looked at her intently and saw that she was carefully pay-ing attention and seemed to be responding well to what he was saying.

"I know you want to call home now and you want to talk to your son. For his sake and for yours, you have to do what I am saying until things get resolved. Stay in the motel room and com-pletely out of sight. Have your food delivered and don't leave or let anybody but me in here. Do you trust me?"

"You are coming back tomorrow, for sure?" she asked meekly.

Cody nodded his head and diverted another tear from her cheek with his finger. "About eight o'clock tomorrow morning."

That assurance seemed to do it for her. "Oh, I trust you," she said, suddenly smiling bravely. "I saw what you did to that ass-hole Dmitry. He ain't going nowhere anytime soon. You gave him what he deserved. If you can do that, the least I can do is trust you for two more days." She smiled sweetly at him and threw her arms around his neck. The honesty and tenderness he had shown her worked wonders on her disposition. She went from feeling rejected to feeling like she was respected enough to be in on his personal emotional secrets. Now she felt obligated to help him safeguard his feelings of love and commitment rather than try to control him through his sexual urges.

Cody pulled her close to him and gently rubbed her back. He kissed her forehead and squeezed her hand and then left her there on the bed to walk over to the office again and pay the clerk for another couple of nights. As the clerk processed his credit card, Cody contemplated how his life had changed so drastically with so many different types of challenges. *So this is what a real life is about?* Going from smashing some guy's face one night to work-ing hard to consider some broken girl's feelings before he blurted out what he wanted to say? In between all of that he was worrying about getting his jobs done and keeping a schedule, delivering on his promises to customers, and struggling to make time for the lady in his life. *So this is what everybody has been talking about all those years.* He smiled at himself. *Welcome to the real world, Cody.*

He strode across the parking lot looking at the black metal dive watch on his wrist. He had twenty-five minutes to get to the marina before it shut down and Tom and Jenny left for the day. He figured it to be a ten-minute ride, which would get him there just when they would be distracted with closing up the office. Probably the perfect time to launch into some nonchalant talk about the Russians and pick up on whether anybody had contacted them about the counterfeiting.

On the ride, he intended to give some thought as to why it made him feel stronger and more powerful as a man to dry the tears of a broken woman and give her comfort when she needed it than to break the body of a large and dangerously armed man in hand-to-hand combat. He intended to stay the night with Shirley tonight for the first time since they had been dating. Maybe some insight into all his newfound emotional manliness would help him deal with that development.

Through all these years of his casual relationships, Cody had not allowed the women in his life to sleep with him. In his mind, there was something too intimate about sleeping with someone in the same bed to be shared with the ladies he had known in the last decade. He would start out the night with them in his bed but always leave them for another bed in the house after their physical escapades were finished for the night. Sleeping was a time of extreme vulnerability; it was not that he feared for his safety with the ladies he spent time with. It was merely that it seemed to him that the time of vulnerability was meant to be shared with someone of stature and connection in his emotional metrics. None of the ladies of recent vintage had met those criteria. He always dismissed their inquiries into why he would leave them with the retort that sleeping was something better done alone because it saved him from the complicated and potentially hurtful real explanation.

Shirley had asked him to stay with her before on a previous occasion and again tonight. He declined the first invitation, but tonight he intended to stay and sleep all night with his arms wrapped around her. He probably would not sleep worth a damn since he had slept all morning and half the afternoon on top of the strange surroundings of her house, and the newness of being with her in bed would probably throw him off his rhythm and keep him awake all night. Nonetheless, he committed to himself that he would lie there all night and endure it no matter how restless he got. He was going to do this to advance the connection with her and show her that he could give her "normal."

"Normal" was where all this was headed. He had jumped off the crazy train headed for Stupid Island and found an oasis of serenity and pleasure with a woman who captured his interest and attention completely. Being with her was easy. Easier than easy. Tonight, he intended to break out of his isolation and offer his best companionship. He was finished with the extremes and harshness of his solitude and isolation. He had found where he wanted to be and who he wanted to be there with. Shirley needed normal and he would give it to her.

CHAPTER XX

Jake O'Leary stopped his shuffling walk across the marina parking lot to watch Cody ride in on his motorcycle. He had pretty much talked to everyone else at the marina today; having Cody roll up just as he was ready to kick off happy hour was an unexpected bonus. Here was somebody else he could jabber with. There was nothing too trivial for him to jack his jaw about. If he could just get one meaningful nugget of news from Cody or find out something new about him, that would carry over into tomorrow and give him reason for making an entire lap around the marina sharing his news break. Cody had real news value at the marina. He turned around and quickened his pace to catch the rider before he got into the marina building.

Cody was finding a hard spot on the shell parking lot that would support the jiffy stand on the bike when he saw Jake approaching him. He knew he had to act fast and cut the man off before he got started with his inquisition or he would never catch Tom and Jenny before they closed up and left the marina. He found a spot and leaned the bike over on its stand and swung his leg over the saddle just as the older man sauntered up. His face was a little red from hustling over and he was breathing a little harder than normal. The pace of life at the marina was slow; even short bursts of energy expenditure were not the norm for the residents there.

Cody noticed that his body still felt mighty sore from the previous night's activity as he swung his leg over the saddle. He smiled to himself—he half hoped Shirley would take it easy on him tonight. Maybe he should back down a little for tonight, he thought. He mulled that over again and decided that no, he was ready as required for the lady no matter how sore he felt. She deserved it for being so easy to get along with and forgiving about his spotty track record of calls and attention lately.

"Don't make me call 911, Jake." Cody softly laughed without looking up from the bike stand. "I don't think I have ever seen you move that fast. You got something big to tell me or are you just looking for a scoop to put out over the coconut telegraph tomorrow?"

"I just want you to come over and look at the new handlebars I put on my scooter, Cody. They are ape hanger handlebars like you see on all of these Harleys all the time. The Vespa dealer got some in and I had him put them on my little scooter. New chrome handle grips and some stringers, too. Now I get some respect when I pull up at the diner for breakfast."

"Yeah, you showed me those a few weeks ago, remember? Right after you put them on and I started coming here to the marina for that boat job I did." Obviously, Jake didn't remember who he talked to or what he said to anybody. There was no humanly possible way a person could keep all of that straight.

"Well, come over to my boat anyway and have a drink with me. I am just getting ready to kick off happy hour. I've got some Jack Daniel's, for sure."

The older man was clutching his laptop bag and beach bag with all his stock reports after a hard day of talking about company earnings with the other marina residents who liked to trade stocks. They all had their regular little coffee clutch in the resident lounge. It was more gossip and social club than making investments, but they kept up the handy stock ruse to give themselves some cover. Jake was president of their little investment club in which they pooled their money and made some minor monthly investments. It was more social than substantial, but the local rumor was that they actually had a pretty good long-term track record, and some members of the group were talking seriously about stepping up the contributions to it and pooling more capital. Apparently, Jake actually did know stocks and how to trade. Jake had lost his wife a few years back and now lived on his sailboat and messed around at the marina with all of his new friends there. It was a lively, fun life for him since he had so many friends, but he would always eventually talk about his deceased wife if you were with him long enough. He obviously still missed her.

Cody agreed he would stop by for a drink after he finished with Tom and Jenny. It helped short-circuit a long conversation with Jake that he couldn't afford right now and it also would give him something to do until he had to leave for Shirley's house to be there by seven. One cocktail with Jake would be just about right after Tom and Jenny closed the office and left.

Cody swung open the door to the tiny, dimly lit office and settled down into a slouch on the well-worn couch with his legs crossed and hands behind his head. He couldn't look much more disinterested and casual if he wanted to. Tom and Jenny were huddled up looking at the rent roll for the marina and discussing who had paid rent on their slip for the month already and who they needed to nudge for payment. Both Tom and Jenny looked over at him and nodded without saying anything as he flopped down on the couch.

Cody picked up a boating magazine and was flipping through a sea trial article on a mega yacht recently built by some Internet mogul from the West Coast. The boat was a ridiculous waste of money in Cody's opinion, but the finishes were spectacular and he enjoyed looking at the pictures. He might pick up some ideas for a refurbishing job in the future. He was acting heavily engrossed in the magazine when Jenny called out to him.

"To what do we owe this honor, Cody? Was seeing you every day for a while and then all of a sudden you disappear again. You decide you like us again or are you just lost?" Jenny stared at him over her glasses while she took a pull from the huge insulated cup of soft drink that was forever on her desk. The mock seriousness in her expression was betrayed by the twinkle in her eyes.

Tom chuckled and Cody ignored the question. He came around the desk and asked, "You looking at that article on the mega yacht? Did you see the pictures of that nerd that bought that thing? What a Poindexter. It figures that you would have to be into computers to make the money to have something like that built."

Cody turned the magazine around and showed him the galley picture. "Look at this galley. You could feed everyone in this marina out of that." Tom looked good, Cody thought to himself as he made that remark. His color was back and he seemed like his old self again. He closed the magazine and flipped it back on the small table.

Tom motioned for Cody to follow him. "Come with me into the ships store. I have to close up the register and get the night drop ready."

"You make sure you watch him, Cody. Don't let him stuff any of that cash down into his trousers like he tries to do sometimes for poker money. You let him know his big sister is watching. And no drinking in there either, you two. We are running a respectable business here."

The two men filed out of the small office over to the ships store counter next to the cash register. Tom looked at the wall clock to verify that it was five o'clock and pushed the button to open the register drawer. He began carefully counting the money and making notes on a pad when he looked up at Cody and said, "Grab us a couple of those cold Yuenglings down at the bottom of the cooler. It is beer-thirty in my book. I am finally off all that medication now and I can have a beer or three when I want to again. You mind locking that front door, too? I usually lock it up when I am counting the money."

Cody shuffled over to the cooler and pulled out a couple of the beers as requested. He put them on the countertop as Tom laid a bottle opener down next to the register without looking up.

"Here is the church key for those," he said with a sly smile. "How about pouring those into soft drink cups from the fountain over there so that Jenny doesn't know we are drinking."

Cody smiled and opened the two beers. He poured the contents into cups and slid one to his friend. It was good to see him back to his normal self. Jenny and Tom were good people and long-term friends.

Jenny opened the door to the ships store enough to stick her head in. "Good night, you guys," she said. "I'll see you in the morning, Tom. Those beers cold enough for you?" She put on a mock face of disapproval as she spied the empty bottles still on the countertop. "At least hide the empty bottles if you are going to go to the trouble of pouring the beer into soft drink cups. Jeez, you men think everybody is as stupid as you are." She huffed out toward the back entrance to the building.

Without looking back she yelled, "You are a bad influence on my kid brother, Cody!"

"She has a point, you know, Tom." Cody looked over at his friend while he counted the cash and made a quick notation. "We should either drink these like men out of the bottle or at least hide the empties."

"It was your job to get rid of the empties, man. Why did you leave them on the counter, for Christ's sake?" he joked. "You got my sister all upset and I am going to be hearing about this all week, now. You know how she worries about me." Tom sipped the beer and changed the subject. "By the way, what do you think of these new logo cups we got?"

Cody nodded approvingly at the cup. "Yeah, that new chiller is keeping these beers good and cold, too. You guys are running a first-rate place here, Tom."

"Yeah, and did I tell you about the Secret Service agent that came by here?" Tom looked earnestly at Cody, relishing the opportunity to tell him the big news. "Some guy came by here investigating some money that we deposited into our account that was counterfeited. The bank caught it in the deposit and alerted the Secret Service. They sent an agent over here to talk to me about it and make some inquiries."

Cody looked intently at Tom. He had hoped that the conversation would head in this direction without having to inquire about it directly. Tom had taken it right to the subject without any prodding. He cocked his head intently as Tom rattled on.

Tom reached down under the cash register and pulled out a business card. "Special Agent John Bond," he announced loudly. He took a long pull on his beer while he looked at the card. "He came in here and said that some counterfeit money had been found in our deposit at the bank and they were investigating the source of it—hundred-dollar bills. He asked us to remember who might have brought in large bills like that during the day of that deposit to help establish the back trail on the money."

Tom paused and looked at Cody with a self-satisfied smirk. "Guess what I told him."

"I couldn't guess," lied Cody. He hated this deception of his friend but he was ecstatic that it had worked so well and so quickly. He only hoped that Tom had conveniently forgotten that he had also used hundred-dollar bills that day and that Tom had not turned his name over to the special agent.

"There was only one customer that day that used hundred-dollar bills, and that was those Russian fuckers. They paid their rent that day in cash with hundred-dollar bills just like they normally do. The day that the deposit was made with the counterfeit bills was the same day that they paid their rent. They are the ones who gave me that money."

Cody chuckled calmly at his friend. He was glad to see him up and around with fire in his eyes again and with his spirit back. "So did you throw them under the bus, man?" he asked Tom.

"Hell yes! I couldn't wait to tell the agent all about their little bullshit routine. I told him how they only used the property late at night, how they pay me in cash, how secretive they are, about the abandoned speedboat we found recently in the channel, the dead fish that started showing up around here after they started using the property. He was taking plenty of notes, too. He asked a few questions and wanted to know more about them. Unfortunately, man, I just don't know anything about them other than this phone number they gave me. We never signed a real lease or anything and I never had them fill out an application. At the time they showed up, I needed the money and they seemed willing to pay me in cash in advance, so it didn't seem like any risk to me to let them use the property." Tom took a breath and finished tucking the balance of the day's register take into the cloth night deposit bag.

"Jenny had one other piece of information that I didn't know about, though. She had been taking down the license plate numbers of the guys that showed up here to give us the money. She had several different license plate numbers recorded. He took all that down and the phone number and said he would get back to me if he needed anything else." He pushed the register drawer shut and finished off the beer.

"Let's get out of here. I got somebody waiting on me over at the fish house for drinks and dinner." Tom turned out the lights and locked the door behind Cody as they walked outside the building.

Cody had the confirmation he needed from Tom about the investigation that had been started on the counterfeit money. He knew if he seemed too interested, it might arouse suspicion, so he changed the subject. "So who you meeting for dinner tonight?" he inquired coolly. He was glad to hear that Tom was getting back to a normal life.

"It's that gal Angela that owns the bakery up the street where I get breakfast sometimes. She stopped by to ask Jenny why I hadn't been in for a while and then came up to the hospital to see me when she found out I was in there. I didn't even know she liked me." He grinned sheepishly. "Hell, if I would have known I was going to get so much good attention, I would have gone crazy sooner."

The two shared a good laugh over that comment and shook hands good-bye at the front door of the marina building. Tom jumped into his truck and drove off while Cody glanced at his watch to check the time. He sighed heavily and ambled off across the crushed shell parking lot surface toward Jake's boat. He had about thirty minutes to kill before he needed to leave for Shirley's house. That was probably about all he could take of Jake's incessant rambling.

He started thinking about the evening ahead with Shirley and smiled with anticipation. He had been missing her and thinking about how nicely things had evolved between them.

Shirley had made it clear to him in several recent conversations that she expected him to start staying with her through the night. She had been a good sport up until now about Cody's nighttime disappearances from her home and the lack of invitations to come over and stay at his home for the night. In her sweet way, she had made it firmly clear that she required a more intimate and connected level in their relationship. Cody had dreaded that expectation; he was not sure how he would be able to respond. He had thought it through, however, and knew that he wanted to make a real effort to give her what she needed. He needed to move toward normal and he knew that the lady had every right to expect a more involved relationship. The timing was awkward with all the craziness he was into, but he couldn't explain that to her. All she knew was that she needed to know she could expect more from him. For now, he just had to deliver for her and work the rest out later.

He had an uneasy feeling in his stomach as he climbed the gangplank to Jake's old trawler. He was greeted at the top by Jake with a strong Jack and cola topped with a large lime section. Cody graciously accepted the cocktail and settled into a comfortable deck chair and an easy banter back and forth with the kindly stockbroker. He decided to relax about the upcoming encounter with Shirley and to treat it like a mission. In his Special Forces training, sleep deprivation had been a critical part of the initial training exposure. If he could get through that, he could easily make it through a night in the arms of a woman as sweet and nice to be with as Shirley was. He chuckled at himself for feeling anxiety over something that most men would leap at the chance to experience.

In reality, she wouldn't know whether he was sleeping or not. All he had to do was stay there with her the entire night. He knew he would have trouble dropping off to sleep, but he didn't have to let her know about it. Besides, the exhaustion he still felt from the previous night and the stiff drink that his host had just served him would probably give him as good a chance as he ever might have to actually get some good sleep tonight in her company. It was going to be an interesting evening, he thought as he tuned back in to Jake's nonstop download on life at the marina.

CHAPTER XXI

The noise and chatter of the men in the cell block were nonstop. Every noise created an echo and reverberations. It seemed like the loudest, most unpleasant place Dexter had ever been in. He knew jail was not meant to be pleasant, but he had never thought about it being unpleasant because of the noise and an irritating, incessant inquisition by one of the other inmates.

"So what's a motherfucker like you in for, man?" The gap in the man's front teeth was striking. It was hard to not notice and stare at the combination of buck teeth with such a severe gap between them. They almost looked like the tines of a forklift protruding from the slender man's black face. They both had the same orange jumpsuit given to all the occupants of the county lockup. The man was staring at Dexter's face with a defiant look. "You ain't no street nigger. I can tell that by looking at you."

Dexter was confused at the man's choice of words and blankly stared back at him, not knowing how to respond to being called a nigger. Like most white people, he avoided the use of that word because he did not want to cause offense. He did not quite know how to deal with black people who used the word for him and for themselves.

"Oh, yeah. You a nigger now, boy. You think you white and that don't make you a nigger. But if you in here, you somebody's nigger now." The man leaned uncomfortably close to Dexter's face as he spewed his jailhouse wisdom.

Dexter silently hoped that the man's interest in him would wane quickly if he just ignored him. He noticed uncomfortably that all the other, much larger and angrier-looking black men in the large cell area were staring at him intently watching the inquisition. Dexter nervously shuffled the deck of cards he had been toying with to try to distract himself from the huge waves of humiliation he was feeling at being caught and arrested in the music store parking lot with his pants off and a lit joint hanging from his lip by six policemen who converged on his car while he was getting a blow job.

He had been arrested for possession of marijuana and lewd public sex acts by the policemen who had seemed to enjoy every minute of his plight. They had all watched and laughed at him when he bleated and sobbed uncontrollably for the officers to let him go without arresting him. He had repeatedly apologized and begged to be let go while the cops made him stand outside dressed only in his underpants where he could easily be seen by passing cars. They had immediately separated him from the girl, too. He knew that they were asking each of them the same questions to see if they really knew each other. She had been taken away without even a glance back at him in the backseat of another squad car. He had been dismayed by what he felt was unnecessary roughness of the officers in arresting him and their enjoyment of his plight. He felt they had delayed the process of taking him to the jail in order to force him to stand outside longer in his underwear for all to see.

No matter what his situation, however, he didn't want to be involved in any conversation with the likes of the guy talking to him now. He carefully stood up and haltingly walked over to a table close to the small television set hanging from the ceiling of the large holding area and sat down at a table where he could watch the local news. He was uncomfortable with the racial tone of the dialogue given that he was the only white person in a cell full of angry-looking black men who kept staring at him. So far, his skinny tormentor was the only one directly addressing him. The rest just glared silently.

"I asked you a question, nigger." The slender man's Adam's apple bobbed up and down and he spat small goblets of saliva when he spoke because of the protruding teeth. He glared angrily at Dexter as he sat down at the new table closer to the television.

Dexter stared transfixed at the television, however. He slowly stood up as he saw a local news reporter standing in front of his house with a fire blazing in the front yard. The reporter was breathlessly giving the details of the fire, and Dexter watched in the background as his wife lugged out his Guitar Hero video game and threw it on top of the blazing pile of furniture, clothes, and other personal items. He heard the reporter mention his name and the arrest from earlier in the afternoon, and he slid into a state of shock at the sudden collapse of his entire life all around him. The fire in the front yard of the upscale neighborhood had made the evening news. His wife had obviously lost it when she heard about his arrest and was now burning all of his things.

Suddenly his tormentor made the association between Dexter and the scene being played out on the television screen. He shrieked out a girlish laugh while covering his mouth and pointing at the small TV screen.

"The bitch be burning the brother's Guitar Hero, man. She mad at you! You ain't never getting back in that house, man." The skinny man went into a hysterical giggle with one hand over his groin, the other girlishly over his mouth as he pranced in circles around Dexter, repeating his foolishness.

"This stupid motherfucker done fucked up, man. You a street nigger now for sure, Holmes. That bitch be putting you out."

Suddenly, several of the other inmates gathered around to watch and started talking quietly to themselves, shaking their heads and laughing at Dexter from behind his back. The skinny tormentor was prancing around holding his groin and shaking his free hand up and down for emphasis as he circled around all the group of men staring at the TV screen.

"One minute the brother be burning some weed in the back-seat of his BMW and getting his dick sucked, and the next minute he standing in here with the niggers watching his wife burn his Guitar Hero. Sheeeet. That's cold, man. That is one cold moth-erfucker, man."

Dexter felt his heart sink as he watched his boss and father-in-law stride up to the house to console his daughter just as the camera panned back to the reporter. The silver-haired man quickly put his arm around the hysterical woman and whisked her back into the house. Several fire trucks pulled up with their sirens on, and the TV reporter remained on site valiantly trying to carry on with her coverage over the sound of the trucks.

Dexter stood there transfixed and oblivious to the hand slap-ping and laughter of the men in his cell block behind him. Despite the grief he knew it was going to cause him, he started to cry un-controllably at the realization of his loss. He wondered if there was any hope left to get his old life back. He promised himself he wouldn't take it for granted again. He sobbed as he painfully concluded that there was no way that would happen. For once in his life, his head was not being invaded by rock-and-roll lyrics.

CHAPTER XXII

Cody carefully pulled his arm from underneath Shirley's head as she slept. He quietly slid out of the bed, being careful to not disturb her any more than necessary while he slipped into the kitchen for a glass of water and some relief from his sleepless vigil over her.

In the kitchen he stood over the sink while running some water. He leaned over and splashed some cool water on his face and dried off with a dish towel. While he was bent over with the towel over his head, he felt the gentle touch of her small, soft hand on his upper back.

Shirley had the gentlest touch that Cody had ever felt. He had grown up without a mother, and his father had raised him by himself for most of the years of his early childhood. Later in life, there had been mistresses, wives, and girlfriends who had all taken some measure of interest in him while they were in his father's life. His father had always been there for him in his own way, but never with a soothing hand to tenderly touch him like Shirley was doing now. Cody had never known a touch like that before. He found himself concentrating on how she gently massaged his back. He kept the towel over his head so that he could close his eyes and completely focus on the slight friction created by the gentle stroking of her hand on his skin. It was a feeling now well-known to him.

She pulled herself near to him and bent over with her arms around his chest and laid her head down on his back. She gently massaged the front of his chest with her hands and sleepily murmured, "Are you having trouble sleeping, baby?"

"No, not at all," he said, acting surprised that she would ask. "I was just up getting a glass of water and splashing some on my face." He pulled the towel off his head as he answered and turned around to take her in his arms. He held her away from him so that he could look at her in the darkness and study her. She looked angelic with her hair slightly tousled and her short nightgown loosely draped over her slender figure.

Cody reached for the water glass with one arm and put his other around her shoulder. As they walked together back to the bedroom, she reached up and kissed his cheek. "I would be happy to give you a nice back rub if you want it," she offered sweetly.

As they lay down together in bed, she quickly turned over and spooned against him again with his arm around her chest. Her small, delicate hand clutched at his as if emphatically locking it in around her body. She smiled sweetly, closed her eyes, and sighed heavily as if content with the rightness of the world. Within several minutes she was softly snoring again and Cody found himself smiling in the darkness. Good thing he didn't want the backrub; he laughed silently to himself.

He lay in the darkness reflecting on the evening. After leaving the marina he had gone straight to Shirley's house for dinner. She had clearly gone to great lengths to prepare a delicious lamb roast dinner complete with soft music, candles, pleasant conversation, and a flan dessert with coffee. The lady knew how to make a house a home and knew her way around the kitchen. She seemed to think about every detail and made it seem effortless.

The most surprising aspect of the evening for Cody was the absence of any questioning or prodding into his absences and spotty record for calling to check in with her since they had begun dating. It almost seemed to Cody that she was too good a sport about it, and he wondered if this was based on her natural personality or simply a fear on her part that too much questioning might drive him away. She genuinely seemed interested in him and continuously peppered him with questions about his early childhood and distant past while remaining respectfully off the more recent times in his life that she sensed he was not interested in opening up about.

She offered a complete review of her own life in exhausting detail as if finding it important that Cody understand every nuance. The product of a very normal and happy childhood and loving family, she had been horrified at the divorce that she initiated with her husband of seven years when she began to question his fidelity last year. Despite the hard times, she had missed him greatly after her divorce and had trouble replacing the connection she had with her husband in the dating arena. She had second-guessed her decision to divorce for many months, and the eventual decision to leave him had been difficult for her despite the transgressions. She indicated repeatedly that Cody represented the first meaningful relationship she had found since her divorce. Cody felt uncomfortable hearing the significance of the relationship to her already given his own history of casual, insignificant connection with the two ladies he had been involved with over the past few years. He felt some responsibility to care for her heart and consider the impact of his actions. This bull rush of responsibility on an area of his life that had been so uncomplicated for so long left him slightly off balance.

Shirley seemed a little disappointed that the complete, detailed revelations she shared about her own life did not elicit a similar response from Cody. Cody carefully managed his disclosures to her to avoid direct questions about his life over the past ten years and left her with vague and cryptic responses to her questions. The woman's perception was impressive; just from watching him move around the kitchen, she had picked up on the soreness in his body and asked him about it. Shirley was working hard to wedge in and become important in his life. Cody knew that he had to be careful about disclosing information because she would compile it and compare it with other known facts until she began piecing things together.

Cody gently pushed his nose up to her hair and enjoyed the natural fragrance of her head as he let it register in his memory banks. He wanted to remember this tender moment and file it away for future recall in case this did not last. He had a gnawing fear that he might not be able to satisfy her quest for information about him, which might alienate her.

He had just cast a glance at the digital alarm clock screen on the nightstand and laid his head back down on the pillow when he heard the vibrating buzz of his cell phone. That buzz indicated receipt of a text message. At 3:30 in the morning, there was only one source of a message that seemed plausible. Someone had just entered his home uninvited. The security system was not monitored by a service, just programmed to send a silent notice to his cell phone. Cody inadvertently jerked at the vibration, which woke Shirley up from her slumber. She softly stroked the side of Cody's thigh and whispered softly with her eyes closed.

"What was that noise?" she asked. "Is someone calling you at this hour?"

"No," Cody offered. "I forgot to turn my phone off. It must be a spam email message or something. I'll turn it off now." He slipped out of bed and pulled the phone out of its holster to look up the message before turning it off. It was just as he suspected; a text message from the home security system alerting him to an intrusion at his back door. He pushed the button to turn the device off and slid it back into the holster attached to the belt on his jeans, which were hanging on the bedpost.

Shirley turned to face him as he lay back down on the bed and sweetly kissed him. "I am ready for that repeat performance you promised." She smiled. She draped her leg over his and slid on top of him with her elbows on either side of his head and stared into his eyes. The woman had an appetite, Cody thought to himself.

Cody's mind was racing at the implications of the break-in at his house. He was sure it was the Russians planning some sort of retribution. He couldn't ignore the lady, though. She was intent on more attention from him, and he would have to defer thinking about it until he finished taking care of the business at hand. He gently put his hand on the back of her head and pulled her down to his lips and then rolled over on top of her. *This is a lot better than lying in bed and not sleeping*, he thought. There would be time enough in the morning to think through his best course of action about the break-in. At the moment he could do nothing about it, anyway. He may as well relax and focus on his "mission" here, he laughed to himself.

"A few minutes ago you were snoring," he joked to her. "Now all of a sudden the lady is awake and demanding service?" He slid his hand under her backside and lifted her up slightly as he positioned himself better between her legs.

"Thanks for staying over with me tonight, Cody." She barely gasped the words out before his mouth covered hers. He was done talking.

CHAPTER XXIII

It seemed strange to be sneaking up to break into his own home. He had no idea what was waiting for him inside. While he had driven back to his house in the early morning darkness from his stay at Shirley's house, Cody had analyzed the possibilities that might be waiting for him when he returned. He had left early in the morning to be able to deal with the home intrusion and then get over to see Karen at the hotel relatively early in the morning to keep his promise to her. He needed her to stay out of sight and she seemed like a wild card. He knew he needed to continue making an effort there or her commitment would wane and she would potentially expose herself. At this point, she would be linked to Cody and that would pose a problem if a connection were made between them. It would lead to Cody's eventual connection in the whole chain of events involving the Russians. She was his weak link and she would require an ongoing investment of time and energy to keep her quiet and hidden.

There were two possibilities from the break-in that he felt required extreme caution. The most obvious was that someone might be waiting to attack him inside his house. The other possibility was that they might have set a lethal trap for him. The third possibility seemed more benign; the Russians just might want to gain more information on him or steal something from him of trade value to get him angry or to use as bait to induce Cody to expose himself again.

There was little in his house that would provide trade leverage and almost no way that they would have found out much about him from the items that he kept in the house. He kept a safe with some cash and weapons stored, but they would have had to blow the safe to get the contents, and that seemed unlikely to him. The first two possibilities seemed the most likely to Cody as he worked through the logical metrics.

He crouched in the low bushes surrounding the back of his detached garage and scanned the yard, drive, and house for any information on what might be waiting on him. There were no signs of entry, no vehicles or strange tracks in the yard or driveway, no lights on in the house or other telltale signs. Cody studied the drive area for cigarette butts, wrappers, or other evidence of a stakeout and saw nothing. As he crouched down he caught a slight scent of Shirley's perfume on his shirt that distracted him momentarily. He pulled the shirt up to his nose and sniffed again. The woman did smell nice, he mused. He rudely interrupted his own diversion and sharply reminded himself to focus on his task at hand. He crouched down again and circled around the back side of the garage and checked the yard and drive area again before scampering over to the back side of the house. He quickly circled the house, stopping at each window to listen carefully for any sounds that might tip him off to an intruder or signs of forced entry. He found no signs of entry and did not overhear any unusual sounds as he finished the lap around the house and returned to his original starting point hidden in the bushes.

Cody did not keep a weapon on his motorcycle other than the standard short piece of rebar that he kept handy in all of his vehicles. He had elected to ride to Shirley's house the night before and had staged the bike about one block away from his house in order to quietly approach his home without potentially tipping anyone off to his arrival. He had pulled the rebar out of the saddle bag and carried it with him now. He needed more firepower than that, however, if there was an armed intruder in his house. He would retrieve the nine-millimeter pistol that he kept stashed in the garage and turn off the security system from there.

Cody touched the keypad and stopped the garage door after it opened approximately three feet. He lay down and quickly rolled inside and then lowered the door again from the inside control button. He felt relief as he pulled the weapon out of the drawer in the tool chest where he had stashed it last. The heft of it in his hand was comforting, like an old friend; he knew he could rely on it if needed. He had a fifteen-round clip of hollow-point bullets in the magazine. He racked the slide and chambered a round with a solid click. He wanted the weapon ready for action as required.

After disabling the alarm system from the garage control panel, he slipped out the side door and slinked across the yard toward the back side of the house. He had grabbed an ice pick from the tool chest which he carefully kept pointed away from himself as he rounded the corner to the back of the house. Cody approached a window in the guest bedroom that had his spare bed underneath it. He jammed the ice pick between the sashes of the window and pulled the ice pick sideways, which rotated the lever to the unlocked position. He repeated the maneuver to make sure that the lever fully rotated to a position which left it unlocked.

Cody carefully pushed the window sash up to the fully opened position using the ice pick in the bottom of the sash for the last few inches. He listened intently to the noises coming from inside the house to see if he could detect anything. After a few minutes of waiting, he heard the air-conditioning compressor kick on as the house heated up from the open window. He quickly threw the gun onto the bed and hoisted himself up through the window. He tucked and rolled onto the bed and recovered the pistol. He felt soreness in virtually every part of his body as he completed the maneuver and stood on his feet. He was going to have to get some good rest and recover from all of the activities of the past few days, he thought to himself.

Cody reached back and carefully slid the window shut to knock down the noise of the air-conditioning condenser unit and allow him to better hear any movement inside the house. He kept a loaded twelve-gauge Mossberg pistol grip pump shotgun under his bed, which was as deadly a weapon as could be found in close quarters. He listened carefully from just inside the bedroom he was in to see if he could detect any breathing, movement, or other signs of an intruder. The house was eerily silent. He felt a sense of rage boiling up from deep inside at the thought of having to enter his own space in this manner and having to fear for his own safety within the only safe sanctuary he had known for the past twelve years. If there was anybody still in the house, he intended to make them pay a big price for the entrance. They would get his full fury, and only one side of this sordid showdown was leaving the house upright.

Cody eased his head out into the hallway at floor level to scan both directions. He saw and heard nothing. Easing up to the doorway, he quickly sprinted for his bedroom down the hall, bursting into the room and rolling up to the bed. He reached under the bed and found the Mossberg with minimal groping, then quickly pumped the slide to chamber a round and waited for any sound or movement on one knee beside the bed. He reached down to recover the pistol and felt himself exhale a long breath. Surprisingly, he felt no tremble in his hand and very little emotion. Nervous excitement was displaced by the anger boiling up inside him at the thought of thugs breaking into his home. While he had never felt great attachment to his home, it had always been his safe sanctuary, and the thought of someone invading it angered him.

With the two weapons in hand, he felt that the advantage had just moved over to his side as long as he didn't walk directly into the line of fire of someone waiting patiently in one of the other rooms. He knew he had to work his way through the entire house, starting from the master bedroom and moving to the front. He carefully entered each room and swept it with his eyes and opened every closet door, looked under every piece of furniture, and checked each room for signs of entry or tampering.

Cody made it to the kitchen—the final area of the house— without finding anything unusual. He was about to let his guard down and relax when he felt his blood run cold and the breath exhale from his body in short spurts. He locked in on the chilling sight of explosives crudely stuck to the wall next to the back entry he normally used to enter the house from the garage. Wires dangled in the low light that had been inserted into the dark matter stuck on the wall. Upon closer examination, he realized that it was C-4 plastic explosive with a crude detonator switch and battery pack fastened to the door.

Cody studied the device for a moment: It was set to trigger the charge when the door opened. The two wires would feed an electrical charge to a detonator cap imbedded in the malleable wad of plastic explosive, which would cause it to explode upon completion of the circuit when the door opened. It was crude but effective against anybody entering the house from the outside. Cody had opened that door without any thought thousands of times. Without the text warning from his security system, he would have opened it for the last time this morning, and very few of his remains would have been found. He involuntarily shuddered at the thought of the sudden eruption that would have been created by the detonation of that much plastic explosive. There appeared to be about a pound of material stuck to the wall. In military circles, it is generally assumed that it takes slightly more than a pound of C-4 explosives to blow up a large truck.

The investment in the security system had paid off. Cody had personally installed the high-tech system and had gone through the aggravating process of installing all the modules that maintained a dynamic linkup to a website which spun out the text message alerts to his phone when an intrusion occurred. While he had fail-safe tested the system numerous times, he had never had a break-in or any real need for the system previously. He was glad that when he needed it, it worked for him as advertised. It also doubled as a home systems control device thorough which he was able to monitor and adjust his hot water heater, air-conditioning, several appliances, irrigation system, and the security system cameras set up around the house. He had found that capability useful when he traveled. When time allowed, he would review the digital recordings stored from the hidden cameras to view the intruders and their activities while in his house. The cameras were activated with motion detectors and would provide him a reasonable understanding of how they broke in, what they did, and when they left. The recordings were stored on a server downloadable only by him through the website with the password he had set up.

The installation of the security system and maintaining hidden weapons in various safe locations around the house had been Cody's lone remaining compromise to his secret past. Although he was virtually certain that nobody could trace him to the contract kills he had committed, he could never rule out the possibility that his identity might be compromised back through the Spaniards who hired him or that, possibly, the Spaniards might eventually feel the need to eliminate him for some security reason of their own. He was glad he had trusted his instincts on that. It had saved his life and put him in a position where he could now surprise his opposition. Dmitry seemed intent on getting him back and would undoubtedly continue trying until he was successful. It was time to counterattack and clear them out before he was identified as an enemy of theirs by the police or killed in revenge.

Cody gently pried one of the two batteries out of the battery pack with a knife, being careful not to spark or pull the device off its mount in any way. He gently pulled out the other battery, which completely rendered the crude device disabled. He clipped the wires and pulled the switch off the door, then pulled the malleable putty explosive from the wall and carefully dislodged the detonator cap.

C-4 explosive was composed of a highly incendiary material known as RDX combined with an additive binder and plasticizer materials. The combination produced a highly explosive material that could safely be shipped, handled, and stored. A substantial amount of energy was required to kick off the chemical reaction that would cause it to explode. The detonator cap provided the explosive charge to produce that energy, and the reaction from the RDX created a rapid decomposition, releasing gases that expanded at over 26,000 feet per second. Without the initial explosive charge from the detonator, however, the material was fairly safe to handle. It would not explode in a fire; some troops had been known to use it as fuel for emergency cooking fires. It could also be shot by a weapon and not ignite.

Cody placed the C-4 in a Ziplock bag and then into a small cardboard box for transport. He would probably eventually burn the explosive at some point, but for now he kept the detonator cap, battery pack, and switch for potential future use. There might come a time when he wanted to rig his own retaliatory surprise against these guys. He could think of nothing more satisfying than using their own explosives against them if he decided to make that move. The thought caused a thin smile to spread on his face as he packed the C-4 into one small box and the detonator cap, switch, and batteries in another.

The cool water felt refreshing as he drained the tall glass. The stress and nerves of the night's events coupled with the long, sleepless night with Shirley had left Cody dehydrated and tired. He gazed out the kitchen window at the garage. The sun had come up during his disarming of the device and the new day was emerging. He grabbed his phone and quickly fired off a text to alert Karen of his expected arrival time at the motel. He had one last stop to make and then he could return and get some needed sleep. He needed to visit with Karen to keep her in position for the time being. He washed his face and hands and shook his hands vigorously to dry them. He rounded the house collecting the weapons and storing the items where they belonged. He packed the nine-millimeter pistol into a case for the return ride to visit Karen. Until he finished this with the Russians, he intended to keep a weapon close at all times.

CHAPTER XXIV

The pain from the broken lower leg bone caused an almost constant throbbing whether Dmitry sat down or stood up. The metal rod the crazed attacker had used on his leg caused a complete breakage of the shinbone and several bones in his hand. His face had been pummeled with complete precision, and the swelling was going down slowly, but the purplish bruising and cuts still remained. As bad as his body hurt, his pride was hurt more. He could feel the difference in the way his gang looked at him. It would have been much better if he had been shot and recovered. With no gunshot or knife wound, it was impossible for his men to ignore the fact that he had been taken down and beaten severely in hand-to-hand fighting by someone substantially smaller than he was physically.

Dmitry was not capable of walking without crutches, and he hated the wheelchair because it made him feel crippled. The crutches hurt his armpits and ribs. He was struggling to keep up a good front of ignoring the pain. He could sense several of the members of his gang of thieves maneuvering to oust him and take over. He was on dangerous ground now and he knew it because he was dependent on his loyal lieutenants to do all of his bidding. In his condition, he could not enforce any of his own rules or get revenge on the man who had attacked him. He was severely compromised and any one of several possible gang members could supplant him as the leader with relative ease. He was in no position to defend himself physically. He was entirely dependent on intimidation and threats with the nine-millimeter pistol he kept nearby at all times.

He had dispatched his loyal lieutenant Vladimir to plant explosives in the man's house. Dmitry was confident that if he could strike back at his attacker and kill him, it would prove that he was still capable of leading his gang of Russian desperados. He was certain the man would not be prepared for the impunity with which he operated. He feared no law, no law man; respected no convention or morality; and he would attack relentlessly until he got revenge. He had no care or worry about who else he harmed in order to hurt back. With a terrorist mentality, he would blow up a building full of people to hurt one occupant. His ferociousness and violence had helped him build this motley group into a gang who did his bidding, and he needed to show that he still ruled and that he would not allow anybody to do this to him and live.

Vladimir had assured him that he had set the explosives up on the obvious entry door to the house. The man was not likely to have been prepared for that type of counterattack, and the amount of explosives he used would have left no doubt about the result of the explosion. No one could survive the detonation of so much C-4 at that range. Dmitry was anxious for confirmation of the blast and kept one of his lackeys watching the local television news for any story about an explosion. Dmitry had confidence in Vladimir; if he said he did it, then it was done just as he said it was.

Dmitry had expected to hear some confirmation about the blast by now and was getting anxious and irritated. He would have to send someone to drive by the house and get confirmation of the hit. Either the man had not returned home yet or the news media were not covering the story. He was certain that the plan would work. No one untrained and unsuspecting would anticipate the planting of explosives like that in their own home.

Vladimir was a skilled thief who could easily break into any house or building without leaving any trace of entry or exit. The detonation device was a simple one that Vladimir could easily install without a hitch. Dmitry knew the plan would work if his target came home.

Dmitry had the men working outside in the print house counterfeiting more money. He intended to break his unit down and move to another location as soon as they got this batch of bills printed. Now that the idiot banker Dexter had gotten himself in trouble and lost his job, Dmitry could no longer count on the cover he needed to run a successful operation here. His hopes of getting the marina property were now dashed and things were no longer going smoothly. His intuition was telling him to get out of the area; things were closing in on him and he needed time to heal his body from the terrible beating he had absorbed. The swelling in his face was receding enough now so that he could see better, but he knew he needed medical attention. He needed to get back to Russia and get some treatment on his leg and get checked for other fractures.

He cursed as he leaned over to grab the crutches lying against the table next to his lounge chair. Grunting in pain, he propped himself up on his good leg, using the crutches to lean against, and hobbled over to the window in the kitchen overlooking the backyard to watch his men working to break down the printing equipment and load it into the box truck. They had completed the last of the printing earlier that afternoon and now were waiting for the ink to dry on the linen paper. The first step in their process was bleaching the one-dollar bills to reduce them back to blank linen stock. After drying and then pressing the bleached paper stock, the printing specialists took over and used sophisticated computerized presses to individually print each bill one side at a time. When the printing process was done, the former one-dollar bill was printed as a one-hundred-dollar bill. It took an expert to discern the difference between the counterfeit bills produced by his team and the real thing. The detailed border pattern, red stripe, and even the holograms imbedded in the bill print were precisely duplicated by the printing process. In the end, the bills were mixed in with the cash given to the Haitian drug dealers in exchange for the product that the Russians distributed with their street-level network in numerous cities throughout the northeast major metropolitan areas. The Haitians accepted a certain percentage of high-quality fake currency along with the real cash.

The counterfeit money was distributed throughout the Caribbean, and the Haitians were careful not to push the counterfeit money up their drug distribution pipeline. They purchased from violent Colombian drug lords who carefully checked the cash given to them with sophisticated testing procedures to prevent accepting counterfeit money. The Haitians were careful to launder the counterfeit cash in a widely dispersed network through cash payroll in local hotels, cruise lines, bars, and restaurants. The money wound up being distributed to so many different individuals so quickly in so many different locations that its source was almost untraceable. The dollars were utilized in legitimate businesses to pay employees who would never think to check the bills for authenticity. Those employees typically spent the money in the local economy at small shops or sent it back to their home economy for saving or to help support their families. Managers of the businesses purchased the counterfeit money at a discount from the Haitians and then took the spread for themselves. They were careful to disperse the fake bills among numerous employees, and the local cash economy easily absorbed the counterfeit bills with no notice.

The Caribbean economy had always supported a high level of counterfeit American bills anyway. The Haitians enjoyed a good markup over the credit they gave the Russians for the fake bills on top of the extremely lucrative profits that they made on the cocaine trafficking. As long as the quantity released was limited, the risk was low. Dmitry had never been a big fan of the counterfeiting effort and he resented linking it to his more profitable drug distribution efforts, but his bosses insisted on maintaining the operation. They ran a diversified crime syndicate involved in drugs, human trafficking, counterfeiting, fraud, theft, and blackmail. He had never been able to convince them to break the linkage between the two activities and just focus on the drug dealing. Once his bosses established a profitable business, they never wanted to stop it. They had no interest in listening to Dmitry complaining about unnecessary risks.

Dmitry had started out in the insurance operation causing minor accidents, and his fraudulent chiropractic physicians assisted them in extorting whiplash settlements out of insurance companies. Through a dedicated commitment to the syndicate and a fearless, violent efficiency to completing his mission, he had advanced to the more lucrative drug trafficking operation with his own team. He had to play his cards right now or he would lose the post he had worked so hard to attain due to his physical injuries and inability to maintain control over his group of rogues.

Dmitry struggled across the room to the kitchen window to check on the progress his lackeys were making. Some of them were downright listless when it came to physical exertion like loading up the print equipment. They were brutal thugs who were not accustomed to physical labor and they acted like surly children when they were forced to break a sweat. Dmitry had Vladimir supervising the operation and he heard him exhorting the others to keep working on getting the sensitive equipment crated to be loaded on the box truck. Several of the tattooed men were congregated around the rear of the truck smoking and trading jokes.

There was an intense exchange between Vladimir and the group which led to some harsh words.

Dmitry cursed under his breath as he felt a shooting pain in his injured leg from nudging the corner of the cabinet. He drew himself up on his good leg to get a better vantage point for viewing the activity outside. He hated not being able to directly supervise the activities himself. Watching the insolent attitude toward Vladimir infuriated him and triggered a rage against the man who had put him in such a compromised position with his own team. He would kill him, he vowed again to himself for the hundredth time. He wanted to know why the explosives hadn't detonated yet. For his own sanity he needed to know that he had his revenge on the man who had beaten him so severely. He would dispatch someone to drive by the house and give him reconnaissance once they had the printing equipment crated and shipped out.

Dmitry positioned himself for a better view out the window to peer into the door of the shed where the equipment was being moved from. As he scanned the scene, his eye caught some movement in the stand of trees on the outskirts of the yard. There in the bushes were two men with weapons, crouched and studying the activities with binoculars. Dmitry felt his heart leap in his chest.

He quickly leaned down to keep his head from being visible from the outside, scooted over to the corner of the window, and peered outside again to scan the entire perimeter of the compound. He cursed as he counted at least a dozen men dressed in black campaign gear. Based on their similar uniforms and flak jackets, he guessed them to be policemen of some stripe. His suspicion was confirmed when he saw the words "Secret Service" emblazoned on the back of one of the flak jackets.

Dmitry hobbled across the kitchen on his crutches, oblivious to the searing pain in his leg. He swore loudly as the crutches banged against the door opening and nearly tripped him. He crashed into his bedroom and flung open the closet door and pulled out the automatic rifle, then slammed a clip into the chamber and leaned the rifle against the wall. Yanking a canvas duffle down from the closet shelf, he kneeled down on his good leg in front of the large safe and was furiously spinning the dial when he heard the bullhorn.

"This is Special Agent John Bond of the U.S. Secret Service." The voice sounded authoritarian and completely confident. "We have your position surrounded. You are outnumbered and out-gunned. Lie down on your stomachs and put your hands out to your side immediately. Drop any weapons or we will shoot you where you stand."

Dmitry flung the duffle to the side and quickly stood on his good leg. After checking to make sure that his pistol was in his back pocket, he snagged the rifle from its perch against the wall. He swept the car keys into his hand from on top of his chest of drawers and hobbled out the door using the rifle as a crutch.

As he burst through the front door and hopped down the few stairs onto the lawn, he heard bursts of gunfire erupt from the backyard. It sounded like his guys had decided to go down fighting rather than be taken alive. The gunfire bursts were short and fierce. Obviously, the attackers were disciplined and well trained. He heard the sound of wounded Russians screaming and calling out to one another as the gunfire quickly subsided. He made his way into his car and heard loud yelling telling him to stop where he was. From his place in the driver's seat he unleashed a burst from the rifle that shattered the window and sent his adversary scattering into the bushes for cover.

Dmitry slammed the electronic key into the slot and pushed the button to start the car. He leaned over and pulled the driver side door closed, and the engine roared to life. As Dmitry brusquely shoved the car into gear, he was unknowingly on the edge of discovering the answers to the mystery that had been nagging at him for the last hours of his life. The explosion that ripped his car literally launched it into the air over thirty feet and blew pieces of it in all directions. In the microseconds of his last remaining consciousness, Dmitry knew that he had been blown up and killed by his own explosives.

Agent John Bond rounded the corner of the house at a full run with his weapon drawn. He saw the burning carcass of the car lying on its roof to the side of the driveway in a blazing inferno. He let out a deep sigh of relief when he saw his agents cautiously making their way out of the surrounding underbrush with their weapons at the ready while they approached the burning remains of the car. He did a quick mental count and confirmed to his relief that all his agents were accounted for and seemed to be fine.

Everything about the raid had gone as well as it could have with the exception of this car explosion. No one from his team had gotten hurt and they had only been forced to wound two of the Russians before they had all laid down their weapons and surrendered. He would have to get with the agents who had seen the car explosion and find out what happened here. There didn't seem to be an immediate obvious answer.

CHAPTER XXV

The long, metal Brazilian *espetos* were triangular in shape to allow the chef to expose three sides of the meat to the hardwood flame. Cody had stoked a hickory and oak wood flame into an intense heat. He had added some mesquite chips to the top to increase the heat and draw up some flame as he laid the long skewers of marinated sirloin over the fire. The metal rack on which the espetos lay kept the meat directly over the heat of the fire but out of reach of the flame. The large nuggets of sea salt dissolved with the juices of the beef and absorbed into the meat before dripping down into the flame.

Cody carefully laid all the skewers out over the flame with an appropriate space between them. He stepped back from the grill and took a long pull on the cold liquid. He looked at the brown bottle of Rail Bender beer and nodded his head appreciatively.

"This is damn good beer, man. Where did you get it? I don't think I have ever heard of it before."

Cody leaned back against the Road King. Dillon had taken the bike for a lap around the neighborhood and had left it out near the grill so that he could admire it. He had just finished the latest installment of his ongoing discussion with Cody about purchasing a motorcycle that his wife would not know about and keeping it in Cody's garage. He had longed for a bike for many years, but Laura would not approve the purchase because of her fear of him hurting himself. Cody allowed his friend to indulge in his daydream without splashing any cold water on it. He suddenly decided to get another bike that he could offer his friend to ride with him when he wanted to. Dillon would never go against his wife's wishes and actually buy a bike.

As a good friend, the least Cody could do was to make one available to him to ride when he needed to get away. Dillon had ridden before he got married; domestic responsibilities and his respect for his wife's wishes kept him from enjoying an occasional ride that would do him good. Cody wondered why he had been so slow to solve this little issue. He had been eyeballing the new Street Glide models anyway, and this gave him a good excuse to splurge on one. It seemed like the natural thing for a guy to do for his longtime friend in need.

Dillon lifted up his bottle and admired it. His feet were resting on the top of the cooler and he was lounging back in one of the two Adirondack chairs that were separated by a small wood table about ten feet from the large grill Cody had made from a barrel he had cut in half and welded legs to.

"Allison from work gave it to me for my birthday last month. I figured I needed to bring some if I was going to talk you into cooking and playing hooky from work with me. I have been going ape shit at the office and I needed to get out of there for a little bit. I can't always explain it to Laura, man. She is a good girl but she doesn't realize how much she asks of me all the time. I almost never get any time to myself anymore. By the way, I think it is a sad state of affairs when I have to call in sick and play hooky from work to spend time with my buddy. What the fuck have you been doing lately anyway? It's not like you to be so hard to get in touch with and not call and check in every so often."

"I know, man. I have been up to my ears in bullshit lately. Sorry I haven't been checking in more. I have all that behind me now, so things should get better from here."

Cody plopped down next to his buddy and slid down in the chair. He let loose a long yawn and casually crossed one leg over the other. "This is a damn good idea, anyway. How come we don't do this more often?"

"Mostly because some of us actually hold a freakin' job and work for a living," Dillon popped off. He stared at his friend with a look of disbelief. "I still can't believe what you told me down in the Keys, Chief. I always wondered about you, man. Glad you decided to come back and join the real world. How is it going with Shirley, anyway? You taking good care of her? Glad you listen to your old buddy every once in a while?"

"We are doing well; much better than I would have thought, to be honest. I haven't had a real girlfriend in so long I forgot what it was like. I am looking forward to getting to know her better. You know it's been a long time for me, bro. It's nice having her in my little world, though. I am getting used to the idea of it. She is easy to be around."

Cody got up and rotated the skewers one-third turn each and elevated his friend's feet to open the cooler lid and extract two more cold beers. Dillon chugged the rest of his beer and slipped the foam insulator off the bottle. Cody gave him a look as he took the empty bottle from him.

"I'd be happy to take that empty from you, sir. Anything else I can offer? Wash your car, clean out your garage?"

"Least you can do for someone who is getting your sorry ass laid." Dillon grabbed the opener from the small table and popped the top off the new bottle. "You bringing her to the party at the marina on Saturday night?"

"Of course," replied Cody. "I wonder what this big announcement is that Tom and Jen have to make. He is definitely looking a lot better these days. I was worried about him for a while there."

Cody took the two empty bottles over to the recycling bucket and gently slipped them into the bottom. He walked over to the grill and rotated the long skewers again. The fragrant smell of the meat cooking over the hardwood flame was making him hungry. He was just launching into a detailed explanation of how to make the jalapeño potato salad that Dillon kept munching on when the sheriff's cruiser slowly pulled into the driveway and stopped.

The two men stared at the two officers in the police car. Without looking at Cody, Dillon quipped, "Anything else you aren't telling me about, Chief? They aren't going to arrest me just for being with you, are they? I got to tell you, man; Laura is going to kick my ass if I wind up in the butt farm this afternoon. She doesn't know I'm not working. I will not be able to explain that."

"Just relax, man." Cody took a nonchalant pull on his beer when he recognized Norman from the martial arts academy. "I know the driver."

"Oh, so this is just a social call, huh? Since when did you start hanging out with cops, Chief?"

"Just let me handle this. Try not to say anything if you can help it."

Cody did not recognize the man getting out of the cruiser on the passenger side. Both opened their doors at the same time and adopted the same unhurried manner. Both wore sunglasses. The passenger did not have a sheriff's deputy uniform on. He was dressed immaculately in a nice suit. He buttoned the jacket as he walked toward the two men.

Cody and Dillon stared silently at the two men as they approached. Norman casually looked around the yard and gave the garage building special attention.

"Nice place, Cody." Norman sauntered up and held out his hand. "Smells good, man."

Cody reached out and shook the big deputy's hand.

"Leave it to a cop to show up when the food is just about ready to serve. Heard you won that fight the other day. Congratulations; I heard it was a knockout in the second round."

"Guy didn't train right and he was exhausted. He ducked right into one of my uppercuts and went out like a light. Learned that uppercut trick from you. It was deadly."

Cody nodded appreciatively. He wondered what this was all about and why Norman showed up with this guy in the suit. He had never told Norman where he lived or even what his last name was. Norman would have had to have done some research to loop all this together and find him; this was a bad sign. Cody resolved to play the whole situation very coolly.

"What brings you out here, Norman? Meet my friend Dillon, by the way. We were just about to head inside and eat some of this steak. Sorry I didn't know you were coming or I would have put some more on so I could feed you guys, too." Cody made it clear that he wasn't planning on hosting uninvited guests.

Dillon stood up and extended his hand to Norman.

"Good to meet you," he said casually. He was behaving himself for once, Cody noted.

The two shook hands firmly and Norman motioned toward the man dressed in the suit with the dark sunglasses.

"This is Special Agent John Bond with the Secret Service. He has been in town on an investigation and he had a few questions for you, Cody. You think we could talk to you for a minute?"

"What's on your mind?"

Bond reached into his jacket pocket and retrieved a small notepad and a pen. Cody was torn between dragging another couple of chairs out for them to sit in or keep them as uncomfortable as possible while they were here to keep it short. He could tell that Dillon was worried about the situation and getting scared for him. After just learning of the things that Cody had done in his past and now to be witnessing an interview by the cops had to completely spook him out.

Bond made no effort to shake hands or set anybody at ease.

216

He referred to his notes and then looked up at Cody.

"I am involved in the investigation of counterfeit currency circulation. My office was investigating a suspected group of counterfeiters who were here illegally from Russia and were thought to have been actively printing counterfeit money in an old citrus grove outside of town. We were moving in for an arrest on their operation the other night, and the leader of their group, Dmitry Medvedev, was trying to escape in his car. His car blew up in a massive explosion with all of my men surrounding him. Fortunately, no one else but him was hurt in the explosion."

Agent Bond looked directly at Cody and paused. Cody returned his stare and said nothing. The pause turned awkward as neither man made any move to offer explanation or ask questions. Dillon shifted his weight in his chair and moved uncomfortably to one side. Cody looked at him and motioned at the grill. Dillon walked over and turned the meat skewers again. On his way back he lifted the cooler lid and pulled out another beer for himself without offering one to anyone else.

"When questioned about the explosion, several of the men we talked to indicated that you had fought with Dmitry and that you might be responsible for planting the explosives in his car."

Bond again stared directly at Cody. The silence became uncomfortable again. This time Norman piped in.

"Nobody is sure if the explosion is related to the counterfeiting or not. Since we believe the car was blown up by explosives that were planted prior to the escape attempt, Agent Bond has looped us into the investigation in case there is a murder that needs to be pursued."

Bond again reviewed his notes in an unhurried manner. He looked up from his notepad and questioned Cody with his eyes. This was one cool customer, Cody thought.

"We wondered what you thought about being mentioned as a

possible suspect in the murder of Medvedev," said Bond.

Cody continued to act unresponsive. He looked at Norman and then back at Bond.

"Is there a question in there somewhere, or are we just making small talk?"

"A murder charge is not small talk," replied Bond. "Let me try this another way. Did you know Dmitry Medvedev?"

"I was involved in a road rage incident with a large fellow who appeared to be Russian. It was early in the morning out south of town on Highway 192. The guy was enraged beyond belief and blocked my vehicle from leaving the scene. We had an angry discussion which led to him physically attacking me. I defended myself the best I could."

Norman smirked and said, "I know a little about how he can defend himself. I am sure it wasn't pretty for him."

Bond shot Norman a cool look and turned back to Cody. "So you fought with him?" he asked.

"I defended myself and defused the situation. The guy came at me and I immobilized him."

"Did you ever know him before? Have you had any contact with him since the incident? Did you exchange any threats of retaliation or suffer any other attacks that might have come from him?" Bond was losing his unhurried pace with the rapid-fire questions.

Cody polished off his beer and took the replacement being offered to him by Dillon as he stood up and made his way to the grill to remove the beef from the flame. "Do you mind if we eat while it is hot?"

His calm manner and limited information sharing was seriously beginning to irritate Bond. The agent was not accustomed to getting this kind of response from suspects he questioned; they almost universally went the other way and tried too hard to make him believe what they wanted him to believe. This guy was acting like he couldn't care less if Bond believed him or not.

Cody purposefully did not offer any food or refreshments to the two policemen. He had plenty and could have served them easily, but he chose not to. He found this questioning highly galling and he was rapidly developing a dislike for this cat Bond with his Mr. Smooth attitude. He acted like he expected everyone to run off at the mouth and spill their guts just because he had some questions.

"So what was the end result of the fight? Did you get hurt? Did you vow to retaliate against him or hurt him at some later point? Did you hurt him?"

Cody accepted the plate of beef from Dillon and walked over to serve himself some of the jalapeño potato salad he had made earlier. It had a serious bite just the way he liked it, and his mouth watered thinking about eating.

"It was not much of a fight, to tell you the truth. The guy came at me and threw a punch, which I blocked, and then I took him down and torqued his shoulder a little bit until he gave up. As you can see, I was not injured. To the best of my knowledge, neither was he. I do not know what this guy's name is or what his story is. I can't help you with anything else on him. I don't know for sure if he is the one you are talking about or not. I guess I will have to see if I get his Christmas card." Cody smiled for the first time at Bond and took a bite of the steak. It tasted as good as it smelled.

"Why do you suppose the other guys in that gang suspect it might be you who planted the explosive?"

"How do you know they are talking about me?" asked Cody. "Are you sure it's me they are referring to? If they are talking about me, the only thing I can think of is that they are trying to divert your attention from some other possibility."

"We are just investigating all the different possibilities. We put a few different things together to come up with your name. We don't see any linkage to you in any other way other than the explosion and the fight you had with Dmitry."

"You mean the fight I might have had with Dmitry. You might want to ask yourself why I would want revenge on him if I won the fight. Neither of us even knows if it was actually him I had the fight with. Do you have a picture?"

"Not on me," said Bond.

"We just have to run down all the possibilities, Cody. Don't get your guard up. We are just here to talk and make sure we look at everything." Norman looked longingly at the food Dillon was eating.

"Be happy to make you guys a plate," said Cody. "Be a shame to eat this and not have a beer, though."

He decided to change angles here with these guys and see if that got a more relaxed atmosphere. Somehow he doubted that either of them cared whether a notorious outlaw like Dmitry got blown up or not. The way they probably saw it, it was one less bad guy they had to deal with and get off the streets.

"I am done working after this," said Norman. "I would take a plate if you are offering. That looks about as good as anything I have eaten in a long time. I don't miss too many meals either, as you can see. I didn't get to be this size eating salads."

All three of the other men chuckled. Cody went over and scraped the meat off one of the remaining skewers onto a plate and then served up a big helping of his jalapeño potato salad.

"How about you, Special Agent Bond, you care for a plate of this?"

Bond looked at Norman, who was already wolfing down his food. Norman looked at him and nodded.

"You better get a plate of this, Bond. You don't want to miss out."

"Well, I guess I better since it looks like I won't be able to talk my partner here into going anywhere else for lunch."

Cody smiled and grabbed the last skewer of meat. He loaded the plate and stooped down to grab beers out of the cooler and handed the beers to Dillon, who promptly opened them. Cody passed the plate to Bond and then motioned for him to sit down in the chair where he had been seated. He ambled over to the house and pulled two more chairs out for the new guests to sit in.

Gradually the conversation shifted between the Russians to fishing, motorcycles, diving, fighting, and sports. After an hour the discussion migrated to women. It turned out that Special Agent Bond was a single man and enjoyed dating. Norman seemed to especially enjoy needling Bond about his interest.

"Yeah, Bond here is quite the swordsman. He has the ladies swooning wherever he goes. He has some little hottie over at the bank chasing him around already. She invited him to some event at the marina here Saturday night. It's a party on some rich dude's boat launching a real estate project. Let's see, there is going to be exactly no deputies there. No deputies invited at all. But Special Agent John Bond swoops into town and gets an invitation from some girl at the bank who already wants to have his children after one lunch date."

Dillon had been carrying the majority of the conversation burden over the last hour with the two law enforcement officers. Cody had been leaning back, enjoying the exchanges, and chipping in with short anecdotes from time to time to stay involved. He had warmed up to Bond after the rough start. It turned out the guy actually had a decent sense of humor and seemed like a pretty reasonable guy. In some ways, he was very similar to Cody. Meeting under other circumstances they probably would have become fast friends and good buddies. Cody didn't quite trust him yet as it pertained to the investigation. He maintained a friendly but reserved demeanor when engaging him.

Dillon piped up. "Yeah, Cody and I are going to be at that party, too. We are friends with the owners of the marina. It sounds like it's going to be quite a party. Our friends have been struggling to launch a condo project at the marina, and they just formed a partnership with this Canadian guy to move it forward. Cody refurbished the Canadian guy's boat and introduced the guy to our friend to see if he could help him. Turned out the Canadian guy is a big real estate developer and he had a lot of interest in the project. He has the muscle to help them get it going."

Cody caught Bond's eyes on him during Dillon's explanation.

"Is that what you do for a living, Cody? You refurbish boats?"

"I do some of that," said Cody. "I would like to do more of it, but I don't get as much of that kind of work as I would like. Mostly, I make custom furniture and do some trim carpentry work. I knew the captain of that boat, and he was familiar with some other renovation work I had done on a similar boat and he got me the job. The owner of the boat needed a hydraulic lift installed to allow him to take his disabled daughter out with him on it."

The explanation of his occupation seemed so ordinary, plausible, and normal that all three men could visibly see the remainder of any doubt about Cody leaving Bond's mind. He began to talk to Cody about a refinishing project he wanted to do on his teak dining room table. Cody offered a couple of simple but important pointers on how to get a good job done, and Bond seemed sincerely appreciative.

By the time the two officers left, all the beers had been drunk, all the food had been eaten, and new friendships had been formed.

Dillon looked at his friend as they cleaned up the last of the plates and dishes from the patio.

"Didn't kill you to be nice to the guy, did it? You notice how he started lightening up on you once you quit being such a hard ass with him. Man, you need some people skills. You don't have to kick everybody's ass every time, do you? Sometimes being a friendly guy like me will get you further than being so defensive."

"Okay, Dr. Phil. I get it. I think I did okay. I had them slamming Rail Benders and eating barbeque before they left here. Did you forget that?"

"Yeah, I thought I was going to have to get your back at first. Having to take on that big bastard Norman while you took out the small guy didn't appeal to me, General Patton."

"Well, Princess, you can quit shitting yourself now and straighten out your panties. We didn't have to take them on. The bad guys left already."

"Yeah, you say that now. I know who would get the first call if they threw you in the pokey." He made a childish face and used a very high voice. "Dillon, can you come bail me out of the butt farm? These bad guys stole my cigarettes and want to make me their husband."

The two men cracked up laughing at the stupidity of the crude joke. Dillon had the uncanny knack of making anything funny if he wanted to.

Cody held out his fist for their traditional fist bump when the two of them agreed on something and was surprised when Dillon didn't immediately respond. He looked up at Dillon's face and found his friend staring at him.

"You have to tell me something, first. Did you blow that Russian bastard up?"

Cody looked at his best friend. He enjoyed the fact that he could tell him the truth if he wanted to. In fact, in comparison to many of the other things he had done, blowing Dmitry up in his car didn't even make the top twenty-five horrible deeds he had done in his lifetime. He knew that he could completely trust his friend if he did tell him. He went through all the metrics in his head and decided to spare Dillon from knowing all the gritty details of everything he had been through with the bastards. There just wasn't a real good reason to tell him. He hated lying to his friend but at this point, there wasn't anything to be gained by telling him. By Saturday night he would know after he saw Bond again whether or not the police were going to pursue anything against him further.

"Would you be offended if I told you that it is better for both of us if I don't tell you everything right now?"

"I am having a hard time understanding that, Code. You know I am not going to tell anybody anything."

"In the end, you are going to know everything, I promise."

"You are just chock full of surprises, my man." He stared at his friend as if he was seeing him for the first time.

CHAPTER XXVI

The gangplank leading to the Sea Ray was festively lighted and the music was comfortably wafting over the dock basin of the marina. The haunting lyrics of Van Morrison taking the party-goers into the mystic perfectly complemented the late summer evening's get-together being hosted by the friendly Canadian Georges and Tom and Jenny to announce their recently consummated partnership. Georges had taken an interest in the condominium project that Tom had designed for the property adjacent to the marina. Tom had agreed to let Georges' organization take the lead in completing the approvals and refining the design of the project.

Cody and Shirley were slowly making their way up to the gangplank to board the boat behind several young ladies Cody had never seen before who were hugging Georges and making nice with the young lady in the wheelchair next to him as they crossed onto the boat. As they drew closer to the crowd, it became obvious to Cody that the girls were friends of Georges' daughter. The animated debutantes all clamored to make an entrance as they loudly exchanged compliments with each other and hugged in greeting. Georges beamed in pleasure at the sight of his daughter's excitement with her friends' arrival. From the sound of the exchange, they were all planning to make a trip on the boat to Jamaica for an extended cruise after the party.

Cody had worn his best Tommy Bahama silk shorts and shirt with some new canvas slip-on boat shoes he had put on without socks. Shirley dazzled in a yellow print mid-length cotton skirt slit open on the sides and a halter top that showed off her beautiful tan. Her toned arms and muscular back were the match of her busty front. It was hard to decide which side of her to admire the most. The bronze color of her skin highlighted her beautiful emerald eyes. She had a simple and elegant natural beauty which Cody never tired of admiring.

Cody extended a hand back to her to help her step down from the gangplank onto the deck of the cruiser. All eyes were on her as they drew close to Georges.

"Thanks for having us aboard, Georges." Cody extended his hand toward the host.

"Meet my friend Shirley."

"Thanks so much for coming and bringing this lovely flower, Cody. Meet my wife Rose."

Shirley smiled sweetly as he shook her hand politely and then looked at Rose.

"Thanks for inviting us to your event, Rose."

Rose swooped in and took Shirley by the arm and began touring her on the boat. Cody hid a smile as he thought of the night they had spent together on the boat. He could tell from Shirley's body language and reaction to Rose that she was not letting on that she had ever seen the boat before. No need to explain that to the nice lady, thought Cody.

Cody admired Shirley from the back as she disappeared toward the bow of the boat. The two women were intently chatting. Within ten minutes they would know each other better than most men would know each other after a year. Cody admired the view as the women entered the hydraulic lift he had installed and went down to inspect the galley. He felt proud to be with her.

"You had better not let Captain Timmons see your lady unescorted, Cody. You know what a swordsman he thinks he is. He will spend the whole night embarrassing himself trying to get her phone number if he sees her alone. What can I get them to make you to drink?"

Cody chuckled as Georges draped an arm around his shoulder and walked him unhurriedly toward the bartender. The elderly Canadian had a comfortable way of making anybody he was with feel like the most special person in the world while in his presence. He was urbane, sophisticated, and kind at the same time. It was a powerful combination that made you want to remain in his company for as long as you could. A simple glance at the bartender brought a hostess scampering toward them to take Cody's drink order.

Once Georges saw that Cody was attended to, he excused himself and rejoined his wife. Cody took a sip of the drink and made note of who else was there at the party. Tom and Jenny were busily talking to Georges and his wife. They were all facing the vacant property and Tom was excitedly gesturing while he shared his vision for the property and some of the history of it. Cody smiled to himself as he thought about his friend and the journey he had taken over the past few months. It was good to see him so alive again and charged up about the potential for his beloved condo project. He and Georges were going to make a joint announcement at the party later to tell everybody officially about their new partnership. It was the first time that Cody had ever seen his friend in a tie and jacket. Jenny had worn a nice blouse and slacks for the occasion, and she was beaming as she watched her brother talk.

Cody was turning to try to find Shirley when he saw Special Agent Bond walk aboard the vessel with a striking brunette. He immediately recognized Cody and strode over to extend his hand.

"Nice to see you again, Cody. Meet my friend Janet. She works at the bank and knows the owners of the marina. She invited me to this fine event."

"Pleased to meet you, Janet. Make sure this guy doesn't try to frisk you for weapons before the night is over."

Cody gently shook her hand and looked at Bond. "You look like you just left South Beach, Special Agent. You been shooting a *Miami Vice* episode? Where is Tubbs when you need him anyway?"

Janet giggled and put her hand to her face. "You are just jealous. He looks nice all the time. That is what I like about him." She inserted her arm into the crook of his and gave him a quick buss on the cheek.

"Just picked this jacket up today, as a matter of fact. Glad you noticed. I take that as a compliment."

Bond refused to get embarrassed about his good taste in clothes. He had confidence in his sense of style and he enjoyed looking his best. He looked at Janet and gently removed her arm from his.

"You think you could get them to make me a mojito, sweetie? I need to chat with Cody here for just a quick second."

As Janet walked away Bond looked back at Cody with a serious look.

"I'm not going to beat around the bush here, Houston." His dark eyes were intense as they stared into Cody's, looking for some kind of response. "There are a lot of unanswered questions here about those Russians and with a persistent linkage to you that nobody seems to be able to understand. I can't figure out why these two guys keep insisting that you must have been the one who put the explosives in that guy's car to blow him up. They keep talking about some kidnapping of your girlfriend, a fight between you and the leader of their gang, and some stolen money."

Shirley was making her way across the deck, smiling demurely at Cody. Cody returned her smile sweetly and looked at Bond.

"Here comes my girlfriend now. I'll just let her tell you how exciting our life has been together for herself."

Shirley walked up to Cody and possessively kissed him on the lips.

"Shirley, meet my friend John Bond. John meet Shirley."

Cody could tell that Bond was duly impressed. He had not expected Cody to be in the company of such a dazzling woman.

"I was just telling John here about that cruise we were discussing to add a little excitement to our life. I told him that you were going to get bored with me if I didn't pick things up soon."

Shirley looked at him sweetly and somewhat quizzically.

"I like our little life together just the way it is, honey. You don't need to take me on a cruise. I would have you over for dinner every night if it were up to me. I love cooking for you. I would be happy to go on a cruise, though, if you just insisted on it. Which one did you decide you were going to book us on?"

"I was thinking we would take the one that stops in Key West and heads down to Mexico. The one that leaves out of Tampa." Cody hugged her and quickly kissed her again before he stared back at Bond.

To his credit, Bond picked up his part.

"I have heard that is a really nice trip. Four nights, isn't it? Takes you down to Cozumel?"

Before Shirley could respond, Janet walked up with Bond's drink and excitedly gushed, "Come on over here with me, John. I want to introduce you to some of my other bank customers." She was clearly excited to have him as her date. She was going to be treating him like a show pony the whole night, thought Cody.

As the two of them walked away, Shirley grabbed Cody's arm and took a sip of his drink.

"He seemed nice. How do you know him?"

"Just met him the other day, actually. We found out that we were both going to be coming to this get-together tonight and chatted a bit. He sure is a good dresser, isn't he? What do you think of his outfit?"

"You would look better in it than he does," answered Shirley matter-of-factly. "I just might have to buy you some clothes like that for our cruise. Oh, look, here comes Dillon and Linda."

Cody had already seen his friend approaching the boat. Tom greeted him and accepted the bottle of wine he was carrying. Dillon spied his friends and waved at Cody as Shirley hugged Laura. Dillon wrapped an arm around Cody's shoulder and inspected his drink.

"Don't you ever get tired of Jack and Coke? Have you ever thought about drinking something else?"

Cody eyed his friend and slapped him on the back. "When I find something that works for me, I stick with it. Kind of like some of my friends. May not know exactly why they hang around, but I sure wouldn't trade 'em in."

"Well, Tom promised me cold beer at this event and I can't believe I don't have one yet. Laura wouldn't let me drink one on the drive over. I keep trying to remember when I lost the right to decide what I get to do."

Cody was arching his eyebrows at Dillon, trying to shut down his friend's complaint just as Laura showed up with a beer for him.

"Here, stud muffin. Drink this and quit complaining. You didn't die of thirst on the way over."

Dillon took the bottle from his wife and draped his arm around her shoulders.

"I was just explaining to Cody here how much I appreciate you saving me from myself and the wicked ways that I would be prone to pursue without your supervision."

"I heard you." She turned her attention from her husband to Cody. "You look nice, Cody. Did Shirley pick those clothes out for you or did you do that all on your own? Your shorts and shirt actually match and they look good with those shoes. Is that just a coincidence or did someone work that up for you in advance?"

"Just trying to keep up with my good man Dillon here."

"Now there is a joke, the two of you in a fashion contest. Let's clear the runway and get an audience for that."

Shirley chimed in. "My man is being good tonight, Laura. Take it easy on him. He was on time to pick me up and he is dressed nice all on his own."

"That may be true, but we should probably keep these two separated because things are likely to go downhill fast if they start drinking together. I have a little experience with these guys, you know."

The evening wore on and Cody circulated on his own throughout the boat. Shirley roamed from group to group, getting attention from all the men at each of her stops. Occasionally, they reunited briefly for a quick kiss and a rub on the back. Cody felt his blood getting up as the memories of his first date with Shirley on the boat flooded back into his consciousness. He was feeling much improved with most of the soreness gone from his back, legs, and arms. He began silently contemplating how early he could drag Shirley away from this little event without being too rude. Just as he began his lusty contemplation, Dillon walked up while unscrewing the cap on a bottle of Moosehead.

"Those Canadians know how to make a beer."

"Looks like you are enjoying yourself. That must be your fifth or sixth beer since you got here. You better take it easy, family man, or you are going to hear about it from Laura when you can't drive her home."

"You know, I have always thought that counting other people's beers is a sorry occupation. For your information, just so you don't spend your whole time here at this fine party worrying about whether or not I have a kitchen pass, Laura has agreed to be the designated driver tonight, and she has agreed that I am going to get lucky tonight if I don't embarrass her too badly."

Cody continued scanning the guests at the party without looking back or responding to the comment.

Not getting a reaction, Dillon continued his commentary.

"I guess we all know we don't have worry about you tonight, Code. In an hour or two you are going to be giving Shirley the hairy puppet show and making the poor defenseless girl fall in love with you all over again."

The two shared a small laugh about Dillon's comment. Cody turned and looked at his buddy and stuck his hand out.

"In case I haven't said it, I appreciate you introducing me to her, by the way. Besides your continued good friendship, she is the best thing that has happened to me in quite a while."

"Oh yeah, now you start with a little appreciation. What, you need to borrow some money or something? You are making me get all misty here. All I really want are some details, Chief. She is looking smoking hot tonight. I bet she is a nasty little wildcat in the sack, isn't she?"

"Now you know I can't go talking about her like that, even with you. I really like this girl, man."

Dillon looked at his friend in shock.

"You are shitting me. You must be getting serious about her. Damn, I am proud of you, Chief. Finally acting like a grown-up."

Cody was looking over Dillon's shoulder and spied Tom and Jenny's niece Karen talking with the deputy sheriff who had been investigating with Agent Bond. Suddenly, his mood changed and he felt the need to casually intervene and find out what they were discussing. He didn't quite trust Karen yet and he saw danger all over this scenario.

"Let's head over and chat up that deputy. He is talking to Tom and Jenny's niece."

They walked over, and Norman smiled and gave Cody a big bear hug.

"How you doing, bro? Let me introduce you to my new friend Karen here."

Cody smiled at the embrace and slapped the big deputy on the back. He could tell Norman had been drinking heavily.

"Nice to see you again, Karen. Cody Houston. We met briefly the other day in the marina office when I picked up that check. You are Tom and Jenny's niece, right?"

Karen picked up her cue expertly and smiled demurely. "Yes, I remember. Good to see you again. The work you did here on this boat turned out really nicely. You must be really proud."

"Thanks, it did turn out well. Glad to be able to work on such a good project for such nice people. Looks like you have been getting your drink on tonight, Deputy. You have a way home or are you planning to crash here?"

Norman laughed boisterously. "Nah, Bond is driving tonight. Speaking of him, here he comes now."

Bond rolled up with Janet in tow. Based on the way she had attached herself to his arm, it was clear that she was enjoying his company. After the proper introductions were made, Janet broke the small pause and looked at Bond.

"We were all just admiring the work that Cody did on the remodel of this boat interior."

Bond studied Cody carefully for a second or two longer than normal before he responded.

"So I heard from the owners. You are quite a craftsman, Cody. Norman tells me you are a martial artist, also. Quite the enigma."

Cody stared back without blinking. "How is the investigation going, Special Agent? Or am I allowed to inquire?"

Bond returned the intense stare and paused before responding. "The deputy and I were just discussing that a few minutes ago. Based on all the information we have been able to gather on the persons of special interest in this case, we have both concluded that all the related parties have been apprehended and we can move to prosecution with what we have. We won't be investigating anybody any further other than those in jail now, isn't that right, Norman?"

Norman nodded affirmatively and drained the cocktail in his hand.

"What the hell are we doing talking about work anyway? I am getting a good buzz on and the last thing I want to do is be worried about bad guys when I am trying to party. You guys need to lighten up. Where the hell do I get another one of these, anyway?"

Karen smiled and took the deputy's big paw in her hand. "Come over here and sit down with me. We can get you another one of those right away. What are you drinking?"

As the two slowly walked away, Cody caught Dillon's glance and smiled at his friend. He had just heard what he needed to know. Neither the Sheriff's Department nor Bond seemed intent on trying to link him to any of the events involving the Russians. Cody knew that he could count on Karen for spin control with Norman because there was no way that she wanted him to know about her call girl activities.

The evening wore on nicely with much small talk and laughter. Georges and Tom made a short public announcement about their new joint venture on the condo project. Georges smoothly gave all the credit to Tom for his visionary pioneering of the project and took none of the credit for the beautiful designs displayed on the artistic renderings of the buildings which his staff had produced. For his part Tom nearly broke down in tears thanking his sister Jenny for her support and belief in him and for supporting him as they faced the challenges of launching the project. He announced a breakthrough in support for the project at the City

Council. It seemed that some of the political metrics had changed recently and now that Georges was involved, with his legal staff and financial horsepower, the commissioners had come around and were now unanimously in support of the project.

Not announced but known to close friends was the fact that the bank was now completely backing the project again with Georges on board as a personal guarantor. They were lobbying to get the construction financing on the project and competing with Georges' Canadian banking relationships to remain in the project. That pesky foreclosure suit was a forgotten mistake, and they were now courting Tom again to stay involved.

Shirley rejoined Cody with a plate full of prawns and a cocktail for him that she had personally poured to his specifications. They had excused themselves from the group and sprawled out together on the same bench seat at the back of the boat on which they had first physically connected. After feeding him all the huge prawns on the plate one by one, she laid her head down on his chest and quickly nodded off in the comfortable evening air. Cody smiled as he looked at the back of her head on his chest. His little party girl had tired of circulating through the guests for admiration and had come home to her safe spot for rest.

As her rhythmic breathing carried on, Cody thought through the events of the past few weeks. His whole adult life had been a series of calculated risks with limited emotional involvement. His involvement in resolving this crazy dilemma for Tom and Jenny had been purely emotional. He got no payment; he neither got nor sought any credit or glory. Self-satisfaction for a wrong righted was his only consideration in the bargain. His special skills used for something other than his own personal enrichment and preservation. He knew that there would be time to fully contemplate the ramifications and angles of what had happened in this small drama.

Right now his arm was draped around a special and unique woman who was fast asleep on his chest. His friends were here and the moon was shining down on him with its comforting glow. Without even realizing it, he had lost his feeling of vulnerability and fear for his safety.

All seemed right as he quietly drifted off to sleep like a baby.

CPSIA information can be obtained
at www.ICGtesting.com
Printed in the USA
BVHW032318280220
573681BV00001B/16

9 781977 210944